JOSEPH O'NEILL was born in Cork in 1964. He is the author of three novels – *Netherland*, which was longlisted for the Man Booker Prize and won the PEN/Faulkner Award for Fiction, *The Breezes*, and *This Is the Life* – and a family history, *Blood-Dark Track*. A barrister in London for many years, he now lives in New York.

By the same author

Netherland
Blood-Dark Track: A Family History
The Breezes

JOSEPH O'NEILL

This is the Life

HARPER PERENNIAL
London, New York, Toronto, Sydney and New Delhi

Harper Perennial
An imprint of HarperCollins*Publishers*
77–85 Fulham Palace Road, Hammersmith, London W6 8JB

www.harperperennial.co.uk
Visit our authors' blog at www.fifthestate.co.uk
Love this book? www.bookarmy.com

This Harper Perennial edition published 2009
1

First published in Great Britain by Faber and Faber Ltd in 1991

A catalogue record for this book is available from the British Library

ISBN 978-0-00-730921-4

Printed and bound in Great Britain by Clays Ltd, St Ives plc

Mixed Sources
Product group from well-managed
forests and other controlled sources
www.fsc.org Cert no. SW-COC-1806
© 1996 Forest Stewardship Council

FSC

FSC is a non-profit international organisation established to promote the
responsible management of the world's forests. Products carrying the FSC
label are independently certified to assure consumers that they come
from forests that are managed to meet the social, economic and
ecological needs of present and future generations.

Find out more about HarperCollins and the environment at
www.harpercollins.co.uk/green

To my mother and to my father,
and to their mothers

ONE

The other day I was queueing up at the bank. The man in front of me, a man in black leather trousers and jacket, had long fair hair which was tied together below the shoulders with ribbon. The hair looked as though it had not been washed for several years, and its strands were so intertwined, so caked with adhesive, that it had solidified. It was impossible to tell which hair was which, or where it came from or led to. The filaments started pretty distinctly, each springing cleanly from the scalp; but once they reached ear level, where they melled, they became indistinguishable from each other and lost in a blur. I stepped back slightly in the queue. It was not a mane that I wanted to get too close to.

I mention the incident because the events I am about to relate are ravelled in my mind like those hairs. Their meanings are twisted and tied together in unfamiliar knots that will not easily undo – at the moment, at the start of this undertaking, I feel like a blindfolded man fingering at running bowlines, marling hitches, sheepshanks and cuckold's necks. This is partly due to my own entanglement in what I am preparing to describe, and the cock-eyed viewpoint that results from such a snarled involvement. Spectators, after all, see more of a play than its players.

What I am aiming to do is run a comb through the matted locks of my memory, run through the facts one more time as I remember them in the hope that, in doing so, as the threads separate and disentangle, a pattern of sorts will emerge.

When I say pattern, I do not mean a swirling motif of significations: I mean a straightforward, ordinary picture of what happened. I am not a philosopher or someone looking for ultimate truths or breathtaking revelations. What I am after is something I can get by with, so that I am able to get on with my life in the way that I am used to: because at the moment I am having difficulty getting on with anything. At work I sit listlessly at my desk, toying with a pair of scissors, snipping meaningless shapes in the air, unable to concentrate. June, my secretary, has never seen me like this before. She suspects that I am lovesick and brings me steaming cups of tea at regular intervals.

'Thank you, June, but I've just had one,' I say. I raise my hands. 'Really, I'm fine.'

She will not be deterred. 'Drink, it will do you good,' she says, bossily pointing at the cup. 'Come on now.' She stands there, arms folded, watching me. I drink.

'Thank you, June. That's a lot better,' I say weakly. When she has gone I return my gaze to my work. Again the print fuzzes over and once more my eyelids weigh kilograms. Again, after leafing through a few pages, I am exhausted and have absorbed nothing.

I will not dwell further on these symptoms, which anyone who has ever worked in an office will recognize. The important thing to note is that never before have I been afflicted in this way. The experience is, for me, unprecedented, and therefore doubly alarming – I, who am so happy in my work, struck down like this!

I must without delay go back to Friday, 9 September 1988 – the day, you could say, when I first began to be hauled from my element and enmeshed by Donovan's quickly unspooling life.

That Friday I travelled to work on the underground. As usual I was reading a newspaper as the carriage hurtled through the tunnels towards the Embankment. Just before we reached my stop (we were slowing down under the riverbed) I read the following piece in a column of ecological chit-chat:

As anxiety grows over the planet's dwindling ozone layer, attention has centred on the case of the European Commission v. The United Kingdom. The argument in the European Court concerns the alleged failure of the government to implement EC directives restricting the use of carbonfluorochlorides (CFCs), substances which, it is thought, damage the ozone layer. The resolution of the dispute has been delayed by an unforeseen snag. Yesterday counsel for the government, Michael Donovan QC, suffered a collapse when he rose to address the court. Proceedings have been adjourned for a replacement for Mr Donovan to be instructed.

Michael Donovan: the name jumped at me from the page. Donovan, collapsed?

Before I had time to consider the matter further the tube clanked into the station, a booming voice warned *Mind the gap* and I had to fold up my newspaper and alight. On my way to work – on the escalator up to the surface, on the gradient past Charing Cross Station up to the Strand and during the three minutes of walking after that – I gave some thought to Michael Donovan for the first time in years: probably two, maybe even three years. Our lives had diverged, and for a long time now we had moved in different circles. That said, there had remained the occasional intersection. I had, naturally enough, seen his name from time to time in the newspapers and in the law reports, and once, years ago now, I had glimpsed him at a function, something which caused me a certain amount of discomfort. Socially, I am unskilful, and one of the consequences that flow from this is that a drinks party usually finds me in a corner listening, reluctantly but inescapably, to a person whose conversation I find uninteresting. A second consequence is that I am filled with uncertainty when it comes to greeting demi- or semi-acquaintances. The degree of warmth or recognition called for by the encounter eludes me completely – is a handshake and a brief conversation necessary, or will a raised, friendly eyebrow suffice? The matter is

3

aggravated if, like Donovan, my acquaintance is more senior than me. Should I, the lesser of the two, humbly make the first move? Or would that not be a little presumptuous?

I find that I am straying from my point, which was that I was not entirely happy bumping into Donovan. This is not surprising (that I have strayed, I mean), because I have never undertaken this kind of enterprise before. Although, due to my training and occupation, I am an adept chronologist, I am not a natural recounter. If, at some gathering, I am casually relating some inconsequentiality or other, and I notice that a silence has descended around me and that suddenly I have an audience, almost invariably I freeze up and forget the point of what it is I am saying and it all ends badly, in blushes.

As I was saying, I did not relish it when Michael Donovan crossed my path (more precisely, when I crossed *his* path – Donovan was the man with the path; me, I have not done it my way, I have gone the way of others). Walking into the building where my office is situated, waiting with a cluster of others for the elevator to descend to the ground floor, I painfully recalled the last time I had spoken to him.

The encounter had taken place seven years before, in 1981, at a party in the Temple. To put myself at ease (it was one of those burdensome gatherings filled with partial acquaintances and characterized by a lot of hesitant eye contact) I had drunk quite a few flutes of champagne. Suitably uninhibited, I spotted Donovan talking to a group of people and felt no trepidation about approaching him, even though it had been some time since we had last met.

The group he was with was bunched into a tight phalanx of suits, and I had difficulty in joining them. I hovered around the perimeter of shoulders for a while, waiting for a chink to appear in the ranks, and just as I was beginning to feel a little foolish one of the suits drifted off and I was able to slip in. I remember chipping into the general conversation with the odd well-received remark and gradually I gained the confidence to speak to Donovan personally when a lull came in the talk.

4

'Well, Michael,' I said, 'how are things?'

Everyone looked at me. Everyone stopped what they were doing.

Donovan said, 'Very well, er – . How are you?' He gave me a blank, though not unfriendly, look. Then he smiled politely. 'How's the, er, work getting on?'

It was obvious to me, and to everyone else, that he did not have a clue who I was, or what I did – in fact, he looked at me as though he had never met me in his life! Now, although I never forget a name myself, I can well understand that a person like Donovan, a big fish, has better things to do than remember all the small fry he has ever met, the plankton of casual acquaintances. He has other things on his mind, he has global problems to crack, issues that affect all of humankind. But forgetting *me* – this was truly extraordinary. I was small fry, yes, I would be the last to deny it – but I was also his former pupil! Only three years previously I had spent six months tête-à-tête with him, locked in collaboration, my side by his side. It was a time of extreme proximity and affiliation. For six months I carried his papers and tidied his room, for six months I researched his opinions, made his coffee, drafted his pleadings and operated his telephone. For half a year I was an indispensable, if extricable, part of his practice – if not his right hand, or even his fingers and ears, then his shoe-laces, his cuff-links. He had counted on me, and in my humble way, I had counted for something.

Since that time my appearance had stayed roughly the same. Admittedly, my hair had thinned somewhat and my face had accrued more flesh – but it was not as if I had grown a moustache or dramatically changed my accent. I had, moreover, dropped him a note from time to time to keep him up to date on my progress. (How stupid of me! I cringed at the memory of those letters, their earnestly informative, self-important tone . . .) How, in all these circumstances, could it be that I, or something about me – my voice, my manner, the way I looked – rang no bells?

'Fine,' I said, 'fine.'

5

There followed an unhappy, a miserable, hesitation. We both looked about the room, brimming with chortling lawyers, to avoid one another's eyes. The other members of the group exchanged glances. I felt ridiculous. Although, as a rule, I am more than content with who and what I am, the incident was nevertheless an unhappy reminder of my unimportance in the legal world. The moral was clear: Donovan was out of my league now. I had no business talking to him. I swallowed wretchedly at my glass. It was empty. When I looked up I sensed that everyone was waiting for me to say something, and I noticed Donovan's eyes were flickering around the room, searching for a getaway. I decided to act, it was time to put an end to this torture.

'Well, it's nice seeing you again,' I said, and clumsily wandered off at the wrong moment, just as Donovan opened his mouth to reply. I turned round to repair my error but it was too late. Along with the others he had turned his back and doubtless had already purged the incident from his mind.

What Donovan had forgotten was that my name is Jones, James Jones. It is a plain, transparent name and, until an unrelated namesake induced a mass-suicide in Guyana, was an unremarkable one. I am a junior partner in Batstone Buckley Williams, an unprestigious firm of solicitors in the West End of London. I have a general, unspecialized practice: quite a lot of personal injury, family, some landlord and tenant, conveyancing, the odd bit of crime. I think it is true to say that, by commonly accepted standards, I am not an especially successful lawyer. I do not regret this, as professional success is not something I set great store by. Of course, it would be nice to wake up in the morning a highly paid and famous lawyer, respected and admired by my fellow men – given that option, I would take it like that, in the click of two fingers. But the pain of actually achieving that type of standing, the sacrifices, the boredom – these are not for me.

By contrast, for those of you who have not heard of him, Professor Michael Donovan QC was, in the autumn of 1988, one of the most triumphant practitioners at the English Bar. He was easily (there is no doubt about this) the top international lawyer in these islands, the possessor of a world-class legal mind. That mind of his . . . It was naturally and freakishly powerful, like a once-in-a-blue-moon tidal wave, or a tree-plucking wind in England. Perhaps this is a pedestrian or fanciful metaphor, but I most easily visualize it as one of those fat Swiss army penknives, deceptively stocked with cutthroats and instruments of severance, disassembly and dissection: razors, scissors, corkscrews, bottle-openers, screwdrivers, magnifying lenses, the lot. In a flash, before you could mobilize a brain cell, he would have dismantled an issue, anatomized its components and analysed its implications. He had all the intellectual tools, and this showed, this shone, in his writings. He was a great academic – innovative, controversial, scholarly – a star. He wrote his books and articles in a simple, transparent style, using short, pithy sentences, which meant that apart from anything else, he was immensely readable. He was the M. J. P. J. Smith Professor of International Law at Cambridge University, and his publications excited interest and envy around the world.

Donovan, then, was equipped for any contingency of legal warfare. For myself, I can safely say that he was the most brilliant court lawyer I have ever seen, and probably the most feared as well. His advocacy, whether in court or at the negotiation table, was – I was about to say brutal, but that word has connotations of crudeness that would not be quite right – inexorable. I for one have never seen anything like it. The only feasible comparison I can think of is with the American heavyweight boxer Mike Tyson. If you have seen this man boxing in his prime you will know what I am talking about. He is not especially tall, so it is hard to pick him out in the crush when he pushes through the bodyguards, photographers and spectators that crowd him on his way to the ring. But when he finally stands disrobed and gleaming in the floodlight, he is unmistakable: black, baggy silk shorts, long bludgeoning arms and eager, focused eyes. Then the bout:

some combinations to the torso, an uppercut, then *bam* – a sickening bullseye to the jaw, and Tyson's opponent is on his back, seeing stars.

I am not suggesting that Donovan's entrée to the courtroom was the same as Tyson's to his forum, or that he disposed of cases in a matter of minutes; but Donovan, like Tyson, had a capability unhesitatingly to unleash inimitable, efficient destruction. He would immediately detect any flaw in an argument, spontaneously expose it, and then carefully cudgel it with spot-on, shuddering verbal blows. There was no holding back, but nor was there vindictiveness: personal feelings, emotions, did not enter into it.

I must return for a minute to what I have roughly called Donovan's inexorableness. It marked everything he did. His actions had an unrelenting shape to them, the shape of things to come. He was streaming forward at such a speed, and so unerringly, that his future seemed a foregone conclusion.

TWO

In short, then, reading that item in the newspaper turned my thoughts to Donovan for the first time in a long time. Going up to my office that morning in the full-up elevator, I worried about his well-being. Collapse? What was it, heart? Stroke? At his age? In his mid-forties?

When I had ascended to the fourth floor I stepped quickly into my office, preoccupied by the business. I helped myself to a black coffee and sat in the chair behind my desk. It was half-past eight, I had about half an hour to myself before everyone would come in. So Donovan had collapsed on his feet, I thought to myself. What did that mean, collapsed? I tried to imagine it: had he fallen over the lectern clutching his chest, powerlessly splashing papers everywhere? Or had he buckled at the knees and slumped to the floor, folding up like an old deckchair? What had happened?

I decided to telephone his chambers at 6 Essex Court to find out. There was no need for me to look up the number because after all these years I still knew it by heart – 583 9292.

I stopped dialling and put the receiver down at 583. It did not feel right – it was too direct, too embarrassing. I would have to find out in due course, the same as everyone else. It was not as though I was a particularly close friend of the man, or family, or especially connected to him. In fact, Donovan did not even know who I was any more.

Of course, there had been a time when Donovan did know me, when he knew exactly who I was. I am thinking of my time as his pupil barrister.

My whole pupillage lasted for a year, and it was the second part of that year that I spent with Donovan. My first six months had also been spent at 6 Essex Court, but with a different pupil-master, a man called Simon Myers. Head of chambers at the time was Bernard Tetlow QC (later, of course, Lord Tetlow of Herne Hill). Six Essex was just as fashionable a set then as it is now. The work flowing through chambers was high-class commercial law: shipping, reinsurance, private international law, banking and so forth. There was no crime, no family, no landlord and tenant, no dross whatsoever. The pigeon-holes of the tenants bulged with lucrative briefs from Linklaters & Paines, Slaughter & May, Freshfields and Herbert Smith, the papers wrapped like offerings in their bright pink ribbons. You certainly would never see any work from my firm, Batstone Buckley Williams, floating about the place.

Simon Myers, my first pupil-master, was good to me. Myers was very punctilious and he scrupulously took pains to ensure that I was properly trained. He gave me some useful habits of mind which to this day hold me in good stead. 'Always ascertain the facts. Visualize what has happened: imagine the people sitting down to write letters. Remember dates. Always make up your own mind about something. And remember, never give a definitive answer to any question: always express clearly the subjectivity of your opinions. Use qualifiers to hedge your bets: "In my opinion, in my view, in my analysis, as I see it, from my perspective." Sprinkle your sentences with phrases like "it follows that" and "accordingly" and "therefore". They lend a veneer of logical force to your argument.' There were also tips of a more general nature. 'Look sharp: a tidy appearance betokens a tidy mind. Here, take this.' He handed me a card. 'My tailor. Get yourself a new suit. And this.' Another card. 'My financial adviser. And this. My stockbroker. Get yourself a pension, you won't regret it. Get yourself a portfolio. And while we're on the subject of investments,' Myers said, drawing a ten-pound note from his wallet, 'here, go put this on Royal Burundi to win the 3.30 at

Haydock. You'd do well to invest a pound or two yourself.'
Then the golden rule: 'Look the part. No matter what, always
look as though you know what you're doing.'

Simon Myers liked me and recommended to the head of
chambers that I be seriously considered for a tenancy. It was
for this reason, I think, that I was allocated to Michael
Donovan for my second six months of pupillage. They wanted
to stretch me, to see what I was really made of.

Donovan had his own specialist, personalized practice –
public international law with a sideline in private international
and European Community law. That is not to say that he
possessed a narrow expertise – not Michael Donovan. Even in
areas of the law he was supposed to know nothing about, like
defamation or insolvency, he would run rings around the
specialist practitioner, tantalizing him with far-fetched hypo-
theticals that would push a principle to its limit and then, after
the other had given up or had proposed an inadequate
solution to the problem, he would supply an elegant analysis
that seemed, in retrospect, blindingly obvious.

So it was an enormous privilege to work alongside Donovan. When I say alongside, I do not mean physically, although
my desk was in his room, next to his desk. In fact we saw each
other rarely – it was not often that we actually laid eyes on one
another. Most of the time Donovan would be away, usually
overseas, at an arbitration or conference, and I was left to hold
the fort in chambers, turning over paperwork and manning
the telephone. But no matter how far away Donovan was, we
never lost touch. It is not just that we spoke daily by
telephone, no, our communications went deeper than that. I
knew what he wanted without his telling me, I anticipated his
every unspoken wish. It was as though some wire, some
humming conductor, ran between us.

And so I was his anchor man. I laboured night and day for
him, unobtrusively ensuring that everything ran smoothly on
the home front. Saturdays and Sundays would find me alone
in chambers, poring over the books in the basement library
until late into the night, my desklamp the only light burning in

the Temple, my face on fire. I worked like crazy. No one at Batstone's would believe me if I told them, but in those days I never stopped. The responsibility was not just stimulating, it was like a dynamo, shooting wattages through me that I have never known at any other time in my life. In the mornings I would shake off the reins of tiredness and feel a great horsepower pumping up inside me. My work was my reward. When an opinion or pleading I had devilled for Donovan went out unchanged bearing his signature, far from being displeased or resentful at this exploitation of my free labour (like most other pupils, I was unpaid), I was gratified – to think that I, James Jones, had produced a work worthy of the brilliant Professor Donovan!

In my new state of excitement I became fired by ambition – real ambition, not just wishfulness. I desired that tenancy at 6 Essex like nothing else – more than anything in the universe I wanted my name, Mr James Jones, up on the blackboard bearing the tenants' names in white paint. I would envisage each letter of my name there when I walked in every morning, fantasize over each brushstroke. It would happen, I knew it would; my visions were so vivid that they could only be premonitions. I knew the room I would occupy down to the last detail, down to the paintings I would buy to hang on the wall. My future was under my belt. It all made sense, it all fell into place: sometimes I would awaken from my work and suddenly the ineluctable nature of my situation would be revealed to me: of course, I would think, this is it. This is how it was meant to be.

Looking back on my time at 6 Essex afresh, I think that I was perhaps too unobtrusive, too quietly efficient, too mole-like, for my own good. Just recently I saw a documentary about moles on the television. Moles work night and day. They never rest. If they are not paddling out fresh corridors of earth they are maintaining their existing galleries and tunnels, snapping and crunching intruding roots and mending the walls. The point is, most of this was not known until they sent down one of those fantastic subterranean cameras. Before that happened, the moles received no credit for their industry. For all anyone knew they were bone idle. Likewise, if I had been a little more prominent about my efforts in the basement, if my profile had been a little higher, then perhaps, just maybe, I would have been offered a tenancy. But I thought there was no need for self-promotion. I thought that Donovan would recognize my worth and stand by me when the decision came to be made as to which one of the seven pupils would be taken on. I thought he would say, Consider Jones, he hasn't put a foot wrong in six months. I thought he would say, Jones: look no further than Jones.

But no. When the chambers meeting came around Donovan was in Alexandria, with the result that at the meeting there was no one in my corner, no one rooting for me. Oliver Owen was taken on, I was not.

The afternoon that the axe fell I was in the chambers library with the other rejected pupils. All six of us were seated around the oval central table while we numbly contemplated our bleakening futures. Oliver Owen was at El Vino's with the head of chambers, celebrating.

Then Alastair Smail, the head of the pupillage committee, the man who had made us and broken us, entered the library, whistling a tune through his bright pink lips as though nothing had happened. After searching and craning among the bookshelves he turned round and asked whether anyone had seen *Westcott on Trusts* anywhere. Receiving no reply, he went energetically through the borrowers' index, fingering the cards and commentating loudly on his progress. Then he looked around and sensed, for the first time, the gloom. 'What's the matter with everyone? It's like a funeral parlour in here,' he said, leaving without waiting for an answer.

While the others just looked at each other, I got up and followed him, eventually catching up with him in the corridor outside. I needed to speak to him urgently about getting a pupillage elsewhere, in another set of chambers. I had neg-lected to take precautions on that score (my work had taken up all my time), and there was a real danger that I would miss the boat completely if I did not act quickly.

'Alastair, I wonder if I could have a word with you.'

'Yes, of course,' he said, still walking.

'About finding somewhere else,' I said. 'I was wondering if you might know anywhere where there might be some space – for me.'

He looked at me with a strange expression. 'I thought you had somewhere. I thought you'd organized something.' Now I looked at him: where did he get that idea from? 'I do know some people, yes, but you realize that, well, that the other pupils do have – priority.'

What? 'Priority? Why?'

'As tenancy applicants, they have priority over pupils who made no such application. You appreciate that, Jones.'

'But I am an applicant, too,' I said. 'I applied for a tenancy too.'

'Did you?' Smail said. 'We received no such application from you. We assumed you had made other plans.'

'But I did apply,' I said. I could not believe what I was hearing. 'I did apply.'

Again Smail looked at me with a strange expression. 'Well, we received no application,' he repeated. 'Nothing at all.'

'I didn't send anything in writing, that's true,' I said desperately. 'But I wasn't aware that a formal application needed to be made. I thought the very fact that I was here as a pupil was in itself an application. No one told me that I needed to apply formally.'

'Nobody told you? Michael didn't tell you?' I shook my head. Smail shook his head too. 'Well, this is unfortunate. And you wish to apply, do you?'

I said, 'Yes.' I said, 'Yes, if it's not too late.'

Smail thought for a moment. 'Leave it with me,' he said. 'I'll get back to you as quickly as possible. Don't worry,' he said with a smile. 'We'll sort something out.'

'Thank you Alastair,' I said. I meant it, I was full of gratitude: perhaps all was not yet lost! Perhaps I was still in with a chance, after all! 'Thanks very much,' I said. 'I'm sorry about all this, but I really did not know about the need to apply.' Smail gave me a smile which said it was quite all right, and walked away.

The next day I received the following letter at home. It was a standard letter which began with *Dear . . .* , and with my name, Jones, inked in over the dots.

Thank you for your application for a tenancy in these chambers. It is my sad duty to inform you that, after careful consideration of the merits of your application, we are unable to place you on the short list of candidates. We wish you every success in the future.
Yours sincerely,

Alastair Smail

Soon afterwards I began sending off applications to other chambers. The only pupillage I was offered was with an obscure landlord and tenant set, and they made it clear that they doubted very much whether they would be able to take me on at the end of it. It was not me, they said, it was simply a question of space: there were just not enough square feet to go round. It was then that I saw an advertisement inviting applications to Batstone Buckley Williams. I attended a brief interview and they immediately offered me a position. Of course, I gratefully accepted. The Bar had, by then, lost its appeal for me. The senior partner at Batstone's, Edward Boag, took me aside the first day I arrived. We went into a corner together and he gave me a piece of advice. 'I want you to forget all the law you've ever learned,' he divulged. 'We don't like intellectual pretensions at Batstone Buckley Williams. And let me let you into a secret.' He looked around in case anyone was listening. 'This business is all about one thing: meeting deadlines. Lots of them.'

I must make it clear that I do not feel bitter about the experience – not in the slightest. I am very happy here, at Batstone Buckley Williams, and in many ways I am relieved that I never stayed at the Bar – the pressure and the workload are simply too great for my liking. And certainly I have no hard feelings for Donovan. It was not his fault that I was not taken on, he was abroad at the time of the decision. A man cannot be everywhere at once: omnicompetent, yes, but not omnipresent. If I were as busy as Donovan, I too might well overlook such things as tenancy selections, or simply find myself unable to devote myself to them, however much I might wish to.

So I took no pleasure in the news of Donovan's collapse. I did not rub my hands in glee at his misfortune or count my lucky stars. No, I thought of him with fondness and was anxious about his health. I was also, well, intrigued. The boundary line between my sympathy and my curiosity was, it must be said, a little indistinct.

But when nine o'clock came around and the telephone began ringing and my colleagues started arriving, my thoughts soon turned to other things. A terrible pile of papers awaited my attention and my agenda was awash with appointments, the conferences, meetings and deadlines flowing in waves of bright manuscript across the pages. My secretary, June, notes down my engagements in my diary using an ingenious scheme of red, green and turquoise inks which I have never been able to understand. Her method is so painstaking, though, that I do not have the heart to tell her this. Anyway, I am sure that my diary is a lot more agreeable than it would otherwise be and I am grateful to June for the trouble she goes to. Without her I would be lost, because I can, sometimes, be something of a dreamy, head-in-the-clouds type of man. I have been known to moon away an afternoon revolving in my chair, mulling over nothing in particular, listening to the traffic below my window, the relaxing grumble of engines and the sounds of the klaxons (once I spent a whole afternoon classifying these as toots, beeps, blasts and honks – the toots outnumbered the beeps, but only just).

Other times I take a ladder to my mind's attic to take a look for anything interesting. I climb up there and rummage around old trunks filled with all kinds of bric-à-brac: I never know for sure what will turn up. For better or worse my head is full of trivia, odds and sods that bear on nothing – the cost of wholly insignificant meals, the names of plumbers no longer in business, the lyrics of bad songs, examination questions on Roman law that I never answered, telephone numbers of women I shall never see again. Some people can simply discard these things like leaky old armchairs or out-of-date suits. Not me. When it comes to the past, I am a real hoarder, salting away every moment I can, even those possessed of only the minutest value, their historicity – the banal fact that they have occurred and will never recur. The difficulty with this is that things stick indiscriminately in my mind; that important things are apt to be lost amongst bagatelles.

All of this does not mean that I am sentimental or prone to nostalgia. On the contrary. I have no wish, on the whole, to turn the clock back, nor do I entertain any notion of the good old days. As far as I am concerned, what is done is done. Admittedly, like everyone else, I do sometimes enjoy reliving certain moments. Sometimes, in a kind of reverse déjà vu, I find in myself the exact feelings and sensations that coursed through me at a particular time, so that for a minute I am, my lurching heart and tingling nerves registering a physiological journey, utterly transported: but that is all.

If my mind is a store-room full of junk, Donovan's was something altogether different. Unlike me, who can barely remember the name of a single case, Donovan's brain housed a huge repository of legal authorities which he could instantly cite; it brimmed like a grain-bin with sweet precedents and nuggets of jurisprudence. He had a party trick where, if you quoted a case to him, he would rattle off the ratio of the decision, the year, the judges and barristers involved and even, if the case was remotely near his field, the page where it appeared in the reports. Everyone used to look on open-mouthed. No one could understand how he managed it. I know that science has uncovered some mnemonic freaks, like the Russian reporter who, with only three minutes' study, could learn a matrix of something like 50 digits perfectly and years later could still churn out the matrix without error. This man could memorize anything you threw at him: poems in foreign languages, scientific formulae, anything. It made no difference whether the material was presented to him orally or visually or whether he had to speak or write the answers. His trick, I read somewhere, was to associate images with whatever it was he was trying to remember – in the way that you might, in trying to remember a shopping list, visualize a pig in a tree so that you do not forget to buy pork. Donovan's memory was not, I think, quite as phenomenal as the Russian's; but where he left the Russian behind was in the use to which he put his memory, the way he subjugated it for his own purposes. Donovan always had his facts carefully marshalled, he never allowed what he knew to get in the way of his thinking. The Russian, by contrast, found that his memory subjugated *him*; his mental imagery was so vivid that it fouled up his comprehension, so that the meaning of a sentence like 'I am going to buy pork' would be lost in a surreal collision of pigs and trees.

What I want to know is this: how is it that, with all his powers of recollection, Donovan could not put a name to my face at the party? I will go further: how is it that he could not even put a face to my face, that he failed even to realize that he *should* have known my name? The man was a walking reference library. Surely he could have accommodated me in his mind's chambers? Surely, at the very least, he could have offered me a tenancy in his remembrances?

Three weeks after I had read about Donovan's collapse I was drinking vodka and tomato juice at the Middle Temple bar. I am not a regular there by any means, but if I drop in I can usually find someone to talk to; if not, I am happy to crunch a packet or two of dry roasted peanuts and read the newspaper.

On this occasion I was leafing through the sports pages when I recognized Oliver Owen sitting by himself on the sofa next to mine, looking incongruously splendid on the faded, bashed cushions. It was the first time I had seen him in years. His washed straw hair arced from his forehead in two gorgeous fountains; his parting cut purposefully through his hair, clean as a road in a cornfield, as though it led to some significant destination. Oliver was wearing a charcoal double-breasted suit that had visibly been tailored to accord with his specific instructions. Golden nodules linked the cuffs of his dry-cleaned white shirt and a handkerchief spilled emerald carefully from his breast. I searched my mind for the word that best described him and came up with it – dashing, Oliver looked dashing.

Like me, Oliver was reading a newspaper. I wanted to speak to him. We had been good friends for a couple of years after we had met in pupillage, and it was only circumstances, and not our volition, which had prevented us from seeing each other since then. Even now, I felt, our friendship was not over but merely dormant.

But I stayed where I was; something in me, some ridiculous internal prohibition, prevented me from leaning over and greeting him like the old friend he was. He's probably got an appointment, I thought, he has the air of someone waiting for another; and did he want to speak to me anyway? Why should he, after all this time? What would we have to say to each other?

'James?'

'Oliver,' I said, putting down my reading. I was delighted.

'Why don't you come sit over here?' Oliver invited. 'My God, it's been years. How are you?'

I told him how I was (fine) and asked if he wanted a drink. I went up to the bar and showed Joe two fingers. 'Two large bloody marys please, Joe.' While Joe mixed the drinks I unintentionally caught sight of myself in the mirror behind the bar. I say unintentionally because, for my peace of mind, I do not look into mirrors unless I have to. Comparing my image with Oliver's eye-catching reflection, I was reminded that I am a man of almost transparent appearance, a man whose presence you would not quickly register in a public place, and in the mirror my face was struggling to make an impact between the brightly labelled bottles of Cinzano and Smirnoff and Gordon's gin and Glenfiddich. My pointy and virtually hairless head poked out anonymously, my eyes, nose and mouth small and mistakable. My most distinctive feature, if I am truthful with myself, is a strange one: there is an uncanny symmetry between the tramlines on my forehead and the parallel lines made by my chins on my neck, with the net result that the top half of my head is just about duplicated in the bottom. You could turn a sketch of my head upside down and not notice the difference.

The drinks arrived and Oliver joined me at the counter as I spooned chunks of ice into the drinks. 'So,' he said, taking the glass I handed him, 'what are we up to these days? Still with, er . . . ?'

'Batstone Buckley Williams,' I said. 'Yes. How about you? How's 6 Essex?'

'Awful,' he said. 'I'm spending far too much time in bloody Hong Kong and Malaysia. I hardly have a moment on home turf any more.' We paused and drank from our glasses. Oliver looked at us in the mirror. The contrast was embarrassing. 'You're looking well, James,' he said with a smile. He patted my lumpish stomach. 'But what's all this? What happened to that sheer wall of rock? Turn round, let's have a look: dear me, it looks to me like there's been some kind of landslide.'

I pulled my waistcoat down over the bulge and shrugged. 'You're looking well too,' I said.

'Who, me?' Oliver inspected his image in disbelief. 'I've aged, James, aged. Look at me, I'm a wreck. It's marriage, it wears you down. You married?'

'No,' I said.

'Two kids, house in Putney,' Oliver said with intentional banality. 'Yes, you've guessed it: dog, school fees coming up. After a while, the statistics start to catch up with you. Amazing how it just happens, isn't it?'

For a moment I feared the talk would turn in detail to the question of educating the children, a subject I am rarely anxious to pursue. It was time to change the direction of the conversation. Happily, something came to mind.

'What's all this I read about Michael collapsing? Is he all right?'

Oliver laughed. 'Collapse? Where did you read that? Collapse isn't how I would describe it.'

'Oh?'

'Do you want to know what really happened? It's not a bad story, I suppose.' Oliver paused as he shaped the anecdote in his mind. He was still a gregarious man, a natural for company. 'OK, here it is. Michael's in big trouble. For twelve days he has to listen to Laurence Bowen putting the European Commission's dreary little case that we're not complying with their regulations about the ozone layer. Can you think of anything more boring than refrigerators and their relationship with the stratosphere? No, neither can I. Day after day, detail after boring bloody detail. Each day, each minute even, is a struggle with sleep, with madness.' Oliver swallowed some more bloody mary, pleased with his phraseology. 'Anyway, by the time it's poor old Michael's turn to say something, his case is about as intact as the ozone layer. Those points made by Bowen have been eating away at his ground like bloody CFCs. In short,' Oliver summarized, 'the UK's in big, big shit. We need a bloody miracle. The only consolation for the government is that if anyone can do it, it's Michael. All eyes turn to him as he stands up. What's he going to say? everybody's asking. How's he going to play it?' Oliver stopped. He saw my expression and grinned.

'And?' I said eagerly. 'Go on.'

'Only if you get me another,' Oliver said. 'Same again please.'

Smiling, I ordered two more of the same. Oliver had not changed.

'Go on,' I said, when I got back. 'Get on with it. Michael stands up to reply: what does he say?'

Oliver grinned again. 'Nothing.'

'Nothing?'

'Not a squeak. All they get is a leaden, ungolden silence. He moves his lips and waggles his tongue but not a word comes out. Not a syllable. He's speechless, he's mouthing like a bloody goldfish.'

'You're joking,' I said encouragingly. 'You're pulling my leg.'

Oliver laughed. 'James, I swear to God, it's like something out of Harold Pinter. Michael's just standing there shuffling his papers, completely dumbstruck.'

I shook my head. 'Michael? Lost for words? I don't believe it.'

'He's not lost for words,' Oliver corrected me, 'he's lost for a voice. You can imagine it: the judges are looking at each other, baffled as hell. They've never seen anything like it in their bloody lives. "Professor Donovan, is there anything the matter?" Donovan points at his throat. "Usher, fetch the professor a glass of water." Enter water bearer. Donovan drinks. He opens his mouth to speak: still nothing. My God, you can imagine the embarrassment all round.'

'What happened?'

'Well, they adjourned of course. Sent everybody home. What else could they do?'

'Well, how strange,' I said. 'What an odd thing to happen. It sounds quite serious, actually. What was it, do we know? You don't just conk out for no reason.'

Oliver saw some blemish in the sheen of his left shoe and awkwardly rubbed the toecap on his trousers. You could tell that he was right-footed. 'James, sometimes I despair at your naïvety,' he said with an exaggerated casualness. He looked up from his shining feet and gazed straight into my eyes, without expression.

I gasped. 'You don't mean . . . Are you saying that Michael . . . ?'

Oliver leaned forward to murmur. 'I'm not saying anything, James, I'm saying nothing at all. But let me put it this way: the government is not exactly prejudiced by the adjournment, is it? All that extra time to reconsider the points against it? Handy, I'd call it.'

This was typical Oliver, scurrilous, slanderous and entertaining.

'That I don't believe,' I said. 'Michael would never stoop to such a thing.'

Oliver leaned his back against the bar, looking to see who was around. He raised his faint eyebrows at a passing friend and turned his face towards me once more. 'You believe what you want to, James.' Then a thought seemed to strike him. 'How about another?' He gestured at Joe.

'I mean, what's he been like since he got back?' I asked.

'Well, he came back to chambers straight away and sat down to work as though nothing had happened. This is about three weeks ago. The only problem was, he found that he couldn't write either. As a counsel, he was completely kaput.'

'Couldn't write as well as couldn't speak?'

'James, you've hit the nail on the head.' Oliver patted me on the back by way of congratulation.

'Well, what did he do?'

'Not much. He just sat at his desk, hunched over his papers, good for nothing – he wasn't even able to answer the phone. Completely incommunicado. After a day or two he went home, presumably to look for his tongue.'

'So he wasn't faking it, after all?'

'I never said he was. But before you make up your mind, don't forget it would have looked rather odd if it had been business as usual as soon as he got back, wouldn't it?'

I said, 'So you think it's all an act, do you? You think Michael's having everyone on?'

'James, whatever gave you that idea?'

'Well, I don't agree. It all sounds incredibly far-fetched to me. If anyone found out, he would be disbarred. Besides,' I said, 'it's not his style. It's not like him at all.'

Oliver made a tolerant face. 'With respect, James, how well do you know Michael? When was the last time you spoke to him, or saw him in court? Things have moved on since you were his pupil.'

Reddening, I said, 'Michael would not have done such a thing. He's got too much intellectual integrity – he has standards.' I put my lips to my glass to drink and then stopped to speak. I was whispering, in case anyone overheard the content of the conversation. 'With his brains he doesn't need to resort to that kind of trick. Michael? Going through a charade like that? Are you mad? We're talking about one of the best lawyers in the world, for heaven's sake, not some under-prepared hack.'

Oliver laughed loudly, as if I had said something funny.

'What is it,' I said, beginning to laugh myself. 'What have I said?'

'Nothing, James, nothing,' Oliver said, still tittering.

I smiled. I still could not see what was laughable. 'So what's the situation now?' I said.

'Funnily enough, he came back to chambers today, singing like a nightingale.' Oliver read the time on the clock. It was half-past seven. 'On the subject of birds, I've got to go back to my cage, before I get into big trouble. James,' he said, reaching for my hand, 'we've got to do this again.' With that he swallowed what remained of his drink, thudded his glass against the surface of the bar, winked, and strode off with his bouncing, light-filled head of hair.

Outside it was drizzling. I decided that the best thing to do about food was to go to eat a quarter-pounder and fries at the McDonald's in the Strand, near Charing Cross. I tramped up Middle Temple Lane and past 6 Essex Court, my hands in my pockets. There was Oliver's name, about half-way up the tenants' blackboard. I walked on. There was no need for me to look. I knew that blackboard by heart, especially those names daubed on it after I had left the chambers: David Burles, Neil Johnson, John Tolley, Robert Bright, Alastair Ross-Russell, Paul St John Mackintosh and Michael Diss glowed in my head in big mental capitals like the neon names of the theatre stars illuminating the Strand on my walk to McDonald's. There was a time when I would have wondered why I, James Jones, went incognito while these people, on the whole no more able than I, enjoyed this billing – but those sentiments were far behind me, and in any case I was relishing the meal ahead. When it comes to food I am not very choosy. I rarely cook – unless you count heating up tinfuls of mushroom soup or making salami and tomato sandwiches as culinary activities. Usually I dine at some cheap eatery or takeaway, not because I cannot afford anything better, but because I feel a little self-conscious, sitting in a good restaurant by myself, under the scrutiny of the waiters. Other nights I ring up for a curry or pizza to be delivered at my door: I eat with a tray on my lap and the television remote control by my side, and sometimes finish off a bottle of wine opened the previous night. My diet, then, basically revolves around cheeseburgers, shish kebabs, fried chicken, vinegared fish and chips, spring rolls, jacket potatoes and fillets o'fish.

A friend of mine of around this time, a girl called Susan Northey, used to lecture me on the deficiencies of my eating habits, drawing particular attention to the amount of saturated fats I consumed. According to her – and she was armed with all sorts of figures to support her case – I was on the way to a massive heart attack. Occasionally Susan would cook for me, but her efforts rarely met with success. The idea of preparing my food depressed her, especially if I arrived at her flat slightly late.

This happened the night after I had spoken to Oliver. It was a Friday night, and after we had finished eating she started crying.

'Why am I doing this? I feel like a housewife. Jimmy, look at you, you've come in and sat down and wolfed your plate clean without a word.'

I stared guiltily at my plate. 'Here, I'll do the washing up. Leave that to me,' I said.

'I've got a migraine, my head feels as though someone's split it open with an axe.' Then she suddenly snapped. 'Don't touch those dishes, I'll do them tomorrow.'

I said, 'No, let me . . . ' but Susan angrily barred my way to the sink, so I retreated. I said, 'That was delicious, Suzy, thank you very much.'

'It was terrible, it made me feel sick.'

'Perhaps it did need a little more olive oil . . . '

'I don't believe what I am hearing: I cook you dinner and all you can do is criticize?' She was furious. 'Why don't you cook, if you're so good at it?'

'I wasn't criticizing, Suzy, I was just trying to be constructive. That was delicious, my love, I swear it.'

'Don't lie to me, Jimmy, I can't stand it. It was terrible, and you know it. You just ate it because you're a pig. You'll eat anything you find in your trough.'

At this point I should have kept quiet. 'Well, all right then, I've tasted better tuna salads,' I conceded. 'But there's no need to get so worried about it, it's only a meal. Let's put it behind us, shall we? I'll do the cooking in the future, all right? It obviously upsets you if you do it. Suzy?'

Susan was not speaking. She pulled on yellow rubber washing-up gloves and began brushing down the knives and forks that sprouted from her foaming left hand. I made a noise of protest but stopped when I saw her expression. Then I said something but received no reply. She just continued scrubbing down plates. I sighed: I hate scenes.

I decided to give it time and to wait quietly on the sofa. Hopefully things would blow over. Just as the programme on television caught my attention and I began concentrating on it, Susan spoke again. She said things were not working out and that perhaps it would be best if I went. I reflected for a minute and found that I agreed with her. There was little point in prolonging the evening. I collected my things and quietly left. I suppose that you could say that we broke up at that point. I walked to the tube station feeling – wonderful. Coasting along the buoyant pavements with a warm city breeze in my face and a navy blue, starred sky overhead, I felt I was being returned home on a yacht. I was breathing in and breathing out, and it elated me. It is a simple thing, my elation, but then again, is not quite as straightforwardly obtainable as it might sound. My life is so shot through with distractions, so plagued with interferences, that only rarely am I conscious of something as simple as the action of my lungs, of the fact that I, James Jones, am here, kicking around on this amazing planet. By avoiding the mazes of family life and the side-tracks of ambition, I have tried to take an undeflected, eventless route through the days, to dodge the clutter of incidents that bear down on me from every direction. There is only so much I like to have on my plate – too much at once, and everything begins to lose its flavour. When it comes to personal experiences, I prefer to eat like a bird.

It will be appreciated that, by my standards, this last year has been a complete blowout. On top of my usual diet of occurrences I have been forced to feed on the jumbled broth of Donovan, his father, Arabella, her lawyers, Susan and all their unpalatable, over-rich problems. It must be understood that I am not regurgitating all of these matters to indulge myself. It is not as if I am suffering from some kind of empirical bulimia. Despite the fact that, like most people, I enjoy the odd trip down memory lane, I am not one of these people obsessed with bygone days, those who compulsively inhabit the past as though somehow it housed the real world, as though newly minted, uncirculated days rolled around at a dime a dozen. No, you would not catch me relegating the solid, wonderful here-and-now in favour of the olden times. The only reason that I am chewing over these last months is that I want them digested and over and done with, because at the moment they continue to spoil my stomach for everyday things. The office seems drab and unreal, and still I am numb and listless and fatigued. So much so that June is beginning to show signs of impatience, and rightly so. She has enough to do without worrying about me.

'Come on now,' she says. 'Stop moping.'

'I'm not moping. I'm thinking.'

'Well then, stop thinking then,' she says. June will take no nonsense. 'Start working instead. I'm getting a little tired of fielding these complaining phone calls.'

'Who's been complaining?'

'Mr Lexden-Page for one. He's rung three times this morning already.'

I groan, but this news does nothing to invigorate me. I take up my scissors and start snipping the thin air again. June thinks of saying something sharp but decides against it. Instead she emits a scolding humph! and struts back to her desk and clamorous telephone. But her disapproval has no effect on me. The fact is, my energies only return when I go back to these last months and, specifically, to the moment when Michael Donovan re-entered my life for real, in the flesh.

28

On Friday night, then, Susan and I split up. The following Tuesday (4 October), I returned to the office from the kiosk where I buy the prawn and mayonnaise sandwiches I eat for lunch. On my desk June had left a list of telephone callers: Mr Lexden-Page, Miss Simona Sideri, Mr Donovan, Mr Lexden-Page again, and Mr Philip Warnett. Systematically I returned the calls (I derive a satisfaction from ticking these things off) until I reached the name Mr Donovan. Irritatingly, there was no message beside the name, only a telephone number.

'June,' I called over to her, 'what did Mr Donovan want, do you remember?'

'I don't know,' her voice came back. June sits out of my sight in an antechamber annexed to my office. From where I sit I can just hear the tip-tapping sound she makes on the computer keyboard and, if it is quiet, the small din of her teaspoon whirling sugar in her drink. 'He just asked if you would call him back.'

Usually in such a case, when I have no idea who the caller is or what he or she wants, I leave the ball in the caller's court and wait for a second communication. That day, however, I was anxious to get as much done as possible and scrupulously I dialled the number June had written on the scratch-pad. My call belled three or four times, then I heard the click of an ansaphone whirring into action. A throaty and charming voice, a woman's voice, said, *I'm afraid no one is in at the moment, but if you would like to leave a message, please speak after the tone. Bye!*

I dislike these gadgets and leaving the frozen little communiqués they demand. I spoke stiffly into the mouthpiece. 'Yes, this is James Jones of Batstone Buckley Williams. I am returning Mr Donovan's call. Kindly contact me' – I hesitated and, acutely aware of the irrevocable recording of my every silence, stumbled out an inelegant, incoherent finish – 'if you wish to, to avail yourself of my, my firm's services or otherwise.'

After that misadventure my face and torso felt hot, and I walked over to the kettle to make myself a coffee for which I had no thirst to take my mind off the incident. As I waited for the water to boil, my telephone sounded.

'I have a Mr Donovan for you.'

I groaned to myself. He must have been using his answering machine to filter his incoming calls.

The voice said, 'James, it's me, Michael.'

Michael? 'Ah yes, how are you?' I said. Michael who? I thought.

'James, I need your services. You do family law, don't you? Matrimonial? You know your way about it?'

'Yes, I . . .'

'Good,' he said, 'then you're just the man I need. When can we meet? Thursday – does Thursday suit you? Could you squeeze me in at, say, three o'clock?'

I was in danger of being steamrollered into an appointment with a stranger who claimed to know me. Then it clicked: that self-assured, irresistible tone? Surely not . . .

My tongue stumbling in my mouth, I said, 'Excuse me, but I wonder if I might set something straight in my mind: I'm speaking to Michael Donovan of 6 Essex Court, aren't I? It's just that I have a bad line and I can't hear you very well.'

'The very same. Sorry, I should have explained; you've probably forgotten me after all these years.'

I laughed nervously. 'No, no, no, it's just that the line is poor . . . Now then,' I said, changing the subject quickly, 'Thursday you said? Let me just check. Yes, that would be fine.' What was I saying? Thursday was not fine at all, the page in my diary was turquoise with meetings. Thursday was terrible. 'Three o'clock? Yes, I can manage that. No problem at all.'

Donovan said, 'Excellent. See you the day after tomorrow, then.'

The harsh tone of the disconnected line droned in my ear. Michael Donovan! Michael Donovan had telephoned me!

My head suddenly weightless, I went to make myself that coffee, this time because I felt like drinking it. Back in my revolving chair with a hot mug warming my fingers, I spun round towards the window. I put my feet up on the window-sill, my toes in line with the rooftops across the road. I basked. So Michael had not forgotten me, after all. He knew that I was right here, at Batstone Buckley Williams. Joyously I swung my feet off the sill and walked over to the basin to rinse the coffee stains out of my mug. Of all the solicitors available to him, Donovan had turned to me. So, I had impressed him with my work. My long hours of painful, unpaid, meticulous research had made their mark, the mole had finally received his dues. Donovan remembered me, even after all these years, as someone he could trust; someone he could count on.

'June,' I said brightly, 'please arrange Thursday to accommodate a three o'clock visit from Mr Donovan.'

'What about Mr Lexden-Page? You know how he is.'

'Mr Lexden-Page, June, can be rescheduled.' Lexden-Page had tripped over a protruding paving-stone and was pursuing the responsible local authority in negligence for (a) damages for pain and suffering in respect of his small toe, and (b) the cost of an extra shoeshine arising from the slight scuff his shoe had received. Lexden-Page could wait.

I returned to my desk and rested the back of my head on the pillow my hands made. What could Donovan want? I asked myself. Then I thought about something completely different, if at all.

The morning of that Thursday saw me relaxed and confident. I wore an attractive blue shirt and my best pure wool suit.

Although my desk was an iron one and my carpet was worn down by the chair-legs, it struck me that my office was not unprestigious. It was spacious and it enjoyed a fine view. Looking around it with a freshened eye, I felt a little pang of pride: there were more inconsequential stations in life than the one I occupied. With this office and with customers like Donovan, you had to admit that I was not doing that badly.

But I grew jumpy as three o'clock drew nearer and nearer. Drinking coffee after coffee, I watched the office clock show fifteen-hundred, then fifteen-ten, then fifteen-twenty-five. When, at a quarter to four, I returned from a visit to the lavatory, there it was, Donovan's silhouette against the window.

'Hallo,' Donovan said, standing up with a smile. 'Sorry I'm late. I want you to have a look at this.' He reached into a slim briefcase and handed me a sheaf of papers. 'It came two weeks ago.' Then he sat down.

I moved into the room. It was as though the last decade had never happened.

I read what he had given me. It was a Petition for divorce. The Petitioner was Arabella Donovan.

'I see,' I said.

I leafed through the documents for a second time. The marriage had broken down irretrievably, alleged Mrs Donovan. The Respondent, Donovan, had behaved in such a way that the Petitioner could not reasonably be expected to live with him.

'Yes,' I said.

Then I suggested a cup of coffee and picked up the telephone to speak to June. I could easily have simply raised my voice for some, but that would have been undecorous. 'Do you still take it black, no sugar?' I asked.

'That's right,' Donovan said, with a note of something – admiration, I think – in his voice.

June came in with a steaming tray and a splashy, red-mouthed smile. June is a tall black girl who used to long-jump for England when she was eighteen, and when she enters a room with her long, spectacular legs she tends to bring things to a standstill. While she poured the coffee, I took another look at Donovan, who was patiently waiting for his cup to fill. He was sitting with his legs crossed. His green eyes, and the skin around them, appeared rested, and his black, thick hair was positively glossy. His unexceptional, off-the-peg suit hung well on his large frame. What really caught my eye, though, were his hands, folded in his lap. They were in perfect condition. They were like the hands that hold the cigarette packets in the advertisements, manicured yet manly, good hands, hands you felt like shaking – the hands of an airline pilot or a surgeon, someone you could trust with your life.

How well he looked, I thought. And then it came back to me. His calmness. I had forgotten that Donovan was, above all, calm. And it was the best kind of calmness, profound and reassuring – it was a tranquillity, a serenity. Don't worry, it communicated, everything is in hand. Everything is going according to plan. It also said, implicitly, leave everything to me; leave everything to me and everything will turn out well. It was this stillness that gave Donovan his authority, that subtly turned his suggestions into commands. Even then, as I watched him waiting for his coffee cup to fill, I felt the impulse to yield, to drop the reins.

When June had gone Donovan retrieved the papers from me and pointed to a passage in one of the pages. 'I'm not experienced in this area, so I'm curious to know how often you come across these kinds of allegations.' He was referring to the section in the Petition headed *Particulars*. Here Donovan's culpable behaviour was particularized and broken down into sub-paragraphs (a), (b) and (c).

I was nervous. I said, 'I must say, they are not commonplace. But I would not say that they were unusual, either.'

Donovan smiled at me and stood up. He began walking unhurriedly around the room. Hallo, I thought. He never used to pace around. Or did he?

He spoke gently. 'I intend to contest this petition.' He paused, indicating the arrival of a different point. 'In my view there are good prospects of defeating it. My wife will not be able to substantiate her allegations, which in any case are unspecific, arguably to an unacceptable degree.' He looked at me over his shoulder with his green eyes and resumed his pacing. 'I think you will agree that the tone and content of the pleading are unconvincing.'

I broke a silence. 'Yes,' I said.

He continued slowly striding, and for the first time I noticed the inefficiency of his physical movements. He was not clumsy (this would have not been surprising, given that he was a biggish man), he was simply uneconomical with the way he transported himself. He took irregular steps across the room, he swung his arms by his sides with no particular co-ordination.

I cleared my throat. 'I don't have to tell you what my standard advice to clients is in this situation. Contesting a divorce is an expensive and usually fruitless business. We must try and settle this thing as quietly as possible. The last thing we want is a courtroom confrontation.'

Donovan smiled. 'Yes, I'm aware of the standard advice.' He picked up his coffee from my desk and regained his seat. Would it not have been simpler for him to sit down first and then pick up his coffee?

The conference, meanwhile, was becoming untidy. It had an unsatisfactory shapelessness about it. We were making confused advances. It was time to get systematically to grips with the issues, the nitty-gritty. I wanted to go back to what Donovan called the standard procedure in meetings of this kind. There were things I needed to know. I needed to know the history: what had prompted Mrs Donovan's departure from the family home? How much, if any, truth was there in what she alleged? Were there any incidents which his wife might seek to rely on? What were the main obstacles to reconciliation? Was Mrs Donovan in employment? If so, how much did she earn? I needed to know about the financial arrangements of the parties, about the prospects of reconciliation. I needed to know the facts, all of them, and set them out in a row so that I could understand them. Divorce is an extremely complex area, factually.

So I said, 'Michael, before we go any further there are certain things you need to tell me about Mrs Donovan – about your wife – so that I am able to advise you properly.' I took out a pen and a fresh pad and wrote *Donovan v. Donovan* on the cover. 'Now, firstly, where is your wife at the moment?'

'At her mother's house. James, I would love to go into the details but I'm afraid that I've got to rush in a minute or two.' He looked at his watch. 'Perhaps we could arrange another con – I'll get Rodney to ring. In the meantime, I wonder if you could serve this on my wife.' Donovan dipped into his briefcase and brandished some documents. 'It's an Answer to the Petition. I've left it in general terms for the time being – simply denying her allegations, not making any counter-allegations of my own. There's no point in restricting our options by pointing any fingers right now.'

I read the Answer. It was exactly what was needed, and I opened my mouth to say so.

'As regards reconciliation or settlement,' Donovan said, 'I think it would be wise to shy away for a while. My wife is not, I should imagine, in a particularly constructive mood at the moment. I think a low-key approach is called for, at least for the time being. Let them make the running. What I have in mind is this: we are more than willing to talk, but only with a view to reconciliation. Certainly, I will not contemplate settlement on the basis of consenting to the divorce. Apart from that, we play it by ear. Take no initiatives unless instructed.' Donovan opened his case, replaced some documents, and shut the lid with a dull slam of leather. 'There's nothing else, is there?'

'No,' I said, standing up, thinking, Yes there is, there's a lot else.

'Good. James, you've been very helpful.' Donovan began putting on his coat and scarf.

Feeling that a little bit of small talk might be appropriate at this juncture, I asked, 'How are you feeling? I hear you've been unwell recently.'

'Have I?' He buttoned his navy blue coat. 'Oh, yes – that. Yes, I'm a lot better now, thank you, how about you?'

'Fine, fine. Couldn't be better.'

'Just look at that rain,' Donovan said.

When Donovan left I walked over to the window and watched him hail a taxi. It was four o'clock and already the headlamps shone from the cars. The sky was brown, the rain brilliant under the street lights and, suddenly, everything had become palpable and atmospheric. This was the thing about Donovan – a brightness followed him around, a clarity, it was as if the man moved with Klieg lights tracked down on him . . .

Arabella Donovan was a nice name. Arabella Donovan, I said to myself; it was almost a supernatural name, you could call a spangled mermaid Arabella Donovan. That peachy voice on Donovan's answering machine, that must have been Arabella's voice. I went back to my desk and looked at her photocopied signature on the Petition. It looked a functional signature to me. The letters were printed clearly and regularly. There was no indulgence about the signature, no squiggles or sequins. It was a little disappointing. It seemed a waste of such a nice name. June – June would have done the name justice with her turquoise ink and her fancy, wavy manuscript.

How on earth had Donovan allowed Arabella to slip through his fingers? And what had made Arabella leave someone as eligible as Donovan? What had happened?

I turned once more to the salient points of the Petition. Paragraph 1 said that the Donovans had married on 5 July 1981. Paragraph 4 said that there were no children born to the Petitioner during the said marriage or at any time. Paragraph 6 revealed that the Petitioner had quit the marital home on 14 July 1988, and at Paragraph 8 it was alleged that Donovan had behaved in such a way that Arabella could not reasonably be expected to live with him. Then I looked again at the Particulars of this allegation.

The Respondent has throughout the marriage treated the Petitioner cruelly and/or unreasonably by inter alia

(a) persistently degrading the Petitioner by his conduct so as to make her feel worthless and/or by

(b) injuriously neglecting the Petitioner by according unreasonable priority to other matters inter alia his occupation and/or by taking no or no sufficient interest in the Petitioner's welfare and/or by

(c) persistently maintaining prolonged and unreasonable absences from the marital home.

I had my doubts about the logic of the pleading and the vague language it employed, but I could guess at the gist of Arabella's complaint. Donovan, she said, was a cruel and neglectful husband. That was what it boiled down to.

I regained my seat. On balance, Donovan was right to feel he had a case. The pleadings did not specify the form of the degradation from which Arabella was supposed to have suffered, nor (apart from the matter of the excessive hours he put into his work) were examples given of any maltreatment. Allowing for the customary emotive exaggeration of Petitions, no tangible or damaging misconduct was immediately revealed. There was no suggestion of infidelity or physical violence or of something you could get your hands on, like alcohol or drug abuse, and there was generally an unconvincing amount of huffing and puffing in the pleading; in general, the tactic is to make your case as precise, and therefore as strong, as possible, thereby strengthening your hand for out-of-court negotiations. In this case, the only thing revealed was that Donovan had devoted too much time to his work, hardly the most malevolent of transgressions.

But that was where my understanding screeched to a halt. I rely on information, not intuition. Ferreting out facts from clients, a matter of technique and persistence, I am usually good at. Dates, events, examples, these are things I happily manage. In this case, however, I hardly knew any facts at all. Donovan had disallowed my interrogations, and I was forced to fall back on guesswork: and when it came to sensing the unsaid, to divining what lay beneath the surface, I was weak. I am not, it must be said, greatly interested by those parts of a personality known as the depths. I am happy to take people at face value, with the result that sensitivity to concealed thoughts and emotions is not my strong point. I am a magpie in this respect, drawn towards trinkets and sparklers – more attracted to a person's superficies, with its gaudy bijouterie of individual traits, than to his or her 'deeper' self. Underneath the make-up and knick-knacks, I must confess, I tend to find people wearisome and monotonous, burdened as they are with the same luggage of troubles. And as a solicitor, of course, faced as I am every day with personal problems, I must keep a certain distance. It would not do to become involved.

Going back to that rainy, brown-skied dusk, I stood up and switched on another light to combat the entering darkness. Doubts began to beset me. My situation was not ideal. Donovan was a personal acquaintance and this might cloud my judgment and hamper my conduct of the case. Should I not advise him to seek another solicitor? Moreover, things were rolling along just fine at work. I was busy but not too busy. Donovan would be a demanding client, and the time I would spend thinking about the case would not, I knew, be translated into efficient profits. Was it necessary for me to involve myself?

Of course, even as I asked myself these questions I knew that there was no question about it. It is ridiculous, I know, and shameful, but I was flattered by his attentions. His proximity elevated and enlivened me. This was, of course, a weakness on my part – but what can I say? Faced with Donovan, my normal instincts went haywire. Like one of those Turkish beach turtles that mistake the glow of cafeterias for the luminous sea, I was completely disoriented by him.

FIVE

After that, I did not see Donovan for a while. He was back at work. This meant it was just about impossible to contact him, which was inconvenient for me. I had Arabella's solicitor, a rather abrupt man from the firm of Duggan & Turnbull called Philip Hughes, breathing down my neck. He had rung several times to make tentative approaches, and each time, in accordance with my instructions, I refused his advances. He was becoming impatient. On 31 October 1988, he telephoned me again.

'Mr Hughes, as I've said, I'm afraid I am unable to discuss any questions of settlement. I have had no instructions in that connection from Mr Donovan.'

'Well, I suggest you get some instructions,' Hughes said. 'Pick up the phone and get some instructions.'

'I can't do that, I'm afraid. Mr Donovan is abroad at the moment and I have no way of getting in touch with him. He's a very busy man,' I said. 'He travels all the time. He could be anywhere.'

Philip Hughes sounded exasperated. 'Frankly, I don't care if he's in Timbuctoo. Just leave him a message. Tell him,' he said in different tone of voice, 'I have a proposition that may interest him.'

I said nothing.

Philip Hughes said carefully, 'Why don't I just tell you what we have in mind? What could be lost by that?'

'I doubt very much that any proposition for settlement

would interest Mr Donovan if it involved him accepting the dissolution of his marriage.'

'You're certain about that?'

'Mr Donovan does not believe that his marriage has irretrievably broken down. He thinks that his marriage could be saved.'

Philip Hughes changed the tone of his voice again. This time he spoke in a man-to-man, off-the-record, you-know-it-makes-sense tone of voice. 'Mr Jones,' he said. 'Look. Let's be sensible. There is no way – and, let me be absolutely clear, by that I mean *no way* – that Mrs Donovan will go back to Mr Donovan. Frankly, she's had enough. As far as she is concerned, her marriage is dead and buried. She never wants to lay eyes on her husband again. That is a fact that won't go away. I know it, now you know it.' Philip Hughes drew breath. 'The point is, I would also like Mr Donovan to know it. I want you to make it plain to him that there will be no second bite of the cherry. Frankly, it's *finito la musica*. It's over between him and his wife.'

I could see how Hughes was thinking: I've got Donovan all worked out, he was saying to himself. At the moment he's having difficulty in accepting what is happening to him. He's denying reality, and that's understandable, even inevitable – after all, he's a human being, it's a normal reaction to a major blow. But, Hughes was thinking, Donovan's also a lawyer. He's a reasonable man. Once the truth – that Arabella was gone for ever – sinks in, he'll quickly see that further resistance would be irrational, that at best it would achieve nothing but a painful and expensive delay of the inevitable. Once he realizes he's surrounded, he'll strike a bargain and come out with his hands up in the air. The key, Hughes was saying to himself, was to get Donovan to appreciate one thing – Arabella wasn't coming back.

'Mr Hughes,' I said, 'I will tell him that as soon as I am able to. I must say, however, that I have my doubts about whether that will change anything. Mr Donovan's views are very firmly held.'

'Well, yes, they would be, wouldn't they?' Philip Hughes said slyly.

I told him that I would do what I could, and we hung up. Then I did what I could: I rang up Donovan's chambers and left a message with Rodney, his clerk, to telephone me. Trying to contact Donovan directly would almost certainly be futile: I was not exaggerating when I told Hughes that Donovan was a busy man, and hard to track down. For a start, Donovan did not put any time aside for time off. While his colleagues, even the busiest amongst them, were indulging in hours of leisure, Donovan was pushing himself to the limits of his energies. One minute he was in The Hague, appearing at the Peace Palace, the next he was in the Gulf, arbitrating a dispute. Then, before you could blink, he was on his way to a conference on the Law of the Sea in Stockholm to deliver a lecture on the problems of delimiting fishing zones along indented coastlines. He was an adviser to United Nations legal committees on the pacification of space and the resolution of border disputes. He was always working. Any moment to spare – say he had been delayed at an airport, or a free evening had accidentally fallen his way – was not spent catching his breath or kicking his heels: he would use the time to update his textbook (*International Law*), which was famously the most lucid and original work of its kind, or to write an article or case commentary. His academic activities did not end there: let us not forget, he had to squeeze the obligations of his professorship into his schedule. Like an opera star he was booked up for years at a time. So getting in touch with Donovan was not just a question of picking up the phone and asking for an extension number. You had to plan in advance, you had to be patient.

And you had to be important. The other thing to bear in mind, before you asked Donovan to drop what he was doing and listen to what you had to tell him, was that your message had better be urgent. I did not think that what Hughes had to say was significant enough for me to bother Donovan with it. His minutes were like rubies, they were so precious, and misappropriating his time, or wastefully burning up his golden joules of energy, almost amounted to a species of theft. Sometimes, when I spoke to him, I felt dizzy at the thought that the time he was consecrating to me he could otherwise charge out at a rate of thousands of dollars an hour – sometimes, in my excitement and immaturity, I would feel strangely *enriched*, as if his gratis words represented some kind of windfall.

So I left a message for Donovan with Rodney.

Four days later, on the Friday, I received a reply. The telephone rang in the office and the voice of Rodney was put through to me.

'Hallo, sir.' Rodney still called me sir – it was a throwback to the days when I was a pupil barrister in his chambers, and the ironic deference he had shown me then. 'How are you? I've got a message for you from Mr Donovan.'

'Yes?'

Rodney hesitated. 'He says you're to meet him at his house tomorrow night. He says it's to do with some private litigation he's engaged in that you will be familiar with.'

I could not believe my ears. 'Rodney, did I hear you correctly? He wants to confer with me at his house? On a Saturday?'

Rodney did not say anything.

I felt like saying, Rodney, I know that Mr Donovan is a busy man, but I'm afraid some alternative appointment will have to be made. I mean, it is most unsatisfactory, meeting a client at his house, and at such short notice, and at the weekend to boot. It's just not on, I felt like saying.

I said, 'That's not particularly convenient, I'm afraid.'

Rodney still said nothing. He just cleared his throat.

'Look in your diary,' I said, 'there must be another date. There must be some way to accommodate both of us.'

'You see, that's just it, sir. Mr Donovan flies back from Strasbourg tomorrow and leaves for Geneva first thing Sunday morning. Saturday night is the only time he is able to put aside.'

'How long is he staying in Geneva?'

'He's down for two weeks, sir. Solid.'

'You see, at the moment,' I said, hoping my annoyance would tell in my voice, 'I'm otherwise engaged.' I hesitated. 'If it is really urgent, Mr Donovan could always telephone me.'

Rodney coughed. 'Mr Donovan has authorized me to say that he is prepared to pay double the ordinary fee, sir. For your trouble, sir.'

'I see.' Now it was my time, not Donovan's, that carried a price-tag. I had no idea what could be so important – *Donovan v. Donovan* had not even been listed for trial yet – but it was clear that, for whatever reason, he badly wanted to see me. I forced a laugh. 'I'm afraid I am not open to financial inducements, Rodney, however tempting. You see, it's not a matter of money, it's just that I am doing something else.'

He coughed again, and then he said, 'Treble, sir?'

'Treble? Treble what?'

'Your ordinary fee, sir.'

I was – yes, thrilled: I, James Jones, in such demand! Whereas a minute or so previously I had sat perched forward, put out by Donovan's summons, now I leaned back luxuriously, kicking off my desk to send my chair into 360° twirls. When I saw June walking in, I mimed drinking and stirring – the signal for my sweet cup of tea – and she smiled and nodded. She could tell I was in a good mood. 'Rodney,' I said, 'the importance attached by Mr Donovan to the proposed appointment is becoming clearer to me.'

'Oh yes, sir,' Rodney said. 'It's extremely important. Mr Donovan asked me to stress that. It's extremely important, sir.'

June came back with my tea. I gave her a thumbs up and dipped my mouth to taste the drink. Then I gave her another thumbs up. 'Rodney, if that is the case, if you really are in a fix, then it may be that I am able to accommodate you.' I pretended to look in my appointment book and made doubtful, muttering noises. 'Yes . . . I see . . . Mmmm . . . Well, I will have to make some phone calls, of course. And a lot will depend on my being able to extricate myself from my previous engagements: you appreciate that.' This was untrue – I was only due to see Susan for a casual reunion for old times' sake, and she would understand. 'But in principle, I should be able to attend.'

'Thank you sir,' Rodney said smoothly. 'Mr Donovan said any time in the evening would be convenient.'

I said authoritatively, 'I think eight o'clock would suit me.'

It was all arranged. I left a message with Susan's office and when, Saturday having wheeled around, the time came to drive over, I found myself speeding in my anticipation. I slowed down and breathed deeply. There was no need for nerves or for haste. I had plenty of time, and I did not want to arrive early and over-eager. The address Rodney had given me was 54 Colford Square, in Notting Hill, not too far from where I live, south of the river, in Stockwell. I calculated that if I took my time, I would pull up in front of the house at about eight-fifteen. That was about right. Although I wanted to keep Donovan waiting, I did not want to be too late, either. I had to strike a balance.

Colford Square is a grand, stylish square where imposing and beautiful Edwardian houses surround a sizeable island of parkland. One hot afternoon in the leafy spring (months after the cold November night I am about to describe), I found myself in the vicinity of Colford Square. It was midday, I was emerging from a hard morning in court, and I felt like some peace and quiet. I decided to take shelter on the grassy island. What I had in mind was half an hour lying on the hot grass in my shirt sleeves, eyes closed, breathing in the scents of flowers, hearing the gentle clacks and slaps of croquet mallets for a change, instead of traffic. But I could not get in. I walked twice around the perimeter but could not find an entrance; the wrought-iron gates were locked and the tall and ornamented railings barred any other entry. It was mysterious, because I could hear voices in the glades and thought I saw some movement inside, the flash of white shirts between the gaps in the trees. I was standing around tiredly in the sunlight, trying to think of what to do next, when a friendly man came up to me. He told me, with a smile, as if it were good news, that I could not enter.

'You have to have a key,' he said.

'A key?'

He nodded sympathetically. Maybe he was locked out, too, I thought.

'How do I get one?' I asked. The man shook his head. His mouth had the shape of an apology about it.

'You have to be a resident of the square,' he said sadly.

'I see.' I felt a little scruffy in my rolled-up, unironed shirt. I wished the sticky jacket of my light-grey suit was not bunched up in my fist. 'Are you sure?' I asked. 'You're sure that there's no access for a member of the public?' The man nodded. He was sure. 'I see,' I said again. 'You live here, do you?'

He gave his head another regretful shake. 'I'm afraid so,' he said. Then he touched his trousers around the pockets, patting for something. 'I'd let you in if I could, but I don't seem to have my key on me. Only so much a man can carry around. Still, never mind,' he said. 'There are much nicer places to go to. It's just a boring old garden really.' Then he stood there in a friendly kind of way, in the way of someone passing the time of day. I was on the point of speaking – of saying, By the way, my name is James, James Jones – when I realized that he was waiting for me to move on. Which I did, of course. I slung my jacket over my shoulder and walked off into the fuming streets.

That is what Colford Square is like. It is an exclusive place, and people like Donovan, not like me, live there. The residents of Colford Square matter, their actions ripple with consequences. I sensed it straight away as soon as I rolled up that Saturday night in November, at ten past eight, five minutes ahead of schedule. I always arrive ahead of schedule. At parties, for example, I am always the first to show, despite the fact that I find the jangling, ice-breaking atmosphere a real trial; the full bowls of cashews, the conversant hosts, the lucid thickets of glasses waiting in the kitchen. But it is stronger than me. I dread being late or untimely, it makes me physically unwell, and the appointed hour tugs at me with the force of a huge magnetic horseshoe.

I decided to park further round the block and wait for a few minutes where I could not be seen from the house. I reversed into a space, creaked the handbrake on, switched off the lights and waited. It was cold, the rain was rivering down the windscreen. I checked the appearance of my face in the rearview mirror – pasty, freshly shaven – and sat still.

My shoulder muscles were like rocks and my stomach fluttered with pains – I had to smile at myself, I was exhibiting precisely the symptoms of some adolescent on a hot date. My psychological ploy was rebounding on me: I was the one on tenterhooks, not Donovan. He was probably relaxing in front of the fire right now, sipping a whisky and water. Why did I not just step out of the car and go? Instead of putting myself through this torment?

Still, now that I had taken this course I had to see it through. I switched on the radio. A financial analyst was making exotic predictions about March gold and April nickel, and, not having any money in futures, I reached over and tried to find another station.

Unexpectedly I tuned into a pop song. The reception was pure and stereophonic and, ridiculously, the music went straight to my head. Maybe the surroundings – glamorous doorways, high windows burning in tall white houses – played a part, I do not know, but suddenly I was intoxicated, light-headed, as if I had inhaled my first cigarette in years. I began daydreaming. I saw the running windscreen as a cinema screen and my looming face in close-up upon it: there I was, the cool, brooding hero poised for significant, resonant action, the cheekbones twenty feet across, the eyes purposeful blue slants; that song on the radio, that was my theme song, my soundtrack. I turned up the collar of my raincoat and started smoking a cigarette. I turned the volume dial so that the sound pumped and flooded out of the loudspeakers, the music slowly contacting my prickling skin like water entering a wetsuit. It was amazing! There I was, a man of thirty-three, buzzing and aswarm with adolescent fantasies! Somehow the song, which was utterly unconnected with my situation, was imbued with mysterious poignancy and meaning. Somehow the lyrics, about a jilted, disbelieving lover, hit the spot exactly. Although I have never experienced romantic rejection, I sympathized with the singer, I knew what he was going through when he sang *Tell me that it isn't true*. For a moment I, too, had been thrown over, I ached with loss too. What sensitized me to the singer's predicament, of course, was not his song, which was nothing special. It was Donovan, waiting for me only half a block away. His proximity opened me up like a house visited for the first time in years; inside me doors flew open, inside me rooms lit up.

I switched off the radio and stepped out into the rain.

I doubled over and began sprinting along the street, occasionally flashing a look at the numbers on the houses to keep track of where I was. I tried, where I could, to run below arches and overhanging branches, and to sidestep the pools rising before my eyes in the hollows of the street – but it was no good. I was drenched before I had gone a hundred yards. I should never have parked the car so far away from the house, I thought furiously. I should have brought an umbrella. Now the evening was ruined – I would show up at the doorstep like a drowned rat, my shoes filled with water, my hair in strands, a mess. Damn, damn, damn.

The countdown of houses seemed interminable: 74, 72, 70, it seemed to go on for ever, and with every panting step I took what felt like a fresh litre of water went straight through the fabric of my coat. Finally, my side racked by a stitch, rivulets running down the gully of my back, I reached number 54. I ducked up the steps and ran straight into a man.

'Rodney,' I gasped. I straightened my back, combed my fingers back through my thin hair and stamped my feet on the ground. I was breathing heavily and needed a moment to gather myself. Only then did the obvious question occur to me. 'Rodney? What are you doing here?'

Rodney did not look happy. He was hunched under the doorway, hands in pockets and a red fog on his cheeks. It was clear that he had been standing outside for some time. 'Mr Donovan told me to meet you here. He can't meet you himself.' I stared at him. 'He asked me to give you this.' Rodney passed me an envelope. I accepted it in a daze.

'Where is he? Why can't he make it?'

'He was called away urgently, sir. To Geneva. He flew in this morning from Strasbourg and just had time to nip into chambers before going back out.'

'Called away?' I began to splutter. Why hadn't I been told earlier? I had come all this way in the pouring rain – look at me, I gestured to Rodney, I'm soaked to the skin – and he could not make it?

Rodney looked at his toes. He was not to blame. It was not his fault, he was simply following instructions. Poor devil, I thought, spending his Saturday night on a cold doorstep. Where was it he lived – Bromley? That was miles away, a forty-five minute drive minimum – more, in these conditions. I sighed. 'How long have you been here?'

'Not long. Since just before eight.' It was now coming up to half-past eight.

I sighed again. 'Well, we'd better have a look in here.' I opened the envelope, and read:

James, you will find the key to the house in a cavity in the 4th railing down on the right. Could you go into the house and check if there are any letters/messages from/re my wife? Phone me in Geneva if you think it's necessary. M.D.

I was numb. I disbelieved my eyes: no, this could not be happening, this was impossible. Sacrificing my Saturday night for this errand, this schoolboy's chore. Silently I handed the note to Rodney. He read and nodded at the same time, as if he was in complete agreement with what was written. After he had returned the paper to me neither of us said anything for a while – what could we have said? Then Rodney spoke up.

'I'm off then,' he said evenly. I looked at him. He had a stoical expression on his face; quite possibly he was not unused to this kind of thing. 'Good-night sir.'

'Good-night,' I wished him. He ran down the steps into the downpour and jumped into his car. As he played with his ignition key and started the engine I remembered the key to Donovan's front door, hidden in the railing. At that moment I felt like throwing the key into the Thames. My evening, my precious Saturday evening, was ruined! (What I now want to know is, why did Donovan call the meeting in the first place? Could it be – I know this speculation is a little harsh – that he never intended to show up at all?) I decided on another, more realistic, course of action. I would cut my losses. I would go inside and dry myself out. I would help myself to a whisky and make some telephone calls. Maybe Susan would still be able to come out.

I knelt to look for the key. The nerves in my fingertips were not functioning properly in the cold. I blew warm breath into my fist, rubbed my hands together and tried again. This time I sensed my fingernail knocking into something. I withdrew my hand and extracted a light bunch of keys from their hideout.

SIX

I made the mistake, when I unlocked Donovan's front door and stepped through into the house, of shutting the door behind me, with the result that I straightaway stood in utter darkness. I could not see a thing – not even my hand, raised an inch from my face. Edging forward, I felt my shoes kicking against something: mail; envelopes. Running my fingertips along the wall, my arms outstretched like a somnambulist's, I groped for a light switch. Then, when the hallway lit up, the first thing I did was neglect to examine the post, which lay in a brown and white pile at the foot of the door. Instead, I headed for the drawing-room door. Donovan could forget about his post; me, I had only one thing in mind: his drinks, where did he keep his drinks?

Before I go any further, I want to make it clear that I am not a snooper, or a Nosy Parker. I mind my own business and keep out of other people's affairs. It must be said that this is not a matter of ethics, or of principle, although maybe these things play a part; the simple fact is, other people's private goings-on do not interest me; what I do not need to know, I do not want to know. For example: I never once read the diary of my brother Charlie, with whom I shared a room in my childhood, although night after night he left it on his desk with its pages open and his innermost thoughts and his darkest secrets before my eyes. Never once was I even tempted to sneak a look. Indeed, if my brother had offered to read out a passage I would have told him to stop, or blocked my ears. As far as I am concerned, people can keep what they do behind doors to themselves. I am not one to spy through the keyhole.

I think it is clear from what I have said that the last thing anyone could call me is a busybody. I never secretly steam open envelopes to read their contents, or press a glass to the wall to eavesdrop on conversations in adjoining rooms. My life is complicated enough as it is. I am at pains to say this because, contrary to my usual habits, I spent the evening in Donovan's house reading his private notes, notes he had written for his eyes only, and listening to tape-recordings he had made for his ears only.

I could not help it. I was looking for something to drink when I came across a pile of sky-blue notebooks, tall rectangular ones of the type preferred by barristers. What had happened was that I had found no liquor downstairs, not a drop. When I opened the door to the drawing-room I received a shock. The furniture was spookily draped in white sheets, to protect it from dust I presume, and phantomish sofas and armchairs hovered in the half-darkness. I quickly pressed the light switch and four or five lamps scattered around the room illuminated simultaneously. It was a little startling, but looking around I spotted a drinks cabinet and took heart. As I walked across my footsteps clopped like hooves on the long floorboards: the rugs had been removed too, it seemed, and stored away somewhere. Anyway, the drinks cabinet proved a dead end. The only liquid I found was a neglected inch of pale sherry in one of the crystal decanters. I did not feel like drinking sherry, I wanted something a little stronger, like a glass of whisky with rocks of ice in it. So I went to the kitchen to have a look there, but again, no whisky, no ice-cubes, no anything for that matter. The multi-storey refrigerator, installed with racks, trays and receptacles for every kind of foodstuff, was bare and greasy: a dried-out half of an onion, a tub of margarine flecked with Marmite. Elsewhere, a stack of delicately interdependent washing-up – spoons, cereal bowls, coffee cups – was poised in the sink. A nasty smell arose from somewhere. No one had been around for weeks, that much was clear.

I decided to try my luck upstairs. By this time my craving was more than a simple thirst for alcohol, it was a profound, irrational need for some consolation before I went back home, some compensation for my spoiled evening. For some reason I had taken it into my head that the outing had to have some tangible benefit, and that the benefit should take the form of a drink (this was, I hasten to say, not like me at all – normally I can take or leave alcohol as I please). So I continued my search. It was impossible that there was no whisky, or gin, or cognac, anywhere in this huge house. But the first floor seemed dry as well, with dust coating everything, and walking through the abandoned, creaking hallways, I felt I was treading the sidewalk of one of those corny ghost towns you see in Westerns, the ones with tumbleweed rolling down the main street.

But then I opened the door on a room where the atmosphere was different. If every ghost town has its stubborn old-timer who refuses to leave, who sits tight with his mule in an old shack on the mountainside, certain that the geologists are wrong, that a bonanza waits in the rock, then this room was that shack. It showed clear signs of life. Books were opened and marked with yellow tabs, newspapers lay crinkled on the floor, and a shallow pile of sky-blue notebooks sat up on the desk. Clearly this was Donovan's study. Periodicals and law reports lined the walls: the *Common Market Law Reports*, *Weekly Law Reports*, *Recueil de la Jurisprudence de la Cour*, *Cambridge Law Journal* and so forth. Then I spied it. In the corner, alongside an overflowing waste-paper basket, was a bottle of Bushmills. I congratulated myself: I knew it. I knew I'd find something if I kept looking.

I found a glass in the bathroom and poured myself a double shot. It was nine o'clock, and although the cloudburst seemed over, rain continued to fall, making a racket on a plastic surface somewhere. There was no point in rushing back home, not in that weather. I leaned back in Donovan's functional chair and drank deeply. That's better, I thought, as the liquor made a hot path through my insides. That's more like it.

It was about then, after the first, satisfying mouthful, that my eyes focused on the notebooks. There were about four or five of them in a stack. My thoughts elsewhere, I took one down and fluttered the pages with my thumb. I was not trying to read anything, I was simply fidgeting with the first thing that came to hand. Whenever I make myself comfortable with a drink, I compulsively reach out to manipulate the nearest object I can get hold of – a newspaper, or the channel controller for the television. That night at Donovan's was no different. The notebook that I picked up – well, to my mind it was no different to a magazine you instinctively pick up at the barber's or the dentist's. How was I to know what it contained?

Although I was not concentrating, although the pages moved under my thumb in a blur, I did notice that there was something unusual about them. There was an inordinate number of lists, and I thought I saw entire sentences, whole paragraphs even, written down in capital letters. Then there was the question of the handwriting. I knew Donovan's handwriting, a scribble in biro that only became legible with practice – how many tens of thousands of his words had I read in my time? – I knew his every quirk in that department. The script that I saw in these pages was similar to his but nevertheless different; the words were too legible, the lettering too neat and tidy. The script, in the blue-black ink of a fountain pen, belonged to someone taking care about presentation, someone making a calligraphical effort. That was not like Donovan; the Donovan I knew was a scrawler.

All in all, then, the autography on the pages I saw did not strike me as his, nor did their contents appear to square with what one might expect to see in an international lawyer's notes. There was something different here, something unusual. I decided to take a closer look.

The first page of the top notebook had a date written at the top right corner: 23 September 1988. (Leafing through the pages, I realized that the entries in the book were chronological – and that the books themselves were piled in calendrical sequence.) And then came the strange part: a row of squares was drawn along the top half of the page; below that row was a row of triangles, and below both of these was a further row of triangles placed on top of squares: they looked like children's drawings of detached houses, only without the little windows and front door you normally see. Now, in most circumstances diagrams like these would fall into the category of mere doodles; but here the drawings were so systematically and carefully arranged that I received the clear impression that they represented something else – an exercise of some kind.

Why would Donovan want to practise drawing these kindergarten houses – if that was what they were?

I turned the page. More diagrams, this time slightly more complex: a series of polygons rolled down the page, each with more sides than the last. At the top was a pentagon, below that a hexagon, and so forth.

I did not even try to understand that. When it comes to spatial or mathematical IQ tests, to detecting the common feature in a series of numbers or shapes, I always emerge with a dunce's score. I am lost when faced with this sort of problem, my brain runs on to the rocks. So instead of foundering on these mysteries, I poured myself another drink and turned the page.

Page three of Donovan's notebook was dated 24 September 1988. A row of words descended the page:

A
aardvark
aardwolf
Aaronic

aasvogel
abaca
abba

I could see straight away that this was an alphabetical list. What was unclear to me was the language – was it English, or maybe Dutch, or was it a mixture of several languages? And again, I was baffled – what on earth was Donovan up to? Why was his handwriting so fastidious, like a schoolchild's aiming for a gold star? The next page, the fourth, made things even less clear. It was dated 25 September and all it said was *See Tape 1*.

Tape? What tape? I searched around me, lifting the scattering of papers and pamphlets. Then, in a drawer of the desk, I found a dictaphone, and next to the dictaphone, in a purpose-made rack, three small cassettes. Quickly I extracted Tape 1 (its number was marked on it in red felt-tip), slotted it into the dictaphone and pushed the play button. Then I pressed the dictaphone against my ear.

The tape went through some preliminary crackles and I heard the recording mechanism coming on. I was tense with expectation – what was I about to hear? What revelation was at hand? – when a cough sounded in my ear, and then another cough. I did not immediately recognize these noises for what they were (the recording was unclear, there was a certain amount of acoustic distortion) and just as I said to myself, someone's coughing, a voice started speaking.

What it said threw me completely. I had to rewind and replay to make sure that what I thought I had heard was right.

Second time around there was no doubt about it. The voice said, flatly and distinctly, *ducatoon, exert, fletch, ocean, tectiform, virtuose*.

I stopped the tape and closed my eyes. I tried to think. Although it was difficult to be certain, that sounded like Donovan. I had used dictaphones before, and knew they had a neutralizing effect on voices. But what made me hesitate was the tonelessness, the dullness of delivery. The words were devoid of any inflexion whatsoever, which was not like Donovan, who spoke with emphasis and vigour. The slow, deliberate voice on tape could have belonged to a teacher of English as a foreign language.

I opened my eyes and took a deep breath. It was gone half-past nine, time to be making for home. The rain had stopped, too, although I could still hear water guttering somewhere. The sensible thing would be to drive back now. I felt tired, around my eyes especially. There was no way that I could read all of these notebooks, or listen to all of these tapes, now, in a single evening. And yet there was also no way that even I, with my aversion for puzzles, dramas and the private lives of others, could leave matters as they were, up in the air.

I turned the tape back on. I'll give it five minutes, I determined, no more. Five minutes, and then I'll be off.

The tape scratched, indicating a pause in recording, and then restarted.

A box of mixed biscuits, a mixed biscuit-box, Donovan said twice. Then he said, *Red lorry, yellow lorry, red lorry, yellow lorry, red lorry, yellow lorry* at rapid speed, without hesitation or slip-up.

Tongue-twisters! He was rattling off tongue-twisters!

The sixth sheikh's sixth sheep's sick, Donovan said clearly. *The sixth sheikh's sixth sheep's sick*. He paused. *She sells seashells on the seashore, but the seashells that she sells are not seashells I'm sure.*

Donovan, the voice on the tape, started laughing. He laughed for about three seconds, then abruptly stopped the recording, cutting himself off in mid-cackle. I did not get it. What was so funny? I asked myself. Where was the meaning in any of this?

How was I to know then that, in all probability, Donovan was not drunk, or out of his mind, but simply happy? That he was laughing from simple joy? Like I have said, when it comes to cryptic clues, to inklings, I am a numbskull at the best of times. I need data, lots of data, and I need a systematic overview – my mind is not designed to take short cuts or frog-leaps. Step by step, that is how I like it, one thing at a time, *a*

57

and then *b* followed by *c*. Of course I should have worked out what was going on in no time at all, I do not dispute that. I should have cracked the problem right away. But that is not my method, and besides, I was exhausted and nervous; I felt ill at ease in that house, doing what I was doing – I felt like a trespasser. It was cold and dark, my clothes were still damp, and the sound of Donovan's voice echoing in the silence made me jumpy. The dripwater was no help either, tapping and ticking on the window-pane like drumming fingers. I started hearing noises – slamming car doors and scratching sounds like the sounds of door locks turning. What would I say if Donovan came in now?

Suddenly I became overcome with guilt. What did I think I was I doing, poking and peeping around Donovan's private belongings? Had I gone mad? Feeling slightly sick, I covered my tracks as best I could, watering the Bushmills in the bottle and putting the tapes back in their rack. All I wanted to do was leave, quickly. When I had finished, I stood still for a moment and made myself think: was there anything else? Had I forgotten anything? No, but I did need to visit the lavatory, badly.

The lavatory was large and comfortable, with a mahogany seat and an interesting variety of illustrated magazines within easy reach; some embroidered prayers were pinned to the wall. As there are few things more tranquillizing and inducive of meditation than an easeful spell in a soundproof cubicle, I found their presence entirely congruous. I sat down with a sigh of relief and rose five minutes later feeling infinitely better – freer, less oppressed. I helped myself to a generous portion of paper and it was not until I tugged the chain that things began to go wrong: a feeble dribble of water flushed down, barely enough to soak the paper I had used. I pulled up my trousers, fastened my belt and waited for a few moments for the tank to replenish itself. There was no need to panic, a second flush would do the trick. But when I pulled the chain the gushing cataract I was hoping for did not arrive: in its place came an ineffectual trickle which made no impact whatsoever on the brown and white mound in the pool at the bottom of the basin.

The water: Donovan had switched off the water supply before he left.

This was a disaster. I had to do something, or Donovan would come home to a pile of faeces, my faeces. I ran down the stairs to the basement in a sweat. A switch, or a tap, there had to be one somewhere. Walking down a steep and rickety wooden staircase, I came into a room like a refinery, full of gurgling boilers, tanks and mechanisms. As there was not the slightest prospect of pinpointing the water tap, I activated the likeliest looking appliances that I could see. Then I ran back up the stairs.

Nothing. Not the smallest percolation. Oh no, I thought. Oh no. I picked up the toilet brush and tried forcing the material under water, down along the curved swan-neck of the bowl and out of sight. This met with only partial success: parts of the excrement disintegrated and floated back up to freckle the surface. Now the water had an unmistakable brown colour. There was only one thing for it.

The scoop was in a broom cupboard downstairs. It took me half an hour to pour the lavatory's soiled contents into a bucket, and then to pour the contents of the bucket out of a window into the garden. The paper I put into a plastic bag which I planned to dump in the first wastebin I saw on the way home. It was a horrible, dirty job, but it was almost wholly effective. Someone had taken the precaution of stocking the lavatory with a whole range of odorizers, and aerosol cans with redolent names waited on a pine shelf: *Fragrances of the Forest*, *Alpine Breeze*, *Meadow Sweet*. I sprayed a fresh aroma into the air and wiped the seat clean. With luck, Donovan would not notice a thing. Then I went back down to the cellar and moved the levers back to their original positions. I washed my hands in a drop of tapwater and in my relief poured myself a final whisky for the road.

A burning down-in-one later, I made for the front door. The mail, I thought. I had almost forgotten all about it. I bent down on a knee and rummaged around. There was nothing of interest as far as I could see. Recent portions of law reports, letters from the bank, unexciting brown envelopes and junk mail. Nothing from Arabella or her solicitors. Then, straightening up, it occurred to me that I should check the ansaphone. Perhaps the solicitors, or Arabella herself, had left a message for Donovan there. Donovan would want me to satisfy myself on that score, I reasoned.

There was only one message, spoken in a mild Irish accent. 'Michael, this is your old man. Son, I'm coming to London on the 6th of November. That's a Sunday. I'm just over to do one or two things. I'll be staying at the Savoy for a week or two. Could you give me a ring as soon as you can? Bye, son. Thanks.'

The 6th. That was tomorrow. It looked like Donovan Sr was out of luck, because his son would not be back for weeks. He sounded friendly enough, I thought, as I walked to the door. Then I thought that it was a funny thing, Donovan having a father. This was a silly thing to think, I know, but Donovan was not a man you associated with mundanities; the idea of him as his father's son had never occurred to me. In the way that you never see a movie star straining on the lavatory, there were certain human functions which seemed to pass Donovan by, at least in my observation. He defied, as far as I was able to tell, the forces of gravity that anchor the rest of us down to earth, the downward tug of the kids, the dishes, the emotions. Donovan was up there in the atmosphere, in that azure above the weather zone, occasionally touching down to resolve the frictions of nations. It seemed almost unnatural, unwholesome even, for a man like that, an astral sailor, to be earthbound by something as prosaic as a father.

I did not ponder it any further. All I wanted was to go, to leave the whole evening far behind me. I replaced the key inside the railing and in my urgency began jogging along the dark and wet street towards my car – when it struck me that all those whiskies had put me over the limit. I would have to take a taxi. There was no question of a man of my position, a lawyer with a reputation to protect, being convicted for drink driving; and besides, the minimum disqualification period of one year deterred me in any event. The car I could come back for tomorrow.

SEVEN

It is a Sunday morning. I am sitting in a chair in my back garden, watching the insects clocking in and clocking out on the flowers, envying those bees their job sites. Although I am no gardener, I take pleasure in this little patch of nature that is mine. My predecessor took great pains to introduce to the soil a varied and durable flora, and he conveniently inserted small plastic identification-tabs next to the shrubs he planted. That is how I know, for example, that over there that is a forsythia which blooms in those yellows. Without those tabs I would not know what was growing in those beds. Behind the forsythia, at the back of my garden, is a crumbling brick wall which separates my property from the neighbours'. Wild and acrobatic cats, real down-and-outs with chewed-up, clawed-at fur, are always running along the wall, looking for trouble, trapezing over fences erected in their paths or rolling up into orange balls for a snooze.

Taking my cue from those tomcats, I close my eyes for a moment. The sun heats my ears. Somewhere a dog barks, somewhere else someone is hammering at wood, sinking the nails with sharp reports until they disappear. Blat, blat. Blat, blat. There is, I realize with surprise, a cacophony in the air. The tweetering of urban birds in the skimpy trees and on the rooftops, the conversation of a gang of churchgoers, the sounds of water falling down a drainpipe, a hullabaloo of sirens from the direction of the tower blocks, the yelps of children, another dog barking and, now, Edith Piaf resounding from an open window.

This morning I envy goldfishes too. Living in the pure present, swishing and circling around their bowls, each minute a brand-new world. I am tempted, in this untutored early spring warmth, to forget all about this Donovan business. To close my eyes on the past. To wake up, to live in the here and now. That is, after all, where I used to live. Susan remarked upon it once. We were walking from her flat to the tube together one morning. We walked side by side, holding our briefcases. We overtook a couple in their mid-twenties on their way to work. They had reached the crossroads at the end of the street and their paths were about to diverge – he was going right, she left – and they were kissing. It was an old-fashioned spectacle; he held her in his arms and she was on tip-toes, her mouth turned upwards and expectant. I had seen these two together before and knew they could not walk down the street without continuously hugging, squeezing and making eyes at each other. It was the man, in fact, who made the nuzzling, pawing advances; the woman made little attempts to take avoiding action, wiggling and ducking until, delightedly, she allowed herself to be snared and kissed. She would then push him away and then, after a few paces, the whole thing would start again. According to Susan, this was how they were every day, first thing in the morning. Anyway, that particular morning we saw them break from each other at the crossroads and head off in opposite directions along the avenue. Susan and I were on the other side of the road, but we could clearly see the two of them. With every five steps they took they turned round, cocked their heads and sent each other a little wave of the hand. Maybe this set Susan thinking, because she frowned and said, 'Jimmy, you know, I think we live in different . . . ' She paused, struggling with her words. 'I think we're not living at the same time as each other. Do you know what I mean?'

I hesitated. I was not sure what she meant. 'Yes,' I said. I had to admit it, there were times when I did have the impression that we inhabited different time zones. Some-times, when we spoke and our words overlapped and interfered with each other, it was as though we were speaking on the telephone from different corners of the globe and were not where we were, in bed together in England. It felt as if it was morning where she lay and that I lay twelve hours away, in the middle of some intercontinental night. But I was not sure that this was what Susan meant.

'Where would you say you lived, Jimmy? In the past or the present or the future?'

We were walking past a newsagent's and we stopped while I bought a newspaper. Susan's question took me unawares. It was, I suspected, a very good question. It went straight to the heart of something – quite what, I was unsure, but it flew like an arrow. I paid the newspaper man his money.

'How do you mean?' I asked.

She was frowning. Like me, Susan is not blessed with particularly fetching looks. Her hair is shoulder-length and falls in mousy, lanky strands, like rain. Her ankles are on the thick side and although she is small, due to her slightly bulging physique she is not petite. Her best feature is her skin, and her eyes, too, are pleasantly bright when she removes her glasses.

'I live mainly in the future, but also in the past,' she said. 'I'm not like you. You're lucky, you just live from day to day – I bet you don't even know what you're doing tomorrow, do you?' She was right, I did not. I had no plans for the next day. 'I'm not very happy with things,' Susan said simply. 'That's why I have to look forwards and backwards to things.'

This was Susan all over. This was the sort of thing she always thought about. It put me under pressure, all this talk of happiness, all this analysis.

'Cheer up,' I said, and touched her shoulder. She was sad, and when we turned into the tube station she wordlessly boarded her packed train. I kept my eye on her in the carriage as the windows clouded up. She forced herself between pin-striped commuters, gripping a stainless steel bar an inch from her face. The train rolled off. She was on her way, heading for her office in Hounslow. She worked in the office equipment business. Her job was to follow up on the photocopiers and computer terminals and telephone systems that her company had sold, and to make sure that everything was to the clients' satisfaction. It did not sound like a very fulfilling job to me, especially for an intelligent person like Susan. How perceptive of her, for example, to note that she lived in the future! She was right, as well. She was continually preoccupied with upcoming events – 'It's my birthday four weeks on Tuesday,' she would announce. 'The bank holiday is sixteen days away. What are we going to do?' Or she would ask: 'This time next year: I wonder what I'll be doing this time next year? Or this time ten years from now?' Poor Susan, I thought, as I stepped on to my train. Poor thing, I thought. I found a seat, opened the newspaper and read about Donovan's collapse in court.

I would like, then, to put all thought of Donovan out of my mind, but I cannot, not even on a balmy morning like this one, full of easy distractions. So perhaps the best thing would be to take a robust, broad-brush approach to it all, so that I can be done with it, quickly and once and for all? Surely all I need do is state the main facts and draw the necessary conclusions? There is, after all, a limit to how many conclusions one can sensibly draw from events of this sort. And I know that I am no great analyst of human affairs, but is it really necessary, even for me, to go through all the facts at such length?

It is, of course. The truth is, I am miserably incapable of quickly picking out what matters, what is salient and what is not.

Enough asides and irrelevances; seated at my garden table in my dressing-gown, I return to the morning of another Sunday, the morning after my trespass in Donovan's house. I awoke like an adulterer, racked with guilt, and stepped straight into a powerful shower to cleanse myself. I dressed quickly and caught the tube to Notting Hill. By lunchtime I was back home with my newspaper and a creamy coffee, and everything was back in its place. Enough of Donovan, I thought. No more escapades.

On Monday morning, too, all I wanted was peace and quiet, a return to normality. The last thing I wanted was anything to do with Donovan.

'James, I have a Mr Donovan for you,' said June.

A surge of nausea passed through me. He knew. Donovan knew that I had been snooping around his house. Somehow he had found out.

'I'm not in,' I said. 'Tell him I'm out. Tell him I'm in a meeting.' I had to stall. One of the pieces of equipment the man carried around in his head was a polygraph – in cross-examination he registered lies and evasions instinctively, uncannily – and with my hopelessness at deceit, he would sniff the truth and the whole truth out of me in two seconds flat. It was imperative that I did not speak to him.

I listened to June decisively stalling Donovan. She has a natural talent for that type of task – speedy, unhesitating deception.

'What did he want?' I asked.

'He wants to have lunch with you. He left a number for you to ring at the Savoy.'

The Savoy?

'June, did Mr Donovan have an Irish accent?'

'More American, I thought. But yes, he did have a bit of a brogue too, come to think of it.'

I exhaled with relief: that was not Donovan, that was Donovan's father. Next question: what did he want?

'I want to talk to you about my son's divorce,' said Mr Donovan when he called back. 'There are one or two things I feel we ought to discuss.'

'Mr Donovan, you're aware that my relationship with Mr Donovan – your son, that is – is confidential. I'm not allowed to discuss what we have discussed together, if you understand me.'

'I know that. But let's put it this way: I've certain things to tell you, and all I'm asking is that you listen. Now, that's not unethical, is it? I won't be asking you to disclose anything you feel is between yourself and Michael.' I hesitated. 'Mr Jones,' said Mr Donovan, 'I would be very appreciative if you could come, because I know your time is scarce. But I really do think it would be in everybody's interest if we met. Do you have any problem with eating here? At my expense, of course.'

The Savoy is only a step or two down the Strand from where I work, so there was no difficulty in meeting Mr Donovan as arranged, at one o'clock. I walked in and looked around. He had told me to look out for an old man in a wine-coloured polo-neck shirt and a grey tweed jacket. That was what he looked like, he said.

I saw someone who matched the description reading a newspaper in an armchair. What made me sure it was Mr Donovan were the hands that gripped the pages: they were like the hands of his son.

He rose with a beam across his face. Fergus Donovan was about sixty-five years old, I guessed. He looked very fit and trim, and his skin was like a yachtsman's, darkened and flecked by the elements. His hair was white and distinguished, and his eyes were pale green, paler than his son's. He led me briskly to our table and immediately began cross-examining the waiter about various items; finally he ordered a pamplemousse followed by a baked potato and a salad of raw cauliflower, Californian lettuce and cucumbers, a meal not offered by the menu. He ordered further that olive oil and lemon juice be brought to the table with the salad so that he could concoct his own dressing. He drank Irish mineral water.

When the waiter had gone, Mr Donovan leaned towards me with twinkling eyes, as though he were about to tell a joke. 'Jim, I want to ask you a question. You don't mind, do you?'

I shook my head. June was right, there was a slight transatlantic inflexion to his speech. 'No, please do, Mr Donovan,' I said.

'Fergus – call me Fergus. Jim, how well do you know Michael?'

Not very well, I explained, and briefly went through the history of my relations with his son.

'And what do you make of him?'

'Well, he's a fine lawyer, of course,' I said. The question made me uncomfortable. 'He's a very gifted man.'

'What else?' Mr Donovan still wore his friendly, expectant smile. It was a grin, in fact.

'What else? Well – I mean, he's . . . he's a remarkable person,' I said. I could think of nothing else to say without becoming too personal.

'He's remarkable all right,' Mr Donovan said vehemently. 'He's a remarkable dope, that's what he is.'

Mr Donovan had a resonant voice, and his remark caused one or two heads to turn in our direction. Without changing the expression on my face I reprimanded myself. Stupid. I was stupid to accept this invitation. Look where it had got me, lunching with a crackpot.

'Yes, well . . . ' I said.

'You think I'm just a crazy old man. I know you do, I can tell by looking at your face.' I began to make a gesture of denial but Mr Donovan waved me down. 'But I've known Mikey longer than you have, and take it from me, he's a dope. When it comes to law, maybe not. But when it comes to life, he's got nothing but rocks in his head.' He unfolded his napkin carefully and placed it on his lap. Then he vigorously broke up his bun, making remarkably few crumbs, and buttered a piece. Chewing it, he said, 'Now I don't know much about anything.' He spoke with his mouth full, but in a strangely wholesome and appetizing way. I crumbled my bread and took up my napkin. 'I'm just a druggist. A quack. I'm full of bullshit, I know that. But that doesn't disqualify me from seeing what's in front of my nose. And you know what I see? Trouble. Trouble with a capital T.'

I said nothing to this, I just dabbed at my mouth with my napkin.

'You know why?' Mr Donovan said in that rhetorical, American way. 'You know why I see trouble? Because Michael is taking charge of the whole action. He's calling all the shots. And if I know my son, which I do, it'll be his foot he'll be shooting.' He paused in satisfaction. The waiter made a timely arrival and served the pamplemousse. I had not ordered a starter. I was watching my weight.

'You seem to have forgotten, Mr Donovan, that when it comes to legal matters, Michael is peerless. He's more than capable of looking after his own interests.'

Mr Donovan stopped segmenting his pamplemousse and stared at me in disbelief. 'You really think that?' he said. 'Is that really what you think?'

I smiled at Donovan's father. He obviously had no idea how skilful a lawyer his son was. 'Yes,' I said. 'And besides, I don't think it's quite right to say that Michael is calling all the shots, as you put it. I am there to advise him, and I can assure you that I am not without experience in the field of matrimonial law. There's really no need to worry, Mr Donovan,' I said.

'Jim, you'll forgive me if I say this,' Mr Donovan said, 'but you're exactly the push-over he said you were.'

'I'm sorry?'

'He's got you eating out of his hand,' Mr Donovan said excitedly, 'like this!' He demonstrated with a piece of his grapefruit, popping a piece into his mouth with his fingers. 'Look at you: you've allowed his big-shot reputation to intimidate you!'

I stiffened. There is a limit to how much abuse one can take.

Mr Donovan said, 'Don't get upset, Jim, I'm sorry I said that. I take that back.' He looked apologetic and pushed aside his fruit. 'I've got a big mouth,' he admitted. 'But it does strike me that you're allowing Michael to dictate to you what the plan of action is. How do I know? Because I've spoken to Michael. And you know what he says about you?'

Something rolled inside my belly. Across the table, Mr Donovan was scrutinizing my face. 'I'm not sure how that matters, Mr Donovan,' I said.

'He says you can be relied on to carry out his instructions.'

More food arrived. Mr Donovan decisively helped himself to a blade of butter and inserted it into the two steaming crevasses that criss-crossed his baked potato. He began tucking into his food, swallowing and chewing with great relish. His eating habits were strikingly neat and tidy, and he forked and knifed and manipulated his food with an infectious precision. He made his potato seem delicious.

'This may surprise you, Mr Donovan,' I said, in what I hoped was a cutting tone of voice, 'but the function of a solicitor is to carry out his client's instructions. Reliably. It is not my role to decide for Michael where his interests lie.'

'I haven't come here to knock reliability. It's a great quality to have, especially in a solicitor, Jim. But this situation calls for more than reliability. It calls for something extra – leadership.' Mr Donovan put down his cutlery. 'You see Jim, what Mikey knows about women you could write on a postage stamp. This divorce – it's not about law, it's about feelings, human feelings. Now Mikey doesn't have a clue about what to do with his feelings. He's always been that way, ever since he was a snot-nose. When it comes to emotions, I'm telling you he couldn't find his ass with two hands.'

Mr Donovan started eating again. 'A few days ago I spoke to Arabella's solicitors.' He noticed my interest and said, 'Yes, that's right, Jim, Arabella, my son's wife – soon to be my son's ex-wife unless you people – unless something is done. They told me that you are refusing to talk to them. Is that right?' He looked at me accusingly. 'You're not talking to them?'

'That's not quite accurate, Mr Donovan,' I said defensively. 'I have been in regular communication with Mrs Donovan's solicitors. Moreover – '

He interrupted me. 'Regular communication? Is that what you call it? You've been stonewalling every time her solicitor – what's his name, Hughes – speaks to you! What's going on, Jim? Maybe I'm stupid, Jim, maybe I'm just a dummy. That's a distinct possibility, I'll grant you that.' Mr Donovan made a gesture of concession with his hands. 'But as far as I can tell, if you were trying to smash the marriage for good, you couldn't be going about it a better way!'

Mr Donovan took a swallow of water and started speaking in a calmer voice. 'The thing is, Jim, that if Michael took some time to talk to Arabella, I'm sure this whole thing could be resolved. These silences must stop. We've got to start opening up the communication channels. Talking, I'm a great believer in talking.'

'Yes,' I said. Then, in my iciest voice, I explained that the only thing we refused to talk about with Philip Hughes was divorce. We were more than ready to talk about reconciliation.

Mr Donovan said, 'OK, but is that smart? Believe me, Jim, it's time to shake things up. This is serious. I promised myself I'd get over here and light a fire under your ass, so you'll forgive me if I've come across a little strong. But what you've got to realize, Jim, is that we can't leave this matter in my son's hands. He's bound to screw up, the headstrong gobshite.'

I made a discreet gesture of impatience with my eyes. The meeting was becoming most irregular.

Mr Donovan kept talking. 'What am I driving at? I'll tell you. Number one: be careful about following my son's instructions. Take them' – Mr Donovan searched around the table and then picked up the salt cellar – 'with a pinch of this stuff. Ask him what he wants. Watch him like a hawk, he's more deceptive than he looks. Number two: keep me informed about what's going on. Number three: stop the divorce. Whatever you do, Jim, stop the divorce. Whatever it takes, get Arabella back. That means start reconciliations. Now. Tell Mick to say he's sorry. Let's have none of this standing on his honour crap, tell him to go to her on bended knee. This is no time for pride or pettiness. Jim, I can't stress what a disaster it would be if she left my son. He would fall to pieces.'

I scratched my eyebrow sceptically. Number two, especially, was most unsatisfactory.

'Enough said about all of that,' Mr Donovan said. 'I'll leave you to think about it. You're smart, you'll make your own mind up about what I've just said.'

I said nothing. I did not want to give Mr Donovan the slightest sign of encouragement.

'I'll be here for some time yet,' Mr Donovan continued. 'If anything comes up, be sure to call me.' He chortled. 'Now, what about some dessert, Jim? That trout can't have filled you up. Mind you,' he said, eyeing me, 'by the looks of you you'd take some filling up.'

'No thank you, I'm fine,' I said coldly. If I were in better company I would certainly have considered a small pudding. Instead, I lit a cigarette.

'Exercise. I find exercise is the key to health. Look at me, I'm seventy-three years of age. Are you going to make it to seventy-three, Jim? Ask yourself that question. And if you're not going to make it to seventy-three, what are you going to make it to? Fifty-five? Sixty? Then ask yourself this question: how many years does that leave you with? Let's face it, it doesn't add up to a lot of time, does it Jim?' He eyeballed me again, up and down, as if I were a specimen of horseflesh. 'How old are you? Thirty-fivish? I'd say you're well past the half-way mark.'

My neck felt tight in my collar. 'That may well be so, Mr Donovan, but I cannot see how that has any bearing on your son's case.' I glanced ostentatiously at my wristwatch.

'Golf, Jim. You know what I do with my time? I play golf. Every free morning God gives me I'm up and going at those links. Do you play golf?'

I saw that I would have to answer. 'I have played,' I said.

'Well, we should have a game sometime. When I'm at home I'm on those fairways every day, rain or shine. I play Ballybunion. Do you know Ballybunion? Marvellous course. When we came back from Switzerland, my wife wanted to go back to Limerick, I wanted to move to Ballybunion. So we compromised and went to a place called Askeaton. I live in the Old Rectory there. The old wreck, I call it. My wife's dead,' Mr Donovan said. 'She's been dead for six years now.'

Mr Donovan stopped talking to think about his dead wife. After a long silence, I decided to change the subject, and then to leave as soon as the next pause in the conversation arose. 'Switzerland, you said?'

'That's right. Geneva. I worked in Geneva from 1946 to 1977. Thirty-one years. I was with the Glayer Corporation –

you know, the American outfit. Nowadays they're probably the biggest pharmaceutical company in the world, but in those days, when I joined them, they were just chickenfeed.' Mr Donovan laughed. 'Anti-anxiety drugs, that was my racket. Jesus, the crap people swallow these days.' He folded his napkin into a neat triangle. 'Mikey went to the International School. A grand school. They taught him three languages, French, Italian and German.' He chuckled and began to boast. 'He creamed the French at French and the Germans at German. He wiped the floor with the Italian kid at Italian. He skipped two years. He took his baccalaureate when he was sixteen. *Mention très bien*,' Mr Donovan said proudly. 'Three months later he got a scholarship for Cambridge. He had a great future ahead of him. That's what everybody said. "Fergus, your son's got a great future." What the hell does that mean, a great future?'

He paused to reflect and I seized my chance. I thanked Mr Donovan for the meal and rose to go. He did not just shake my hand, he gripped it. 'Don't forget what I said,' he said, looking me in the eye. 'Use your initiative. Stay in touch.'

Walking back to the office, I resolved to avoid Mr Donovan like the plague.

EIGHT

Two days after my meeting with Mr Donovan, events took a bizarre, if not grotesque, turn. I was at work and Mr Lexden-Page was sitting at my desk. I was trying to dissuade him from continuing his ill-judged action against the local authority responsible for the paving-stone he claimed to have stubbed his foot on.

'The likelihood is that your claim will be struck out as frivolous and vexatious,' I was explaining. 'You will be forced to pay not only your costs, but also the costs incurred by the council. I can assure you that these will not be negligible. They could easily run into thousands of pounds.'

Lexden-Page said, 'I don't care how much it will cost me. I'm not in this for the money. There's more to life than just money, Jones.'

I tried another tack. 'Let's take the best possible scenario,' I said. 'Let's say we win.'

'We will win,' Lexden-Page asserted.

I spoke slowly. 'Now, even if we manage to show that the council was negligent, we will be in great difficulty over damages. For a start, we have no medical certificate from a doctor regarding the injury to your toe.' My words, I saw, were making no impact. Lexden-Page sat with his arms folded, gazing at the rooftops behind my head. 'Then there is the question of the shoeshine you're claiming for,' I persisted. 'There's a problem with causation here: would you not have gone for that shoeshine in any event? Who's to say your accident caused you to have a shoeshine you would not otherwise have had?'

'It's a matter of principle,' Lexden-Page said. 'I don't care how petty the damages will be. I'm going ahead with it.'

'Mr Lexden-Page, litigation is, for better or worse, all about money. The courts are unsympathetic to plaintiffs who simply seek to air a grievance. I advise you in the strongest terms to settle this matter or, better still, to discontinue it altogether.' Lexden-Page plundered his ear with his little finger, which he then pointedly examined. Clearly he was having difficulties hearing me, so I decided to use more graphic language. 'If you will pardon the expression, any money you pour into this action is money down the lavatory bowl.'

I froze.

'Are you my solicitor or the council's?' I heard Lexden-Page say. 'I pay my taxes, same as everybody else. The courts belong to me, d'you hear? Those judges are my servants.'

The episode in Donovan's lavatory. The plastic bag full of turds and toilet-paper. I had left it in his house.

'Why should I not be able to sue the bloody council just because I haven't broken an arm and a leg? Was I the one who left the pavement in a shambles? A man can't even walk down the street any more. What's the point in living in a democracy, what's the point of freedom, if a man can't even walk down the street? Eh?'

I would have to go back. Hopefully the key would still be in the railing. The prospect of Donovan discovering the plastic bag did not bear thinking about.

'Look here, Jones, you know what I want and I've heard your spiel. Now let's get on with it. This whole business has been delayed enough.'

Feeling slightly unwell, I returned my attention to my client. Lexden-Page was about twenty-eight, although his puffy, rosy face suggested a younger man. He was wearing a tweed suit and circular spectacles. A transparent moustache grew hesitantly from his nostrils. He made grimaces as he spoke, twisting his mouth and wrinkling up his eyes into unpleasant, irritating contortions. He snorted.

'Well? Are we going to see something happen or not? Or do I have to take my business elsewhere?'

He curled his nostrils, and I realized to my surprise that he filled me with loathing. My clients rarely made an emotional impact on me. 'Whatever you say, Mr Lexden-Page,' I said coldly.

I would leave for Colford Square immediately after work.

The keys were where I had left them, in the rust-cavity in the railing. Furtively I fumbled at the front door, trying the locks until the bolts gave way and clacked satisfyingly in the woodwork. I spotted the plastic bag immediately, a white translucent heap against the wall. Thankfully there was no smell. Quickly I picked it up and turned to leave. Then I stopped. Upstairs, I remembered, were the tapes and the notebooks.

Don't go up there, I said to myself. Don't do it. Just walk out of the door and go home.

Maybe it was the tension of the situation, I do not know, but all of a sudden I found it difficult to balance myself on my feet. My head spun slightly and I swayed from side to side, as if the house keeled and rocked on foundations of waves. So I stood still, leaning against the wall, breathing deeply. Then everything suddenly accelerated. Before I knew what was happening I had released the bag and was transported up the staircase, up to Donovan's study. I found myself overtaken by events; I found myself in my raincoat, quickly inserting into the recorder the cassette I had played on my last visit. I replayed Tape 1, dated 25 September 1988, until I came to the tongue-twisters and the eerie, disembodied laughter, the point where I had stopped listening on that last night.

What I heard next was Donovan speaking in French. To my ear the accent was flawless and the sentences perfectly cadenced and modulated. It was practically a joy to listen to. I could not make head or tail of it.

I continued playing the tape. An authoritative chunk of German issued from the machine, followed by what sounded like a fluent outpouring of Italian (I could not be sure, my knowledge of these languages is almost non-existent). What was he saying? What message was he relaying?

Then everything fell into the place.

Tired of trying to decode the incomprehensible foreign utterings, my mind turned lazily, almost by way of recreation, to the dates of the writings and recordings – the last week of September 1988. It came to me instantaneously.

September 1988: it was in the beginning of September 1988, on the 8th of September to be exact, that Donovan had lost his powers of communication; that was when his ability to speak and write had deserted him, in Luxembourg, on his feet in the European Court of Justice. Of course, of course, I thought, of course! These notebooks and tapes were exercises in communication! The drawings of the squares and triangles, the list of words taken from the opening of a dictionary – they were all self-imposed writing drills, a systematic relearning of the ABCs! It fitted in, even the tapes of tongue-twisters – they were verbal circuits, designed to lick his speech back into shape. With these recordings Donovan was exercising his vocal cords for the first time in weeks, putting his pharynx, larynx, lips and glottis through their paces, forcing his organs of speech through the oral equivalent of squat-thrusts, sit-ups and star-jumps.

I switched the tape back on with a new sense of purpose.

Indiscriminately, senselessly it seemed to me, Donovan began articulating extracts from treaties, slowly quoting provisions of multilateral conventions – it was hard to say, from the tone of his delivery, whether he was relying on recollection or whether he was reciting from books at hand. What was clear was that he was plainly enjoying himself; in all probability this was the first time he had spoken properly since his breakdown in court. He was eating his words. Like a starved man at a banquet he pigged himself with vocables of any kind. He was wolfing down vowels, phonemes, diphthongs and consonants, making a meal of sibilants and alveolars and slowly regaling on labiodentals. He was licking clean the platter of pronunciation, and so palpable was his gastronomical relish that it almost made my mouth water. In the same way that his father's enthusiastic eating habits gave me an appetite, hearing Donovan like this made me feel like saying a few words myself.

So I was right, then. I allowed myself a grunt of vindication. Oliver Owen was wrong. Donovan had not, after all, faked his collapse. It had been a bona fide breakdown.

The recording came to an end. Sweating a little (I was still in my raincoat, I was not planning to stay long) I went back to the notebooks to steal a last glance at their contents before I went. I picked up a fresh one dated 26 September 1988 – the day after Tape 1 had been made. When I saw what was written, I took off my raincoat. This I had to read.

The first thing I noticed was this: Donovan's handwriting had progressed from the careful, scuttling script of the previous notebook. He wrote more cursively, in the semi-legible fashion I recognized from my pupillage, the letters small and purposeful, and I could tell that he was at ease with himself. Then I thought: what was it he had written down so flowingly?

Cases. Set out, for twenty-seven pages, and in no particular order, were law cases. It was an extraordinary sight. There were decisions from just about every field of the law I knew something of, cases in company law, contract, tort, conflicts of laws, criminal law, insurance law, road traffic law, public international law, commercial law, Islamic law, employment law and constitutional law. There must have been thousands of authorities on those pages – and not just famous ones like *Donoghue v. Stevenson* or *Salomon v. Salomon*, but piddling, minute cases nobody had ever heard of, like *Lochgelly Iron & Coal Co. Ltd. v. Crawford* and *Re Euro Hotel (Belgravia) Ltd*. In awe I realized what Donovan had done: effortlessly, as though he were emptying his pockets, he had turned his mind inside out. What was remarkable was not simply the number of cases on view (not many lawyers could, off the top of their heads, name more than a hundred), but the fact that there was no mnemonic device that I could spot: no numbers, no alphabetical sequences, no classification according to subject. Yes, he knew those cases like the back of his hand. In fact, so fluid and complete was Donovan's grasp of his legal materials that it did not seem as though his powers of recall came into it. He had not remembered these names, he had taken biological possession of them; it was as though they had entered him intravenously and now ran through his veins.

This blood relationship was illustrated by the next two lists, which organized the cases into, firstly, calendrical order, then into thematic blocks. I shook my head. Surely no one had ever known so much law so well! In a daze I turned to the last list – the names, I guessed, of all of the actions in which Donovan had ever received a brief. Again, this was an extraordinary feat – the equivalent, I would say, of naming every person you had ever met, in order of appearance.

I breathed deeply and sat back in my chair. I knew, of course, the purpose of these lists – they were a continuation of the training programme that Donovan had imposed on himself to regain his fighting fitness. This was like Mike Tyson pumping iron in the mountains. I marvelled at his self-discipline and his determination. With all his natural talent, still he drove himself to the limit of his abilities.

Closing the notebook, I happened to look down. There, in the corner of the room, I noticed for the first time a large terrestrial globe. It was not a political globe. There were no borderlines or territorial delineations or colour schemes denoting spheres of political influence. The cartographer was concerned only with the natural features of the planet. Mountains, oceans, gulfs, continents, rivers, deserts and volcanoes were given their names, but there was no sign of states, cities, duchies, sheikhdoms or dioceses. Submarine gradations and profundities were particularly detailed, with the continental shelves shown in silver-white, the abyssal plains in cobalt and the deep ocean trenches in delft blue. All in all, the world looked pretty good like that, I thought. (It was only later that I realized the globe's significance to Donovan.)

Then, looking further around, I saw, among the rows and rows of law reports that ran around the walls, a section of the shelves filled with miscellaneous law books. I recognized a few names – Lauterpacht, Jennings, McNair, Brownlie, H. L. A. Hart – but nothing unusual caught my eye. Nothing, that is, until I saw a stack of computer paper of the continuous, perforated kind, on the bottom shelf. I stood up and went over. The sheaf of papers was at least four inches deep, and on the top page were printed the words *Supranational Law*.

A book – it was the draft of a new book. Carefully, making sure my fingers did not leave a smudge, I leafed through the sheets. Yes, there was no doubt about it. This was a major new work.

Here I have to stop. Here I have to call a halt to this headlong gallop of words, because it is from here on in that things begin to get a little less straightforward. Until now the going has been easy, until now it has been a canter: but the moment has arrived to proceed with caution. In cowboy films you sometimes see a group of riders, a posse, after some outlaw. For a while their man is visible in the distance, a puff of smoke among the buttes. Then the terrain changes. The land starts to undulate and the riders lose sight of the outlaw behind hills. They are forced to dismount, to study the ground for his trail. Now perhaps I am being a little fanciful, but right now I could be in that posse, hot on the heels of Donovan's mystery; and, likewise, I am going to have to start looking out for tracks in the dust. Why? Because I am approaching the moment when the incomprehension that afflicts me begins to set in, when things start knotting mazily in my head. My problem is not that I am not sure exactly what occurred next. I have an outline of the facts in my mind right at this moment. If the telephone rang and someone asked me to relate the events that followed, I could do so without any difficulty at all. No, I have no doubts at all about what took place: only I am beginning to think that there is a difference between what took place and what really happened. Now it may be that I am splitting hairs – maybe, as lawyers are fond of saying, I am drawing a distinction without a difference. But I do not think so; because the facts, on their own, lead me to confusion. Somewhere, during this last year, I lost track of Donovan, which means that somewhere there is a spoor that I have missed.

As I have said, leafing through the sheaf of papers I had no doubts: this was a major new work. I made a calculation: Donovan's last book (the third edition of his text-book) had come out in 1980, which meant that he had been working on this new book for almost ten years.

I went cold. I had to have a copy.

I began searching around the office. I opened drawers and ran through heaps of documents. I scoured and rummaged and exhaustively ransacked (I cringe when I think of my molestful, unconscionable actions!), and at last I uncovered the floppy disc I was looking for. Quickly I activated the word processor. Up flashed the Introduction to the book, showing up on the monitor in green, painful letters. The Introduction, which was twenty-three pages long, would have to be enough. There was no question of printing out the whole text.

Minutes later I switched off the computer and slipped into my raincoat. Under my arm was the bundle of papers that I had printed out, and it was time to be on my way. Then, instead of leaving, I behaved disgracefully.

As I walked out of the study I saw that the door to the adjoining room was ajar and that inside was an unmade double bed. Without the slightest hesitation I went in. It was their bedroom. By the high windows Arabella's toiletries filled the surface of a dressing-table. Shamelessly I surveyed bottles of scent, mascara sticks, cotton buds for cleaning ears, several powder brushes, lipsticks and bottles of baby lotion. (Yes, unbelievable as it may seem, that is what I did. As I write now and feel myself back in that house, grubbily sifting through those private belongings with my sweating, blotchy hands, rifling around in breach of trust, in my raincoat, a hot, ineradicable shame fills me to the brim. Inexcusable! My behaviour was inexcusable!)

I looked around. On the bedside table stood a photograph in a glass frame. I picked it up and studied it. It was a strange photograph, really. It showed the top half of a woman. She was wearing a huge circular straw hat, and its disc covered almost her entire back. There was no sign of her face or her hair, and what revealed her to be a woman were the bare, bangled arms that protruded outwards and upwards from the side of the hat, fingers outstretched – slender, hairless arms that could only belong to a woman. Arabella. It had to be. She was looking out to the sea, the bar of blue with a sun-burned, yellow-rocked island on its rim. It was clear that this was a holiday snapshot, but that was all that I could deduce. I tried to read more into it, but all I came up with was that this was Arabella on holiday. Any guesses or theories I entertained (about her looks, about why Donovan might like this picture) just bounced off the photograph as though it were a mirror.

Feeling locked out and frustrated, I put the photograph down and went over to a big white wooden cupboard. Its well-made door slid open with just a push of the finger. One half of the cupboard, with the exception of two dresses, a thermal vest and some tinkling clothes-hangers, was deserted, while in the other half were suspended some suits and shirts. Some more clothes were scattered about the room, including a clean, wrinkly mountain of whites by an opened ironing-board. A bathroom joined the bedroom and I went in there, too. Inexplicably (what could I have been thinking of?), I rooted around the aftershaves and moisturizers and tooth-brushes. Of course, I found nothing of interest. Undeterred, I climbed the stairs to the third floor. What could a childless couple do with such a big house? I asked myself. Unsurprisingly, the rooms were simply used as guest rooms or as spare rooms filled mostly with books and suitcases. What did I do? I rummaged around. I opened trunks and unpacked boxes, I pried and snooped and intruded. Needless to say, my discoveries were banal: old clothes, tool-boxes, old novels, spare rugs, bicycle tyres.

(Why did I not stop to think about what I was doing? And anyway, what was I expecting to find? Secret doorways? Diaries? Treasure? A message? Who did I think I was, one of those teenage sleuths in children's thrillers, the ones who crack drugs rings on their holidays? What – no, *who*, possessed me that I did these things? I have said that Donovan unlocked me like an old house: who moved into me? Who was the new lessee?)

My intrusiveness did not end there. Before I left I went down to the telephone answering machine. You never know, I figured: there just might be something important. I depressed the button and, apart from Fergus Donovan's old message, heard the following, spoken in ripe, emotional tones that I recognized: *Michael, this is Arab.* A hesitation as the speaker thought of what to say. Then, almost ferociously, *Stop it. Just stop it.* Another hesitation. *Bye.*

NINE

Given the way of things, it was some days before I actually perused Donovan's work. Away from the heightened atmosphere of his study, I was disinclined to muster the concentration and time that was needed for the task. Also, I had other preoccupations which I could not simply brush aside. Foremost amongst these was my date with Susan.

The meeting was Susan's idea, not mine. She telephoned me at work, out of the blue: to see how I was, she said. Then, awkwardly and bravely, she had suggested we meet. Not wishing to rebuff her, I quickly said, Yes, of course, good idea – and that was that. I had committed myself.

Saturday night, therefore, found me in a taxi on the way to a restaurant in Leicester Square, uneasy and a little anxious. I was profoundly unsure about the whole encounter. We had originally arranged to see each other the previous Saturday, but I had been forced to cancel because of my appointment to meet Donovan in Colford Square. I had telephoned Susan beforehand and begun apologizing profusely. She breezily interrupted me. 'There's no need to explain anything, Jimmy,' she said. 'If you can't make it, you can't make it. That's all there is to it.'

I hesitated. It was unlike Susan to make so light of such a thing.

She registered my surprise and said, 'It's not as though we owe each other anything, is it? The days of making excuses are gone, Jimmy.'

I hastily agreed. If one thing was clear in my mind, it was

that I did not want us to resume our old relationship. That was over and done with, and a good thing too. In my recollection the inconveniences had clearly outweighed the satisfactions. What made me qualmish in the taxi was that Susan's intentions were less clear. I suspected that what she wanted was, at the very least, some form of discussion about, and examination of, our time together. That was how she was, she had an almost archaeological approach to our relations – she liked to disinter them, hold them up for inspection, label and analyse them. It was a habit I had found tiring and disconcerting, and it was one reason why I associated Susan with a terrible weightiness; by the end I felt in her presence like a man deeply submerged, the air a far-off roof of light, the water like concrete. I made up my mind to take a firm grip of the evening. The talk was not to take any untoward direction.

I arrived at the restaurant, a place called Garfunkel's, in good time. I had suggested the place. It was not a romantic venue: synthetic tabletops, harsh lights and a floor over-crowded with an unappealing clientele (students, parents with troublesome children, downmarket types generally). The food (steak and chips, scampi, beefburgers etcetera – 'honest' food, I think it is called) was on the fast side, which meant that the meal would not be lengthy. I took a seat at a table and ordered a bottle of house red. By the time Susan arrived (at eight on the dot) I had drunk two glasses and smoked three cigarettes.

I watched her peer around the numerous tables with squinting eyes until she spotted me. When she started walking towards the table I really began to feel nervous. It was our first face to face meeting since our split-up – our first meeting for one month and twelve days, to be exact. Rising from my chair I saw that she had awkwardly extended her arm, and for the first time in our lives we shook hands. I caught the waiter's eye as soon as we sat down and we ordered before conversing.

'I'm still in Hounslow,' Susan said positively when I asked her about her work. 'But I'm looking to start afresh somewhere after Christmas, once I've picked up my bonus. There are one or two things in the pipeline.'

'Good,' I said encouragingly. It must be said that I bore absolutely no ill feelings towards Susan. Quite the contrary, I wished her well. I wished her every happiness.

I loosened my tie. Although we were sitting at a spacious table for four, I felt peculiarly claustrophobic. My trousers felt tight around my thighs and my jacket constrained my shoulders. Recently I read one of the poems they put up on the underground nowadays, among the advertisements for secretarial agencies and skin creams. The poem was by a man called Muldoon, an author with whom I am unfamiliar (I do not read poetry as a rule). Although I did not understand the second half of the poem, its first half was clear enough and has stayed in my mind. It is about two people sitting down for a meal and cleverly describes how there was barely enough room at their table for themselves plus their former selves. The same applied to Susan and me – not only were we seated at the table, but also pulling up a chair were myself as her lover, herself as my girlfriend, the James Jones that had bored and irritated her, the Susan Northey that had caused me anxiety and all the other people we had been together – jokers, cooks, drinkers, travelling companions, tired employees and lustful sexual partners. I sensed them flapping open their napkins and picking up their knives and forks. They were elbowing me in the ribs and crowding the space under the table with their feet.

The food arrived. 'What about you?' Susan said.

'I'm still at Batstone's,' I said glumly. 'Some old boring stuff really.' I wanted to impress upon her how dull my life was, and how fortunate she was to be out of it. To remove any doubt about my unattractiveness, I had taken care not to shave and wore an unflattering suit which revealed my corpulence.

We chewed our food in silence. I could hear the iceberg lettuce crunching and resounding in my mouth and the cutlery clanking against the plates. I decided to steer the talk to a neutral topic which would, with luck and careful management, see us through a significant part of the evening. I said, 'There is one case, though, which is rather interesting. But you must promise not to tell anyone what I'm going to tell you. It's confidential.' Then I ran through the Donovan story, taking it from his collapse to my second, clandestine visit to his house (concerning the latter I told only of my discovery of the manuscript, omitting my shameful searches thereafter).

When I finished there was a silence. Susan had not asked any questions during my discourse and she bore an indifferent expression. Obviously she could not see the significance of what I had said. I realized that she did not grasp Donovan's greatness. 'What you've got to understand,' I said, 'is that Donovan is the kind of lawyer who comes along once every hundred years. What happens to him is, well, history.'

She looked at me doubtfully. After a pause she said, 'Jimmy, I'd like to talk about us.'

'Us?'

'Yes, us – you and me.' She fixed a determined gaze upon me.

I looked down at my plate. A guiltiness passed through me. I could think of nothing to say.

Susan spoke. 'I think that things ended rather messily between us, don't you? I'd like to, you know, talk about it a little – tidy things up a bit.' She laughed anxiously. 'I mean, we had some good times together, didn't we Jimmy?'

I stopped sawing out a triangle of medium rare steak and looked up. Susan was suddenly looking uncertain and vulnerable and I said quickly, reassuringly, 'Yes, we did. We did have some good times. Of course we did, Suzy.'

I was visited by a flashback. Susan and I had, from time to time, gone away for weekends – to Lincoln, to Paris, to Dublin. What I remembered was walking up the cobbled hill at Lincoln and also along a leafy bank of the Seine on blazing days, and on each occasion Susan clutching me suddenly and pressing herself against me, saying, 'Oh Jimmy, I am so happy.' At the end of the weekends she would say, 'Oh, we've enjoyed ourselves so much – haven't we Jimmy? It's been lovely, hasn't it?' And I would say, with all the tenderness I knew, 'Yes, my love, it has. It's been lovely,' and I would reach my arm around her and squeeze hard. I could see her logging away the weekend as a happy one, one with a tick of approval alongside it, two days to be cherished, two days with a future. Always she cried when, bags in hand, we stepped out of the bed-and-breakfast or hotel to leave. Her small eyes gleamed and she buried her wettening face in my chest as the arrival of every new minute brought with it a fresh and tearing dispossession.

I repeated myself. 'We had plenty of fine times,' I said with warmth.

She slowly ate her last morsels of scampi. When she spoke again I saw once more that determined, gritty look. The jaw was set, the mouth pursed intently, the crease between her faint eyebrows deeper. I knew that look from somewhere, and it made me apprehensive. I poured out what remained of the wine. The sooner we drank up and left, the better.

'What went wrong between us Jimmy?' she asked quietly. 'Hmm? What do you think happened?'

This was exactly what I had feared: a reconstruction of our relationship – an excavation, dusting-off, scrutiny and reassembly of the shards. Susan could not leave well alone. Why didn't she just enjoy the dinner? I looked around for the waiter to ask for the bill, but the man was nowhere to be seen.

'I don't know,' I said unenthusiastically. 'Things just didn't work out, I suppose.' A bland smile played on my lips. I saw from Susan's face that this reply was unsatisfactory, so I decided to play for time. Luckily, my legal training came to my help and a semantic device occurred to me. 'I'm not sure that it's useful to talk about what went wrong,' I said. 'I'm not sure that anything, or many things, went wrong. I think it was more the case that not enough things went right.' She looked unconvinced, so I continued. 'You see, when you say that something went wrong, you imply things were right in the first place. I'm not sure that that was so with us.'

Susan considered what I had said then visibly rejected it. That gritty expression settled once more on her face and it came to me where I had seen that look before. She had worn it one day when she had set about unblocking her kitchen sink. I was ready to call the plumber and be done with it, but Susan persisted. She pressed and drove the plunger again and again until finally the plughole yielded up its stubborn contents. She wore that look right now. Unsurprisingly, therefore, when I caught the waiter's eye and gestured for the bill with a scribbling movement of the hand, Susan firmly said, 'And we'll have another bottle of house red, and coffee.' There was to be no escape.

And then it happened. I was powerless to prevent it, the matter was out of my hands. We had more, lots more, to drink, and soon – well, soon, as they coyly say, one thing led to another. First of all the discussion of what had gone wrong was, to my relief and surprise, abandoned, and instead we reminisced; and of course we reminisced about those moments when things were magical: soon we recalled how we first met, at a friend's party, and how exciting our courting days had been.

'At the beginning, every time you rang I felt sick,' Susan said, blushing. 'The first time, when I picked up the phone I nearly swooned.'

I smiled, fingering my glass. We had had this conversation before, but it was always nice to hear it again. How many other girls had ever felt faint at the sound of my voice?

'What about you?' Susan asked. She allowed herself a grin. 'How did you feel?'

'I felt pretty excited, too,' I said.

'How excited? How exactly?'

I gave a shy smile and pretended to give the question thought. 'I felt a knocking in my chest. Thump, thump, thump,' I said. 'It was my heart. My heart was jumping all over the place.'

'Really?'

'Really,' I said. She was blushing with pleasure. 'When I picked up the phone to ring you, my ears were pounding too; it was like I was listening to my heart with a stethoscope.' I poured it on. She loved it when my talk grew lyrical. She revelled in it. 'I could hardly hear your voice my ears were pounding so much.'

'Jimmy, I feel dizzy now . . . Stop, stop it now . . . '

Of course there was no stopping. We talked about what had attracted us to each other, we hinted lewdly at the sexual times we had enjoyed; and the more we drank, the better it all seemed. All the while I was called on by miniature domestic memories – how daintily pleasing her waking-up routine was (after she wordlessly got out of bed I would hear the click of the kettle, then the rushing of water as she performed her face-wash, the second click of the kettle as the water came to the boil, the splat of the tea-bag in the sink, the padding of bare feet, the groan of the mattress as she rejoined me in bed, and, finally, the small slurp she made sitting up to drink next to my sleeping form), how neatly she piled her jumpers in her cupboard, how thoughtful she had always been to ensure that there was enough hot water for my bath. By the time we had finished the second bottle and had ordered a final carafe, I was beginning to see things in a new light. Susan had a lovely colour, and I was sure that she wore a new pair of glasses. Also, her hair was not quite as lank as I remembered it. Now crinkles ran through it, and although the effect was unattractively artificial, I softened at the thought of her earnestly going to the hairdresser and doing her best to enliven her appearance. Poor Suzy!

Emptying the carafe, nothing was really said. We contented ourselves with playing games with our eyes, fluttering and darting little looks and peeks at one another, exchanging momentary but significant gazes. By now the revenants of our old selves had vacated the table and just the two of us were left, breathing in air sweet with oxygen. We paid the waiter (fifty-fifty, Susan insisted) and went to a nearby pub for a final drink. There was a crush of customers but we found an unoccupied corner behind a man with a black, breathless dog. When I returned from the bar with the drinks I squeezed myself between Susan and the dog-owner. Her thigh made tingling contact with mine and soon my arm was around her shoulder and she was bunched up against me, nice and close. She said, Oh Jimmy, and we kissed.

At that moment I was presented with an opportunity to extricate myself from my predicament (I say predicament because, although I was at an advanced stage of intoxication, it was plain to me that the situation was running away from me, and that unless I acted decisively it would leave me behind completely). Excusing myself, I walked carefully and unsteadily to the gents. My head was filled with a fog as I laboured to think of what to do next. Relieving myself, I clumsily tried to identify and weigh up the elements due for consideration. On the one hand I felt a strong desire, an imperative, for a sexual encounter. I recognized that it was not often that such a chance came my way. On the other hand, I knew what disappointment and mayhem this type of encounter would in all probability lead to, given my inebriation and the problematical background to the situation. I looked at myself in the mirror above the urinal and was drunkenly struck by the strangeness of my face: whose visage was that? Mine? Was I inseparable from those eyes and chins? That nose – did I carry it around all day? How on earth did the air that I sucked through it fuel my body? What extraordinary mechanisms I housed! How miraculous everything was! Then, washing my hands, another factor entered my deliberations: I felt sorry for Susan. It is true, I did; my heart went out to her. She had made such an effort this evening, and if anyone deserved a little romantic success, a little happiness, it was her. I splashed cold water on my cheeks and neck and placed my face in the hot jet of air expelled by the drying machine on the wall. It would be uncharitable, I decided, to refuse her advances.

Susan was waiting for me outside, her handbag crossed

over her torso to deter snatchers. She had removed her glasses and was looking, as far as I was able to tell, joyous. At once I hailed a cab and we tumbled together into its dark, comfortable interior.

'Stockwell,' I said to the driver.

A delicious tension held sway between us. Things were acutely understood but left unsaid. We briefly regarded one other with meaningful eyes then sat back to enjoy the ride, swaddled in our overcoats, our hands in our pockets. I always like a late journey home in a safe and roomy black cab on such nights, dark nights sweet and melting as black gâteau, with me in the back luxuriating in the voluptuous swings and curves taken by the big taxi. After ten minutes we rolled up to my front door and I said to Susan, Come on, and unloaded her from the taxi. She said, Just for a coffee then, I really must go. Heavy-legged, we made our way into the flat. Susan fell on to the sofa while I made coffee, spilling sugar and coffee grains on to the work surface. Susan rather uncharacteristically turned on the television and began toying with the buttons on the remote control, zipping between channels and colouring the faces tomato-red then black-and-white. I brought in the mugs of coffee and she said, 'My God, look at that.'

On the screen a match was about to take place between two huge Japanese wrestlers called The Fog and The Sea Slug. They were limbering up. Taking their time, they wandered formidably around, preparing themselves. For whole minutes they threw salt around the ring, rubbed their palms together, slapped their thighs and squatted in mid-air with legs spread, then they straightened and turned their backs on each other to face the crowd, their fat arms and buttocks tremoring. It was spectacular, and we drank in silence, watching. With a final adjustment of their bellybands and a shake of their limbs, the wrestlers crouched down eyeball to eyeball, two great banks of flesh. They leaped at each other. It was over in seconds. The Sea Slug, the smaller man, used the momentum of The Fog against him and simply pushed him out of the ring. That was it. All of that concentration and build-up had come almost to nothing. A glancing collision of bodies, a movement of feet and a push. That was all it amounted to.

If I had had my wits about me I would have learned from the wrestlers. I would have called for a mini-cab or made up the spare bed. I did neither. And so, shortly after we had turned off the television, Susan and I found ourselves in a ring of bedsheets, momentarily clinched and shuddering.

I slept badly. Susan was making a wheezing sound and the bed was unpleasantly warm. I itched below the knee, then behind my ear, then at the back of my neck. What would she say in the morning? What demands would she make? I rolled over to the edge of my half of the bed. I needed space to breathe. Again I scratched myself, this time on the left calf muscle. The air was thickening; somewhere automobiles were accelerating in the night.

When I awoke, at nine o'clock, a great surprise awaited me. Susan had gone. I went to the note-pad by the telephone where she used to leave notes – nothing there.

What did I think? I thought, Phew.

TEN

Like a sailor at sea I have certain routines which I invariably follow: one routine for the morning, another for the evening and another for bedtime. During the week these are mainly a matter of time and motion, designed to remove the pain of constantly having to make decisions and to allow me the luxury of a restfully blank mind. On Sundays I have a routine I treasure so much that it has become a ritual. I lie in until about ten o'clock, then I slip on the first trousers, socks and shirt that come to hand, nip across the road for the newspaper, nip back, undress and climb back into bed, read the sports pages, go to the kitchen and, after some bran flakes in semi-skimmed milk, cook myself sausages, scrambled eggs and toast, wash that down with a grapefruit juice and sugared coffee, finish the newspapers cover to cover, run myself a bath, lie in the water for half an hour, get out and fall asleep in front of the afternoon film.

Thanks to Susan's timely departure, my Sunday morning was still intact, and as usual at midday I sprinkled some fragrancer in the bathtub and turned on the hot water tap. Minutes later, I slid, my heels squeaking against the plastic surface, into a stinging, fumy bath.

The water smelled of apples. Gradually, deliciously, I immersed the top half of my body until I lay neck-deep and buoyant. My knees surfaced like snowy islands. Beneath the taps appeared the archipelagos of my toes. I was in a state of bliss. My pores opened, my neck muscles relaxed, my eyes closed. Purified, utterly released from the night before, I began lazily contemplating what to do with my afternoon; and I remembered my copy of the Introduction to *Supranational Law*. I would read it when I finished bathing, I decided, instead of watching a film. Then I slithered further down the slope of the tub, took a gulp of air and submersed the whole of my head, my cheeks ballooned, bubbles streaming and popping from my nose . . .

Later, wet-headed in my dressing-gown, imprinting the carpet with my bare feet, I lit the imitation coal-fire in my sitting room and made myself comfortable in front of it. The morning was overcast and this had darkened the flat, so the blue flames licked warmly around the dark, fake rocks. As well as the print-out, I had brought out a chunky file of cuttings and clippings and, seeing them spread out on the floor for the first time in a long time, suddenly found myself back in 1974. As I have said, I am not prone to nostalgia, but sometimes, without wishing it, you simply find yourself in the past, you find that you are back there whether you like it or not. This is what happened to me that Sunday. Looking at those notes sledded me straight into another time.

I was a student at university and I dreamed of becoming an international lawyer. It happened in my second year. One afternoon in autumn, when I had nothing better to do, I had opened a law book – a second-hand copy of Donovan's *International Law*. Idly, uninterestedly, I began looking over the first paragraphs. Before I knew what had happened my fingers had turned thirty pages; and to my astonishment (until then I had detested every law book I had ever had the misfortune to pick up), I wanted to read on.

And I did read on. I had no choice, I was hooked. Usually when I read a law book I would stop after a few sentences, gasping for relief from the airless prose. Donovan's prose, on the other hand, was remarkably spacious – his writing brought the subject to life, rather like those aerators that pump oxygen into dead, fishless rivers. Inspired, I tried to read every word that he had written – his articles, book reviews, pamphlets, everything. I read his doctoral thesis, *The Community of Nations* (Butterwells, 1967), I read *The Law of Space* (Butterwells, 1969), and his first edition of *Essays on Space Law* (Donovan, Ed., Butterwells, 1973). Then, the better to understand his work, I scoured everything to do with public international law that I could lay my hands on. I harassed the librarians with remote references, took out dusty books which had not been touched in years, spent hours perched on the library step-ladder going through the contents of obscure shelves. Very soon I realized that Donovan, young though he was (he was only just thirty!) was ludicrously superior to his colleagues. While they lumbered towards tentative and uninteresting perspectives, Donovan explored the field playfully and effortlessly, never neglecting, as others did for lack of scholarship and intellectual capacity, the complex political dimensions of the subject. Late at night in my room, thanks to him, I was animated by difficult, heady questions – what was the true nature of international law? How satisfactory were the voluntarist mechanisms of enforcement? What regimes should operate in contiguous zones?

And, head on my pillow, I was also visited by dreams, by futures. I would join Donovan's chambers and become the junior he could rely on, his trusty number two. I would ride on the coat-tails of his practice and at the same time I would write for the learned journals. Maybe, if I was lucky, some university teaching would fall my way: maybe one day Donovan would not be able to attend a lecture and would ask me to take his place! I saw myself at the podium in the theatre, the students copiously writing down my every word as I strode confidently up and down, my eyes regarding the ceiling, my hands behind my back, my speech unhesitating, wise and humorous. That was how Donovan's lectures in Cambridge must be, I imagined. Then an idea occurred to me: why not go to Cambridge and see him? What was to stop me? So I telephoned the law faculty there. They were very helpful. Indeed, the woman whom I spoke to sounded positively elated at my inquiry.

'As it happens, Professor Donovan is due to give the annual Smith lecture next Wednesday!' she said. 'You are most welcome to attend!'

'Really? I can come?'

'Of course – the more the merrier! It's at the Senate House, at eleven o'clock.'

The journey to Cambridge took nearly six hours, but I did not mind because I slept deeply most of the way (the coach left at four in the morning). Shortly after dawn I opened my plastic lunch-box and breakfasted hungrily on the cheese and tomato sandwiches I had prepared the day before, so that when we rolled in to Cambridge I was refreshed and alive with anticipation. Making sure my notebook and biro were safely in my briefcase (I was not going to miss a word, not a word!) I walked quickly to the Senate House. It was a quarter to eleven, my timing was perfect. Up to the big front door I went, perspiring a little from my exertions. I took a deep breath. Well, I thought happily, here we go. This is it.

I pushed warily at the door. Then I pulled and tugged. It was shut.

I looked around in bafflement. There was nobody around. And yet – I glanced at my watch – the doors should have been open, it was ten to eleven.

Anxiously I walked over to an adjoining, important-looking building where students were walking in and out. By chance it was the university law library, the Squire Library. There was a security man who sat at the entrance.

'Excuse me,' I said, 'could you tell me where the Smith lecture is being given? It was supposed to start at the Senate House at eleven o'clock.'

The man put his book down and took a good look at me.

'Let me see your identification,' he said. 'You're not allowed into the library unless you're a member of the university.'

Ignoring his request (there was no time to lose, the lecture was due to start any minute now) I stopped a student.

'I'm sorry, but do you know where the M.J.P.J. Smith lecture is taking place?'

'What?'

I repeated myself, adding, 'It's being given by Professor Donovan.'

'Who?'

'Donovan,' I said emphatically, 'Donovan.'

She shrugged and walked off. She did not know what I was talking about.

Quickly I went over to some posters I saw on the wall, but they were advertising scholarships and postgraduate courses, not lectures. Then I decided to telephone the law faculty again. I was put through to the same friendly lady I had previously spoken to.

'You're quite right,' she assured me. 'The Smith lecture is not taking place at the Senate House as was envisaged. You see, it's not taking place at all. Professor Donovan was forced to cancel,' she said. 'He's been called away.'

I forced out, 'Cancelled?'

The friendly lady detected my disappointment and suggested kindly, 'I know! Why don't you give me your name and address, and I'll send you details of when the lecture will take place?'

'Jones,' I said hoarsely, 'J. Jones.'

'Sorry?'

'That's all right,' I said. 'There's no need.'

The misadventure in Cambridge was only a temporary setback. Fervently I resumed my studies, so that when I took my finals the following year, I almost achieved a first-class degree (my performance in land law let me down). Importantly, I did well in the international law papers, and it was on the strength of the promise I showed there that I received good references from my tutors. This enabled me to get an interview at 6 Essex Court and then, miracle of miracles, a pupillage. My dreams were coming true . . .

The papers I was sifting through in front of my gas fire were notes and copies I had made of Donovan's writings and the reported cases in which he had appeared. I had started the collection at university, for research purposes, and after I had left 6 Essex I continued to collect, at first because I still harboured hopes of becoming an international lawyer, and later as a hobby or project, I suppose. For years I spent solitary nights and weekends carefully studying Donovan's progress and painstakingly noting my thoughts. Although I had nothing specific in mind, no plans as such, I half-contemplated writing a paper on him – maybe even a book (why not? I reasoned). As far as I am aware, I read every word he published until 1985. It was only then that my monthly visits to the Middle Temple library to hunt for material came to an end. There had not been a conscious decision on my part to stop. I simply realized one day that I had not done any research for the last few months and that I did not feel diminished by the omission. Whereas before if I fell behind or neglected to read a quarterly I would experience guilt and a pressing need to rectify matters, now I felt nothing.

Poor sap! I can hear people say; or, How pathetic! Only a true inadequate would even think of such a cretinous activity!

The terrible thing is, sometimes I suspect that these remarks, if made, would be correct. I, too, can feel like hurling a few insults at the old, younger me: Muttonhead! Imbecile! Dunderhead! What on earth were you doing? Had you nothing better to do with your time? Had you no pride? And yes, when I look back now it is not without some element of shame, of fury even. My fixation was unwholesome: after all, could I really say that I was primarily interested in international law? If Donovan had suddenly switched to specialize in the law of trusts, was there any doubt that I would have trotted in his trail, bleating like a sheep?

Then, when my emotions subside, I find that I can justify my activities in one of two ways. The first is not so much a justification as a limp excuse, and runs as follows. In most respects, I am an untalented man. There is no point in deluding myself about that. James Jones will never attain heights, not in person anyway. People like me have to make do with things like cricket-scoring or autograph-hunting, or some other vicarious, mildly demeaning pastime. There is no point in criticizing myself for this as, since I have little choice in the matter, clearly it is not my fault. Surely I am not to blame for who I am?

Alternatively, I can take a noble and bullish stand: not only are my researches excusable as the inoffensive hobby of an ungifted man, they are positively laudable as an interesting piece of research. Yes, they are not without academic, perhaps even historical, value, because Donovan is truly exceptional, and any contribution to the understanding of his work, however slight, is worthwhile.

I sensed his exceptionality early on, at university. I say sensed because my view originated not so much in mind as in my nerves, guts, heart, liver and bones. Instinctively I knew Donovan to be that rare thing, a man who really matters. Reading his texts over and over again and each time discovering fresh evidence of his powers, I came to the conclusion that he was potentially the greatest international lawyer since Hugo Grotius, the founding father of international law. Grotius (1583–1645) was, in my view, truly a man of genius. Sometimes it is alleged that he was not an original thinker – that he was simply a man of extreme learning and trod paths laid down by people like Suarez and Gentili. That is a slur. Whilst it may be true that Grotius appropriated the concepts of *societas humana* and *jus gentium*, he did so to dramatic and innovative effect. To heat and hammer and pressurize the juridical materials he inherited in the way he did, into new and durable shapes, to produce such a work as *De Jure Belli ac Pacis*, which resonates and bells to this day, is a creative, imaginative feat.

Armed with my accumulating knowledge of Donovan, I began to draw parallels between Grotius, a Dutchman four centuries dead, and Donovan, an Irishman at the Bar of England and Wales. I thought that there might be a thesis in the subject, comparing and contrasting the two men. In many ways they were different. Not only was Grotius a great jurist, he was also a philologist, theologian and statesman of distinction. Donovan was purely a lawyer, and furthermore, although he was absorbed by the academic side of his work, he also relished the pugilism of litigation; Grotius, by contrast, never enjoyed practising law, and was principally occupied as a politician, jailbird and diplomat. And while Donovan was precociously talented and several years ahead of his contemporaries (he graduated from Cambridge with a starred first aged twenty), Grotius was truly prodigious. As a child he published brilliant poems in Latin and Greek, was paraded in front of Henri IV of France, went to university at eleven and was awarded a doctorate at sixteen. He was a Mozart of erudition.

But then I discerned some similarities. Both men had remarkable memories; both possessed relentless energy; both worked unceasingly; and, perhaps most tellingly, both were acutely conscious of the passage of time. Grotius's motto was *Ruit hora*, and it was one which Donovan could easily have shared. Despite his calmness, a weird urgency underlaid everything he did. Once he had performed the task in hand, there would be no dilly-dallying or idle chewing of the fat. He would be off and on to the next item. In some people's eyes this made him poor company. Into the first part of my pupillage, for example, when I was still with Simon Myers, I approached Oliver Owen, who was Donovan's pupil at the time.

'Well, what's he like?' I asked eagerly (I had yet to meet him, having only caught glimpses of him on the staircase).

'Dull as ditchwater,' Oliver said. 'A bit like you really. Don't worry, only joking. No,' he continued, 'he hasn't made a single joke in three months.' He yawned noisily. 'Just thinking of him makes me yawn.'

Philistine! I thought. Doesn't he realize who he is talking about?

'Is he clever?' I asked.

'*Fucking* clever,' Oliver said. 'But, in the final analysis, more boring than clever. Thank God he's away half the time. It drives me bananas, sitting there in the same room as him. All he does is sit at his desk from the crack of dawn and churn out the papers. Never says a bloody word. He's a fucking slave-driver,' Oliver complained.

'So he's not very nice,' I said.

'Nice? James,' Oliver said scornfully, 'Michael's not going to go around being "nice" or "nasty". It's just not on his timetable. He's got better things to do than relate to people. That's far too petty an activity.'

What do you expect? I thought. Donovan sees his pupils come and go every six months. He's hardly going to be on intimate terms with each and every one of them. Anyway, what you don't appreciate is the importance of Donovan's work. A man like Donovan has a responsibility not to squander the enormous gifts which have fallen his way. If his shoes were laced on my feet I'd do exactly the same. I wouldn't have time for too much small talk either.

The trouble with Oliver, I thought, is that, unlike me, he doesn't understand Donovan. Me, I understand him.

In the years that followed my understanding of the man deepened as I kept track with his ideas and preoccupations. They were fascinating. Early on in his career he had developed a peculiar specialty: the law of outer space. He wrote with authority on mainstream issues like the problems of spatial junk and the demarcation of airspace and outer space, but his reputation in the field was sealed by a dazzling, questioning essay on the regime of *res communis* that operates in outer space – a regime which designates outer space as an area existing for the benefit of the whole of mankind (so that a country or corporation cannot own celestial bodies or, for example, mine metals in asteroids for exclusively private gain; another consequence is that weapons of mass destruction – and sky wars – are also prohibited up there; no guns among the stars).

From outer space he moved to submarine areas, a much more orthodox field. He treated the usual problems (economic zones, the exploitation of the continental shelf, the delimitation of territorial waters) but lingered in one unusual area:

the deep ocean floor, also designated by international agreement for the benefit of the whole of mankind. Finally, in the mid-eighties, when I stopped my research, he was looking closely at the notion of the sovereignty of States – in particular, at the concept of exclusive jurisdiction.

What characterized Donovan's contributions was that they were, in essence, questioning. He was not an answers man. Solutions to old problems did not interest him: he was after the problems with the problems. He would take an issue, all weedy and overgrown with commentaries and opaque analyses, and wipe it clean as a washed slate. The resulting clarification was startling, but then, tantalizingly, having illuminated the subject to an unprecedented degree, he would move on to another. It was frustrating for the reader, and led to the accusation that he was essentially a negative thinker and a trouble-maker. But I knew better. I knew that he was keeping his powder dry. I knew that on the horizon was a great, synthesizing work that would bring together all his preoccupations. Indeed I counted on it, because without a revolutionary masterpiece to Donovan's name, the careful comparisons I had drawn between him and Grotius would be embarrassingly unfounded. For years I waited for the great work. Scrupulously photocopying his academic output in the library, I bided my time. If anyone had seen me, my hopeful face flashing over the machine, they would probably have laughed. So be it, I thought. Let them laugh. Let them think what they want.

You see, I had faith in Donovan. I knew that, in the end, he would come up trumps.

But, as I have said, the whole enterprise drifted away from me of its own accord. Even when I began reading the first part of *Supranational Law* and realized that, yes, this was the work I had banked on for all those years, I was not excited so much as wryly satisfied. Nor did I seriously contemplate resuming my thesis. My ambitions along those lines had expired.

The scheme of *Supranational Law* was breathtakingly ambitious. International law as we understood it, Donovan said

(I am paraphrasing crudely and over-simplistically), was out of date. At present it governed the interrelations of sovereign States and did not interfere with the relations of the State with its own citizens and territory. When it came to internal matters, the State had exclusive jurisdiction – this followed, according to the orthodoxy, from the fact that States are sovereign. That was fine, Donovan said, as long as the treatment by the State of its citizens had purely domestic consequences. So, for example, if the Albanians had an atheist, insular, Marxist State, or the Iranians preferred an Islamic republic, that was (putting aside, for the moment, the question of human rights) a matter for them. But what if a State's internal actions had grave *external* consequences? What if, for example, a State burned millions of square miles of rain forest, or punched a hole in the ozone layer, or conducted military experiments that caused irrevocable pollution? Or, to take another example, ordered the extermination of a precious species of animal?

The time had come, Donovan argued, for international law to come to terms with the vital new issue of our times: the prevention of the destruction of the planet. It was true that provisions existed that purported to deal with some of the problems involved. But, Donovan argued, these provisions (i.e. treaties and multilateral conventions) were deeply flawed. Why? Because they remained purely an expression of national interests. This was dangerous, because safeguarding a variety of national interests was an inadequate mechanism for safeguarding the interests of the globe. At present, it was up to a State to determine what its national interest was, and if that meant endangering everyone else, that was tough luck. By law, the rest of the world was not entitled to interfere. It was none of its business.

No, Donovan said. One had to start afresh. For guidance one had to look at the only places where national interest did not rule: extra-sovereign areas like the deep sea-bed and outer space, Antarctica, the high seas. Donovan's thesis was that the concept of the common good which operated in respect of these regions should be extended: surely it was incontrovertible that the rain forests were a resource of the world and not just of, say, Brazil. And States owned airspace, yes, but the world had a vital and legitimate interest in the gases contained in the airspace. The flipside, Donovan said, was that the wealth in the developed countries was also a resource of the world. In order to strike a balance between these two resources, Donovan said, a coherent jurisprudence of supranational law – law founded on the supranational, and not just national, interest – was necessary. His book, he humbly hoped, would supply that jurisprudence.

I tossed the final page on to the carpet. What a project. How on earth was he going to do it? Several huge, and to my eyes insuperable, problems appeared immediately. The function of the State would have to be examined and redefined, and the principle of the self-determination of peoples would have to be shaped afresh. Then there was the thorny question of causation – when a forest in Central America is set aflame, are not some of the perpetrators thousands of miles away, in air-conditioned boardrooms? These were very difficult philosophical, as well as legal, questions – could Donovan deal with them?

Yes, of course he could. He was made for it. He was born to meet the challenge.

ELEVEN

The next day, Monday 14 November, I found in my in-tray a summons for the pre-trial review of *Donovan v. Donovan*. Pre-trial reviews are particularly necessary in contested divorces, in which wild accusations and irrelevant, expensive antagonisms abound. A purpose of the review is to cut these out and to ensure that the trial takes place expeditiously, with no unnecessary slanging matches. It must be said that there was little danger of Donovan coming out with extraneous recriminations. Unlike my usual clients, whom I have often had to restrain from making outrageous attacks on their spouses, he knew what was at issue, which allegations counted and which did not. There was no need for me to spell things out for him. He knew what was what.

I telephoned Rodney and told him to inform Donovan immediately of the summons, which was returnable in two weeks' time, 28 November. That was fine, Rodney said. According to his diary, Mr Donovan would be flying in from Europe early that morning (Donovan's diary! I remember leafing through its crackling, blue-edged pages as a pupil, marvelling at how it was jam-packed for years ahead, how his golden, rock-solid future unrolled there for all to see . . .). He would go to court directly from the airport.

'Is that wise, Rodney?'

'You know Mr Donovan, sir. He likes to keep things fairly tight.'

This last-minute arrangement left me a little anxious. Not only was there the risk of Donovan appearing late, it also gave us no opportunity to confer. This worried me because I still had only an imprecise idea of the circumstances of the case. I was in the dark about almost everything and, as I have said, unlike some people, who seem to possess the relevant bat-like radar, I operate poorly in this kind of darkness, where I tend to bump into shapes that loom suddenly out of nowhere. One aspect of this benightedness was that I was quite unable to see a way out of the deadlock which Donovan and Arabella found themselves in: he would not contemplate consenting to the divorce, she would not consider reconciliation. The dangerous thing about the deadlock, of course, was that the longer it continued, the stronger grew the evidence that the marriage had irretrievably broken down. If Arabella could show that this had happened, she was half-way to getting her divorce.

That said, I should also note that my anxieties about my ignorance were allayed by the knowledge that Donovan, at least, had all the facts in his possession; and that was fine with me, because, in all truthfulness, and notwithstanding Mr Donovan's views, they could not have been in better hands. Clearly Donovan recognized the impasse he had reached and the problem it presented. The only question was, what was he going to do about it? I should say here, for the avoidance of doubt, that I did not resent leaving the conduct of the case to Donovan. Any misgivings which I might have had on that score had been quashed over the weekend, when in reading his new work I had become re-persuaded of the man's legal prowess. There was no dishonour in playing second fiddle to him. Indeed, it was right and fitting for a man like myself to do so. Some people are more potent sources of influence than others and it was only natural, therefore, that events should flow and braid from Donovan's actions more than from mine. That was the way of things.

Two days later I was stepping out of the office building on my way home when suddenly someone intercepted me.

'Why, Mr Donovan,' I said, continuing to walk.

Smiling, his hand on my back in an avuncular fashion, Fergus Donovan steered and deflected me through the doors of the pub we were passing. He said something I could not hear in the roar of cars and, disregarding my unwillingness, he sat me down at a table and fetched me a pint of bitter (he himself drank fizzing mineral water). He began talking to me as though he were confabulating with an old friend. He hunched his shoulders and lowered his voice. He leaned forward, taking me into his confidence.

'Well, Jim, I can't say that things are looking too hot.' He explained himself: 'Yesterday I spoke to Arab. I went round to her mother's place to see if there was anything I could do. We sat down for a coffee, just the two of us, you know how it is.' Mr Donovan pointed at the two of us by way of illustration. 'We talked about this and the other for a while. She seemed pretty relaxed and she was looking well. So, anyway,' Mr Donovan said, 'eventually I stop circling around the subject and I get to the point. I say to her, Give Mikey a chance. Give *yourself* a chance, I said. Talk to him. Speak with him at least.'

Fergus Donovan was making a pleading face, demonstrating how he had looked at Arabella. He shook his head. 'Well, she wasn't having any of that, Jim. She wasn't having a bit of that. It was over, she said. She'd made up her mind.'

Mr Donovan leaned back to analyse her reaction further. Then he leaned forward quickly and said, 'She wasn't angry, no, I wouldn't say that: there was no anger there at all – it was like she was resigned. Like she'd quit and that was that. She said the best thing would be if Michael just let her go. I tried another tack – Jim, let me tell you, I'm not a man to give up easily, I'm not a quitter – I said, Arab, tell me: tell me what Mikey's got to do. You can tell me, you know that, I said. Nothing, she said. There was nothing Mike could do. It wasn't what he did, it was what he was.'

Mr Donovan slumped into his chair. 'For an hour I talked to her, trying to change her mind, but, well, Jim, to tell you the truth, I got nowhere.'

I said nothing. Surely he had not imagined that one pep-talk would be enough to patch things up?

Reading my mind, he said, 'Of course, it was only to be expected. And what can I do? I'm just an old man, what do I know? But you see it's even worse than I thought. I thought – well, I don't know what I thought,' he admitted. 'I just didn't know it was this bad.'

He looked downhearted and, for the first time, he looked his age. The visit to Arabella – this whole business, in fact – was clearly upsetting him. I felt sad for him. At his stage of life he needed peace of mind. He needed everything to be settled, in its place.

I said, 'Michael does not seem to think it's finished. Otherwise he would not be resisting the divorce.'

'You want to know something interesting?' His voice was hoarse. 'You know what else she told me? She told me the reason she didn't want to speak to Michael was that she was afraid. You know why? She was afraid because she knew that, if Michael was given half a chance to talk to her, he would persuade her to go back to him. That was part of the problem, she said. Whenever Arab and Michael had an argument or a disagreement, Michael would always come out on top. It's not that he would *win*: it's that he was always *right*. You see what I'm talking about, Jim?' Mr Donovan asked. 'He was never wrong, she said. He would never allow her the satisfaction of being righter than him once in a while. It's not that they had arguments the whole time – no, they agreed on almost anything! I know! I saw them together! Jim, they were like two doves! – it's that when they disagreed, Mike would always be in the right. And Jim,' he said, 'I'd like you to imagine what that feels like.' Mr Donovan looked at the table. 'Too clever. Too much of a smart-ass for his own good.'

What Mr Donovan said did not surprise me. What chance did Arabella stand in an argument with Donovan? He was a professional arguer. The tricks of apologetics, the ins and outs of pro and cons – he knew them all. When it came to winning over, to logomachy in any form, he was the best. He would be incapable of losing an argument with Arabella for the simple reason that he would only argue if he knew he was demonstrably right: otherwise he would simply agree with her.

'It drove Arab crazy,' Mr Donovan said. 'That and other things, of course. Now she takes him for a monster.'

Drinking my bitter, I began to think that Fergus Donovan's usefulness as man on the inside and tipster outweighed the drawbacks that his intrusiveness presented. He knew this too – which was probably why he was lavishing this information and these drinks on me. Perhaps he fondly imagined that we might together form a mediatory bloc of some sort.

'Does Mrs Donovan work?' I asked (such an elementary question – that was how little I knew!). 'No,' Mr Donovan said. 'She doesn't work.' He sighed. 'I don't know, maybe that's it . . . maybe if she got a job . . .'

'What are her finances like?' I said. I was worried. She could take Donovan to the cleaners.

He regarded me closely, sensing that for the first time I was actively participating in a conversation with him. 'She's rich,' he said simply. 'Leaving Michael won't hurt her, her father left her a packet.'

'Her father?'

'You must have known of him, he was a judge – Lord Tetlow.'

Donovan had married Arabella Tetlow! The daughter of his former head of chambers! Surprised as I was, a potential hazard sprang immediately to my mind: it might be thought by the court that, given his ambition, Donovan had married Arabella to further his career.

Mr Donovan changed the subject. The pre-trial review, he said, was a golden opportunity that could not be missed. Michael and Arab would see each other for the first time since July. He wouldn't be there – he knew when he wasn't wanted – so it was for me to engineer a meeting of some sort. I had to ring up her solicitors and start talks – serious talks, not just mickey mouse exchanges.

I sighed. 'You must understand that there is little I can do. The matter is not in my hands. It is up to Michael and his wife to get together. I'm just a solicitor. I can't snap my fingers and make things happen.' I spoke tiredly but not irritably. 'You must appreciate this.'

'You can *enable* things to happen,' Mr Donovan said urgently. 'You can organize a framework.'

I gave a sad shake of the head.

'Yes, you can!' Mr Donovan was becoming excited. 'You can! You plug away at your end and in the meantime I'll work away at mine. I'll get hold of Michael and talk some sense into him. Then I'll get back to Arab. We may not be able to straighten this thing out, Jim, but we'll give it our best shot. What do you say?'

He was being wholly unrealistic. No amount of agency, go-betweening and bridge-building would close the great, murky crack that divided his son and daughter-in-law. And there was something else he needed to be reminded of.

'I'm afraid that I can't do that,' I said. 'I take my instructions from Michael. I cannot involve myself in schemes behind his back. You know that, Mr Donovan. Another thing,' I continued. 'I must impress it upon you that Michael knows what he's doing. You can rest assured that he has a stratagem which will address all of these problems.'

'A stratagem? What are you talking about, stratagem?' Mr Donovan spluttered. He lost his temper. He raised his voice. 'The time for games is over! We're way past that stage! No more bullshit! Look where all his tricks and wangles have got him today!'

'Please, Mr Donovan, calm yourself. Please.'

'He'll blow it!' Mr Donovan exclaimed. 'Mark my words he'll blow it with his goddamn strategies!'

He must have seen the expression of scepticism on my face, because he expanded on his remarks in an urgent whisper. 'Yes, that's right, he'll blow it. Jim, I've been around for a long time and, believe me, when it comes to blowing it I know what I'm talking about. If Michael blows it, Jim, that's it. There won't be any second chance. When it's over it's over. That's a terrible thing to realize, Jim – that you've had your last chance and you've not taken it. I'm talking about remorse, Jim,' Mr Donovan said. 'Remorse.'

'What do you suggest Michael does?' I said.

'He should come out on his hands and knees and beg for forgiveness!' Mr Donovan whispered furiously, panting for breath. 'He should cut down on his workload, devote himself to what matters – to what really matters. That's what he should do, the idiot, instead of hatching his little plans.' He stopped to breathe deeply. 'He's the one in the wrong – so it's for him to set things straight.'

His outburst completed, Mr Donovan sat back tiredly in his chair. He acceded to my suggestion that we leave. I saw him to his hotel, and on the tube home I reflected that I disagreed deeply with him about the rights and wrongs of his son's situation. Donovan, give up his work for Arabella? The idea was preposterous. On the contrary, it was Arabella who should be making the sacrifices. This was not for the crass reason that she was the wife and he the husband – no, this had nothing to do with sex or with emancipation or subjugation. We were not talking about an ordinary domestic situation here: the ordinary rules and norms did not apply. This is what Fergus Donovan and Arabella failed to realize. What made everything different here was that Donovan was a man of genius, of destiny. Allowances had to be made. History had to be accommodated in the household. Arabella should take a leaf out of the book of Mevrouw de Groot, Grotius's wife. She stuck with her man through thick and thin – she even, if my memory served me correctly, went to prison with him when he was locked up with a life sentence. A man such as Donovan called for special devotion and loyalty. Unlike, say, a man like myself, an ordinary man with ordinary roles in life – shopper, friend, voter, propagator and taxpayer – Donovan's gifts called him to lead an extraordinary and precious life. A woman could rightfully expect a man such as myself to provide her with the mundane benefits – children, money, love, diversion, time. But to expect these things, these niceties, from Donovan? Did these people not realize what a waste this would be? Imagine it! It was like asking Rembrandt to devote himself to the garden, or requiring a great scientist – Fleming, say – to put away his petri dish and concentrate on making his wife happy. Happiness? What was the happiness of one person compared to the advancement of humanity? Donovan was not in the personal happiness business. The rest of us, perhaps – let us be frank, what else are we good for? – but not Michael Donovan.

Let me qualify what I have just said before I give a misleading impression. As a solicitor, the rights and wrongs of a case are not my affair – indeed, I would be remiss if they were. It is not that in my professional capacity I must wash my hands of good and bad, but that, rather like a surgeon at the operating table, I must wear gloves. This suits me well, because I find it no easy matter to reach conclusions about ethics. The variables are generally so complex, the computations so intricate, that rarely do I have the wit or the heart to pursue them. Anyway, I find, you usually finish up by pointing the finger at both sides, so quite often the whole exercise does not advance things very far. But I think it would not be honest if I did not admit that, in this case, my hands were bare, and sticky with the virtues of those involved. I was on Donovan's side.

One of the things preying on my mind in the time before the hearing of the pre-trial review was Susan. Her absence after our encounter was a relief at first, and then, as it persisted, disquieting. When over a week had passed without a word I decided, for my peace of mind, to contact her at work. I was worried that something might have happened. The problem was that when she answered the telephone it struck me that I had nothing to say – or no specific information to convey, at least.

'I was just wondering how you were,' I said.

'I'm fine,' she said flatly. 'I'm also quite busy.' She was eating something and making chewing noises as she spoke.

I hesitated. The occasion was more difficult than I had foreseen. 'I see,' I said finally. When she said nothing to this I added, 'Well, all right then. I'll see you around.'

'I don't think so,' Susan said. 'I don't think we can take things very much further, do you?'

'I . . . Well, you may be right.'

'Goodbye, James.'

So that was that. Exactly what she was thinking I found hard to imagine, but I did understand her wish simply to put a stop to things. It was time to put us behind us once and for all. We had reached, as they say, the end of the road. Now some roads, like tributaries running into rivers, end by merging into other, larger roads, taking on their names and their bright destinations. My road with Susan, though, had not led anywhere special. It had just petered out.

By contrast, the Donovan road has side-tracked me into a wilderness. Lost, I think, is the only fair way to describe my present situation, lost amongst alien places.

Am I exaggerating? Not one bit. Whereas at night, when I am at home reliving the past year, the world is clear and familiar and real, every morning my office grows increasingly strange. At first, when I began to recount these episodes, I was deeply and organically meshed into my workplace. The ecosystem in operation – the social pyramids, the networks of understandings, the unspoken expectations, the subtle pecking orders, the position I occupied in all of this – I was on intricate terms with. The workload? I took care of that with my eyes closed. But with the passage of the days, a foreignness has introduced itself into my surroundings. I do not know where I am any more. The material placed before me has made less and less sense, until, finally, when I went into work today, the letters melted into hieroglyphs. Now the voices that come through on the telephone are speaking pure mumbo-jumbo. The office furniture seems to have changed, too. Now I am uncomfortable in my chair (my chair, where I have swivelled, slept and worked for years, where my body has indented its very contours!); the nibs on my pens are either too thick or too scratchy; the papers on my desk give off an odd dazzle and it tires my eyes to look at them; even June, my dear June – frankly, I barely understand a word she says to me. Two or three times an hour she strides in to place before me a sheaf of typing for my inspection and waits there, arms folded, foot lightly tapping.

'That's fine, June,' I say. I have gazed at the papers and pretended to check them. 'That's just fine. Thank you.'

June says exasperatedly, 'It's not. You've missed four mistakes,' she says, pointing them out. 'Look.'

'Oh yes,' I say gratefully. I circle them with my pen. 'Thank you for spotting those, June; you're a marvel.'

Of course, June will not buy that. Such compliments cut no ice with her at all and she turns tail and rattles away, her quick step signalling her discontent.

I am assailed by fundamental doubts. My occupation is beginning to strike me as a deeply outlandish mode of activity. What is this? I find myself asking when yet another task presents itself. What on earth am I doing? Advise on the effects of this leasehold? Why should I?

Of course, all of this has not gone unnoticed. Batstone Buckley Williams is a small, delicate organization. Unfitting, boat-rocking behaviour is not often missed. Today, shortly after lunch, the senior partner, Edward Boag, took me aside. It was the first time we have spoken alone since my first day at the firm.

'Everything all right, Jones?'

The senior partner is now seventy-three years old and hard of hearing, so he speaks at a disconcerting volume.

'Yes, thank you,' I said.

'Happy with us, are you?' the old man asked.

'Yes,' I said.

The senior partner nodded. He shouted, 'We're happy with you too, Jones. Very happy.'

'Thank you,' I said.

'Oh yes, most happy indeed,' he said. 'Most happy.' He

looked at me. 'Well, carry on then, Jones,' he said, and ambled off, nodding to himself.

It was a clear warning; even in my befogged state I could see that.

TWELVE

At twenty to eleven I arrived at the registrar's chambers for the pre-trial review. There was no waiting room and everybody was made to stand about in the tacky, smoky corridor until the usher called them in. The atmosphere was tense. Children were held firmly by the hand and bunched-up little groups were camped in corners, throwing furtive looks over their shoulders and conferring in low tones. It was not easy for the separating spouses to avoid each other: to stay within earshot of the usher you had to remain in the corridor, and everybody in the corridor could see everybody else. A man was looking carefully at the green wall, closely examining its texture as though he was studying a work of art. Another man was cleaning, or wiping, his hands with a handkerchief. They looked clean to me, his hands, but still he kept wiping them. Mostly people were quiet. You could easily pick out the lawyers: they were the jovial ones with the loud voices. Donovan was nowhere to be seen. He was, I guessed, on his way from the airport.

Leaning against a wall, my ear against a gurgling pipe, I lit a cigarette and tried to match up one of the faces in the corridor with Arabella. I had two things to go on. There was the photograph by Donovan's bed, which revealed only her lovely slender arms outstretched from that disc of straw; and secondly there was the picture that I kept of her in my mind's wallet. Looking around, I saw that one or two women almost fitted the bill, but what dissuaded me from a positive identification was they lacked what to my mind was Arabella's central characteristic: beauty. (Yes, I knew, even at this stage, before I had caught so much as a glimpse of her face, that Arabella was beautiful. And not simply beautiful: I also had a hunch about what kind of beauty she would possess. She would have brown-black, glistening hair that fell thickly past her shoulders, a slim, curving figure and serene big eyes. She would not, in fact, be unlike the tennis stars' girlfriends you see in the guest-box at Wimbledon, the ones in sunglasses perched nervously next to the coach, clapping sweetly whenever their man plays a winner, bravely standing by him when he is knocked out of the championship. Yes, Arabella had taken a very clear shape in my mind.)

None of the women I saw could properly be described as beautiful. One or two of them were desirable, certainly, and not without charms. But none of them possessed the necessary radiance, none of them looked like the heartbreaker I was looking for.

I was on my second cigarette and becoming increasingly flustered (it was eleven o'clock, where was Donovan?) when someone softly tapped my shoulder. There he stood, travel bag in hand, clean-shaven, unhurried and refreshed. His dark hair fell boyishly over his forehead and his smiling face actually glowed. I had not seen him looking better.

The usher called out 'Number twelve, Donovan' and a knot of people trooped into the registrar's small room. There were two rows of desks. Donovan sat at the front and I took my place behind him. As I began snapping open my briefcase a man took a seat alongside Donovan. Philip Hughes, I correctly guessed: I had seen him in the corridor, together with his colleague who now sat behind him, next to me. Like me, she was taking out a notebook to transcribe what was said. As for Arabella, she had not turned up.

The registrar, a woman in her late thirties, emerged from a side door. Then, while intently reading the papers of the case, she listened to Philip Hughes making his application for directions. Then Donovan said his piece simply and unemotionally. He spoke in his usual detached manner, as if he was representing a third party. Instead of referring to himself in the first person singular – instead of simply saying 'I' – he spoke of 'the Respondent'. 'Madam, the Respondent raises no objection,' he said, for example. I would not say that the effect was disconcerting, but it did seem a little strange. When he had finished the registrar reflected for a moment. She looked at her papers and gave what she was going to say some thought.

'I'm deeply troubled by the direction which this case is taking, Mr Donovan,' she said. 'Without in any way passing judgment on the course you have chosen to pursue, I must ask whether you are certain in your mind that you want to be contesting this case.' She looked coldly at me. 'I take it you have been fully advised as to the perils of your position.'

'Yes, Madam,' Donovan said. 'I have.'

The registrar then voiced another misgiving. She said, 'It really is far from ideal, Mr Donovan, that you should choose to represent yourself in this matter. I am extremely surprised that you, of all people, do not appreciate this.'

Donovan said nothing.

The registrar raised her eyebrows and turned to the question of reconciliation. What was being done about it, she wanted to know. Hughes spoke up.

'Madam, I am instructed by Mrs Donovan that the break-down of the marriage is truly irretrievable,' he said. 'Every avenue of rapprochement within the marital framework, if I may put it that way, has been pursued and, I am sad to say, exhausted. That being so, Mrs Donovan cannot see how any improvement could be affected at this stage; Madam, sadly, events have taken us past the point of no return. Indeed,' Hughes pointed out, 'if Mr Donovan would recognize this fact, we would all be spared these painful proceedings.'

'I am sure Mr Donovan is aware of that, Mr Hughes,' the registrar said sharply.

After dealing with several routine matters and grumbling about the Petitioner's pleadings, the registrar fetched the court diary and set a date for the trial: 2 February 1989. Then she removed her glasses. 'There remains little to add at this stage. I must however say this, which I am sure will come as no surprise to all here: namely, that every effort must be made to settle this matter one way or the other. It strikes me that there is room for more, shall we say, realism on the part of both parties. The courts must not be used as a battlefield for marital warfare. The entrenched positions of the parties must, if at all possible' – here the registrar paused for the first time, deciding on the most efficacious exit from the sentence she had started – 'be modified. Otherwise this matter will end up causing a great deal of unnecessary suffering and expense – more, I fear, than at present has been bargained for. That is all.' The registrar put her glasses back on her nose and began writing.

'Michael,' I said, when we had come out into the corridor, 'what – '

'Arab,' Donovan said, 'please. Arab.'

He was, I realized, talking to the woman who had sat next to me in the registrar's room – the woman I had taken to be Philip Hughes's assistant.

She did not reply. She turned her back and began walking away with her solicitor.

'Arab,' Donovan said again, following her, knocking against shoulders in the corridor, 'Arab, wait.' People looked on curiously and the usher walked over to see what was happening. It was his job, after all, to make sure that no ruckuses broke out.

Philip Hughes turned to face Donovan, blocking off the stairway which Arabella quickly walked down.

'Now then,' the usher said, arriving on the scene. A whiff of alcohol came from his breath. 'Now then.'

'Mr Donovan, I think it's clear that my client does not wish to talk to you,' Hughes said.

'Gentlemen,' the usher said. 'Gentlemen. Could you please discuss this elsewhere, please? There's people that want to use the stairs.'

Hughes said, 'For myself, I would be only too pleased to talk to you, Mr Donovan. We're prepared to settle this matter in the most advantageous terms,' he said. 'I really think you ought to hear what we have to offer.'

Donovan gave Hughes a faint smile and said lightly, 'I know what you have in mind. I'm not interested. And I don't think you're serving your client well by advising her not to speak to me.'

Hughes said, a don't-blame-me tone in his voice, 'It's Mrs Donovan who does not wish to speak to you. Those are my instructions.'

'Thank you, gentlemen,' the usher said firmly, 'thank you now.'

Donovan waited for a moment and then turned to me with a smile. 'Come on,' he said.

I accompanied Donovan back to his chambers. I had business to attend in the Temple, I told him. It was a sharp, breezy morning with blocks of sky-blue sky overhead. The Strand was ringing with pneumatic drills and tumultuous lorries, and the air reeked with gases. Workers yelled and hammered on the scaffolding that covered the buildings. Everything was strangely clear, and I walked along in Donovan's slipstream like a vivid dreamer. His gait had not changed. Long, fast strides, eyes front. Struggling to keep up with him, my arms full of flapping papers, trying to catch what it was he was saying before the wind took hold of his words, I could have been back in my pupillage.

We walked through the Temple past Fountain Court and into Essex Court. We stopped at number six.

To my surprise (he had never extended such an invitation to me before), Donovan said vaguely, 'Well . . . Are you sure you don't have time for a coffee?'

I hesitated. I had time. Time was not the problem.

I was about to say, No, no thank you, when I thought, Why not. Yes, why not, I thought suddenly.

I said, 'Thank you, I will if that's all right. Just a quick cup.'

For the first time in a decade I climbed the stone steps into chambers and when I got up I felt a slight wooziness, as though I had just reached some mountain-top. I followed Donovan to the clerks' room and waited by the door as he checked his pigeon-hole and his diary. The clerks' room was the same as ever: the briefs piled up against the windows, the telephones dinning, the barristers rushing in and out. I recognized several of them but decided against offering any greetings. What would have been the use?

Armed with coffees, up we went to Donovan's room, and while he leafed through his mail I looked out of his windows, a briefcase in one hand and a coffee-cup in the other. I still wore my overcoat, unbuttoned. Down in the courtyard the cars were huddled tightly, like metal cattle at a water-hole, around a young tree with a fence around it.

'Well, that was my first appearance in a matrimonial case,' Donovan said. When I turned round I saw that he was sitting back in his leather armchair, still looking at his papers.

I did not want to reply to this. I knew it was his way of making light of the situation and that he did not expect a response. But I felt I should say something.

'Was it?' I said.

I put my coffee on the window-sill and stayed where I was. Apart from a chair right at the other end of the room, there was nowhere for me to sit down. I did not feel comfortable about pulling that chair all that way across the room. At the same time it occurred to me that I could not remain standing by the window indefinitely.

'So, James . . . ' Donovan said, continuing to open envelopes and unknot brief ribbons. Twenty seconds must have passed before I understood that he was not going to follow up on what he had said. He was fully absorbed by what he was reading.

I began to feel an uneasiness. I had never been in this position before. It was the first time that I found myself alone with Donovan in a purely social situation – for that is what coffee is, after all, a social situation. It would have been out of place for me to mention the case, or the hearing that had just taken place. On the other hand, Donovan himself had referred to it, so maybe it was a proper subject of conversation. But then that was his prerogative, I reflected: it was his divorce, not mine. He could bring it up whenever he chose to.

'Busy at the moment?' I asked finally.

'Yes,' he said, after a pause.

I drank up my coffee. Donovan continued reading.

'Doing any books?' I said. I spoke casually. I did not want to betray my snooping at his desk, or my unduly rapid heart.

Donovan groaned at what he was reading and picked up the telephone. 'Sort of,' he said abruptly. 'Hello, Rodney, what's all this about the Amoco arbitration?'

While Donovan talked to Rodney I thought, Why should Donovan divulge the details of his new book to me? My opinion did not matter. Doing up the buttons of my coat, I thought about how little Donovan revealed about his private self to me. His feelings about Arabella, his ambitions, his political views, I knew nothing about these things. Indeed, I received the impression that he would positively obstruct any inquiries that I might make in these areas. I did not resent this – how could I? What grounds would I have for such feelings? – but nor did I find it entirely to my liking. I would have liked a closer involvement with him . . . Not friendship, no – nothing so intimate, one had to face facts! – but maybe something else; maybe a fellowship of sorts.

Donovan continued to talk to Rodney and I waited, buttoned up and ready to go. Still he talked. Then he was put through to someone else. A fresh dialogue began and again I waited where I was, standing by his desk in my done-up coat, my case in my hand. After a few minutes he was still talking so I walked to the door, attracting his attention with a wave and a mimed Goodbye. As he waved back, a kindly expression on his face, I saw that his cup still held a full pool of coffee.

I walked straight back to the office, reproaching myself a little for the unsatisfactory episode in Donovan's room. It had not gone well, and I did not feel that I had done myself justice. An opportunity had slipped through my fingers. (The question which I ask myself now is this: Opportunity? What opportunity? Opportunity for what?) Then, as I stepped along the engine-loud pavements, something dawned on me, something which should have sunk in years ago: Donovan was a poor conversationalist. He had no small talk or chit-chat in him at all. It was ironic, because he was one of the most fluent speakers I knew. I could think of no one more articulate.

I stopped at my sandwich bar for prawn and mayonnaise and tuna and mozzarella sandwiches and another coffee. I sat down at a table and contemplated my recent insight into Donovan. As I have said, I am unused to making discoveries of this kind for myself; usually it takes someone else to point these things out to me. I decided that it went down against him as a minus point – a weakness. It was a forgivable weakness, of course, an understandable one, but it was a weakness nevertheless. And then I thought about it a little more and began backtracking. Why should he be a great conversationalist? I thought. He did not make any claims in that direction. He set out his stall as a lawyer, not a patterer. No, I had momentarily fallen into the same trap as Arabella; I had entertained mundane expectations of the man.

Arabella. I slurped at my coffee and considered my first glimpse of her that morning. Somehow the name had lost its lustre and its magical ring. I could no longer imagine it belonging to a little mermaid, to one who might love her prince so much as to give up her fishtail for tender, excruciating feet. No, she was not as I had imagined her at all. As far as I could recollect, she had worn a practical, brownish suit – not a suit, actually, so much as an ensemble. Her short hair was dark, wiry in texture and greying. She gave a capable, sturdy impression, which was why I had mistaken her for a solicitor. Her figure was trim but unremarkable. She looked like a perfectly ordinary woman in her mid-thirties – the sort of woman, dare I say it, with whom even someone like myself might hope to succeed.

What did Donovan see in her?

I signalled to the waiter to bring me some more coffee. He

knows my face, that waiter, from my innumerable visits, so I receive fairly prompt service from him. It was not a minute before I had my drink and a complimentary biscuit in front of me while others vainly waved their hands. I do not set great store by receiving preferential treatment, but sometimes it can be nice.

Yes, I thought again, Arabella. Then I thought, perhaps a little cruelly, If I were a rich and famous barrister I would hope to do better than Arabella.

I hasten to add that in thinking this I was not seeking to denigrate Arabella. Most certainly not. There was no doubt in my mind that she was an estimable woman, a woman of many valuable qualities, and doubtless, too, she possessed many attributes of personality which made her an acceptable, and indeed desirable, spouse. No, what I had in mind was something else. It simply occurred to me that, in Donovan's shoes, I would seek out someone truly exceptional; I would not settle, if that is not too harsh an expression, for a woman of straightforward and widely available charms: I would try to scoop up the best there was. In other words (I shall be blunt), I would go for a beauty. Arabella, whatever else could be said for her, was no beauty.

It is not difficult to imagine certain responses to what I have just said. Pig! or Brute! might well be among them, and it would not surprise me to hear Sexist! ring out. But can I help my sentiments? And even if I could, can I be blamed? For a start, there are my personal circumstances. Look at me: look at my bald head, at my upside-down face and my small, plump figure: I am not an attractive man. There is very little about me to arouse the interest of a woman full stop, let alone that of a beautiful woman. That is a disheartening state of affairs, because I find beautiful women as attractive as the next man. I hanker after them just like everybody else; my head, too, has turned to lovely strollers during these last, heatwavy, weeks. The difficulty is, I am never going to be in a position to do something about this hankering. My face will always be pressed steaming against the window. Can I be blamed, therefore, for making beauty a particular priority if I suddenly found myself with Donovan's options?

I returned to the office. It was not long before I received a call that I had expected. It was from Fergus Donovan. He wanted to know how it had gone.

'How what has gone?' I said.

'The pre-trial hearing,' he said. 'How did it go? Tell me.'

I sighed. Mr Donovan tired me out. 'Why don't you ask Michael,' I said. 'He'll know all there is to know. It's not for me to tell you what happened this morning.'

It was all right, Mr Donovan said. He had checked it with his son, and he had said that it was all right for us to talk.

'Nothing much happened, Mr Donovan,' I said. I tersely described the morning's events.

Mr Donovan said accusingly, 'You didn't speak to Arab? Jim, I told you to speak to her.' Before I had the chance to reply he was off on another tack. 'Never mind,' he said, 'it can't be helped now. Jim, how would you feel about a game of golf?'

I said, 'Golf?'

'Saturday morning, at Highgate. How about it? I've booked a tee,' he said. 'Eight-thirty, Saturday morning.'

It had been a long time since I had played, I told him. I doubted very much that I would be any good, I said.

'Don't worry about that,' he said. 'You just bring a set of clubs and we'll take it from there. I'll give you shots,' he said generously. 'You can have a shot a hole if you like.'

I did not want to play golf with Mr Donovan. That was the truth.

'All right, Mr Donovan,' I said.

THIRTEEN

The night before the golf game I was attacked by nerves. It was three years since I had last played and, as I tramped around my living-room, I saw with great vividness the disasters that awaited me the following day, and actually tasted the humiliation that would follow: the chagrin and mortification shuddered through me as if I were already on the fairway, not at home, in front of the fire. And there was not just the golf to worry about: Mr Donovan's company for four hours would be no breeze, either.

Nevertheless, when I began polishing my clubs and when I caught the whiff of boiled sweets from the sweet-tin that contained my tees and markers, I began to grow excited (it is ridiculous, really, this excitability of mine). Kitted out with clean clubs and a newly furled umbrella, I began my mental preparation for the day ahead. I opened a manual – *Play Golf With John Greenan* – and refreshed myself about the essentials of the game, intently studying the photographs of the coach's famous swing. Inspired and fired-up by this literature, I drew open the curtain in the living-room, took out a nine-iron and began rehearsing my swing, studying all the while my reflection in the window. I stopped almost immediately. I looked terrible. My round, awkward, contorted body looked terrible.

I turned in early, at a child's bedtime, and like a child I fantasized about all the great shots I would play. In my mind I burned up that course. I did not sleep until half-past two.

The next day, when I had driven slowly past the gates of

Highgate Golf Club and was approaching the clubhouse, the gravel crackling and fizzing under my tyres, I caught sight of a man in shocking tartan trousers taking some practice swings in the net; my playing-partner, Fergus Donovan. I stopped the car and studied him. Even at his age he struck the ball sweetly, and plainly he was a gifted player. What was he doing playing with a duffer like me? He could not have asked me here just to keep him company. He was a foxy old customer and I suspected that, like the law, he did nothing in vain: what did he have up his sleeve?

I drove on. Mr Donovan saw me opening the boot of my car and walked over. 'Jim, good to see you. I'm all set, so why don't you go on and change and meet me on the first tee. Don't worry about green fees,' he said. 'I've sorted it all out.'

It happened then, when I was hanging up my blazer in the locker-room and eavesdropping on the conversation of two members; that was when I saw him. There he was, right in front of me, bending over to tie his shoe-laces.

'Michael?' I said out loud.

He continued tying his shoes, as though he had not heard what I had said or had not recognized my voice. Maybe he thought that another Michael was being addressed.

'Michael,' I said again. This time he looked up. I had taken him by surprise, that was clear from his face.

'Well,' he said, 'James. Well, well.'

I waited for him to finish speaking as he began tying up his other shoe, the power of his burly shoulders showing through his jumper. A lock of his dark hair fell over his forehead and he emitted a soft grunt. Then I realized he had said his piece. He had nothing to add.

I took off my tie and made some banal locker-room conversation. It was a good day for a round, I suggested. There was not much wind and judging by the car park, there would not be too many people on the course. I hoped that my voice sounded normal. I did not want Donovan to know about the emotions surging around inside me.

Donovan agreed. 'Yes,' he said, stamping his feet, 'you

could well be right.' Then he said, 'Well, have a good round,' smiled and strode off.

Surely he realized that I was going to play with him? Apprehensively I finished changing and shouldered my clubs. When I approached the tee Donovan looked at me and immediately began talking to his father in a whisper. I knew what he was saying: What the hell is he doing here? he was saying. What made you ask *him* along?

Fergus Donovan brazened out the situation. 'Jim,' he said, 'I was just telling Mikey here that we should play dog-eat-dog. You know dog-eat-dog? You played dog-eat-dog before?'

Donovan probably did not even know that his father and I had met.

'No,' I said, almost inaudibly. He would probably kick me off the case. If he found out that I had made revelations about the case – if he thought that I had committed a breach of confidence – then he might even report me to the Law Society.

'Well, here's how it goes,' Mr Donovan said, launching into an explanation of a mystifying scoring system. 'You got that? If you haven't, don't worry. You'll figure it out as we go along. You'll see, it's a great game.'

He teed up and addressed the ball. 'Now this is a dog-leg to the left,' he commentated. 'You want to be just to the right of that willow.' Thwack! The ball went soaring down the hill, rolling into perfect position. 'OK Jim, it's you to play.'

I set myself up and stared at the ball. Then, before I knew it, I found myself at the top of my backswing, thinking, Oh no, this is going all wrong, I'm going to lunge at the ball and end up topping it . . .

I lunged at the ball, topping it. It ran miserably along the ground for thirty yards.

'That'll work,' Fergus Donovan said encouragingly. 'That's safely down the middle.'

Red-faced, I went back to my bag. Donovan smashed his ball to the heart of the fairway.

'Shot, son,' Mr Donovan said. 'That'll do nicely.'

Father and son went off side by side down the green, birch-shadowed valley, I headed off in the other direction to look for my ball in the rough. We were off.

Donovan's first shot, his drive at the first hole, was just about the last shot that he hit properly. After that, as sports commentators say, the wheels came off. Almost every shot he aimed, wedges, woods, mid-irons, went terribly wrong. Either he duffed it, flying huge chunks of turf into the air, or, when he did connect, he sent the ball deep into the trees. I could barely watch. A large, strong man like him struggling to swat an immobile white ball; it was, in all honesty, a pathetic spectacle. The situation grew even more embarrassing when, after we had spent ten minutes raking around the undergrowth for Donovan's ball, Mr Donovan began impatiently coaching his son.

'Remember, keep your head down,' he said as Donovan stood over the ball. 'And for God's sake, slow on the backswing.'

Donovan looked silently at his father before turning to his ball. He concentrated for a moment and swished. The ball sliced away out of bounds.

'Slow on the backswing!' Mr Donovan exclaimed. 'How many times do I have to tell you! Slow on the backswing! Look at Jim,' he said, much to my discomfort, 'look at the way he's hitting it, nice and easy. *Jesus*,' Mr Donovan said. Then, at the next hole, when Donovan had fluffed a 4-iron: 'Hit *through* the ball! You're hitting *at* it! Jesus, Mary and Joseph, anyone would think you'd never played before in your life!'

What was interesting was Donovan's reaction to all of this. He seemed completely unmoved. It was as though he was not bothered by his failure at all. This struck me as odd, because to come to grief on a golf course is, to most players, an intense personal disaster. To play like a rabbit, your every gaffe and blunder visible to the whole world, is a crushing experience. That was the reason I had put away my clubs these last years – because the pain of the game was simply too great. Donovan, though, seemed to have some kind of inbuilt anaesthetic. His mis-hits did not hurt him. He seemed completely unembarrassed about losing to me, an inferior, and to his father, a white-haired man in his seventies. There he was, calm as you like, and even when his father goaded him ('You couldn't hit a bull's ass with a banjo,' or, after a fresh-air shot in front of a gallery of members, 'Jesus Christ. That's it. That's the last time I'm ringing *you* up for a game.') he remained unmoved and equable, hardly speaking at all. I could not understand it.

We stopped half-way through our round to sit down on a bench and eat a chocolate bar. Mr Donovan totted up the score and calculated that, at a pound a hole, I had won three pounds and he six. Then there was a silence as we rested. The course was hilly and the steep slopes had tired us. I lit a cigarette.

Then Mr Donovan spoke up. 'Jim, I'm going to let you into a secret.'

I said nothing. I hunched my shoulders and sucked at my cigarette. Sandwiched between the Donovans, I felt uncomfortable.

'Women,' Mr Donovan said, 'are like golf courses.'

I stole a look at Donovan, who was sitting right next to me. From my acute angle it was hard to tell what he made of his father's sudden pronouncement. Probably he had heard it before, because he was staring inanimately out at the horizon.

Mr Donovan warmed to his theme. 'You know what that means, Jim? It means if you want to know what makes a good woman, you look at what makes a good course.' He laughed and turned to me. 'You think I'm bullshitting? Well, just give it some thought. Just think about it.'

We swallowed our chocolate bars and took our shots.

'So, the next question is, what makes a good golf course?' Mr Donovan asked as we walked down the fairway. 'I'll tell you. First and foremost, a good course is demanding – it's tough. It stretches you, it shows up your limits. Number two – and this is less important – a good course looks good. Not pretty – that's not necessary – but good. Ballybunion or Troon aren't pretty, but they're handsome all the same. Myself,' Mr

Donovan said, 'I don't like your tarted-up courses, the type you get in Spain, with their palm trees and their fancy bunkers. Give me a grizzly links any day of the week, something with real character.' Mr Donovan pulled his trolley along. He caught me looking at him and laughed and said, 'Am I right, Jim?'

I smiled weakly, but my unease had by now grown acute. The situation felt all wrong: what was I doing playing golf with Donovan, and what was I doing beating him?

We all reached the green. We took out our putters and stalked around, studying our putts. Meanwhile, Mr Donovan picked up where he had left off. 'A good golf course is hazardous but fair,' he said. 'It rewards you for good shots and doesn't screw you around.' He got down on his haunches and peered at his line to the hole through the curves and borrows of the green. 'On the other hand,' he said, 'if you play badly, then it punishes you. Then it kicks your ass.'

He then said suddenly, 'Jim, my wife, Mikey's mother, she was, you could say, a major championship course. She was like a Hoylake, or an Augusta or Brookline.'

We putted out and walked up a hill and over a bridge to the next tee. A natural silence descended. There was only the sounds of our steps, the breeze, the motorway behind the trees humming like a sea behind dunes. I looked down at my feet, spiking through scrolled, orangey leaves as I walked. Suddenly and queerly everything had become emotional.

'Of course,' Mr Donovan said, 'you don't get many women in that bracket. They're scarcer than hen's teeth. Arabella,' he said hoarsely. 'Arabella is one of them. That's right, isn't it, Mikey? She's one in a million.'

Again I thought: why is it they hold Arabella in such high regard? Apart from being her father's daughter, she was just an ordinary person as far as I could see. Why, then, the big deal?

Donovan did not say anything and at first I could not see any expression on his face. He stood up on the tee and shaped to hit his drive and I pointed my eyes down at my feet. But then, when after quite some time I had not heard the swish of the swing, I looked up. Donovan was furiously gripping his club, and his skin had gone red. Then I saw his eye secrete a drop of clear fluid. It ran down his nose and dripped off its tip, like a drop from a tap. I was taken aback. Some kind of lachrymal activity was taking place, that I was sure of, the tear ducts were visibly functioning: but surely Donovan could not be crying? As another drop leaked from his eye, I came to the conclusion that, extraordinary as it might seem, some form of weeping was indeed occurring. I did not jump to this con- clusion, most certainly not: I was driven and cornered into it by the facts. There was no wind or sand blowing into Donovan's face, nor was there any real question of the fluid being sweat or some other exudative. Therefore either he had suddenly developed a leaky eye (a common enough con- dition, but one I had never witnessed in him), or he was crying. The latter was plainly the more probable.

Michael is crying! I suddenly thought.

He swung at the ball and badly mis-hit it. I shivered with shame and guilt and wished myself back at home, in my bath. I stood still and said nothing. He would hate me for ever for having seen him in his moment of weakness. He brushed his nose with his sleeve and walked quickly after his ball.

My head pulsing with blood, I walked softly behind my playing partners. Old Mr Donovan went into the bushes to help his son to look for his ball. I judged it wise to leave them by themselves and went over to my own ball, forty yards away, and, trying to blend into the background, waited. I watched the two of them snooping around in the under- growth, thwacking away for a long time. From their postures I saw that they were talking – or rather, the father was talking and the son listening.

I was watching a scene of intimacy and I felt ridiculous; in all my life I had never felt so out of place. The Donovans and me: was there ever a more ill-suited three-ball? So why, then, had Mr Donovan asked me to come? Did he hope that the three of us might discuss the case afterwards, in the clubhouse? Or had he planned to reveal another Michael to me, a more vulnerable Michael, Michael the duff golfer? Perhaps he hoped that the spectacle would puncture my admiration for his son. Perhaps he thought I had too grand a vision of him and that this would cut him down to size, thus giving me the confidence to exert greater influence over him.

More fool he! I thought to myself. What did he take me for, a simpleton? My esteem for Donovan was purely professional, nothing more, nothing less. Did he think I was incapable of distinguishing the man from the lawyer? I had no expectations of Donovan on the personal front – he was a normal man on that side of things, an unexceptional man. Indeed, there was a slight uncanniness about this – the fact that his extraordinariness as a jurist went hand in hand with this utter normality. Just as evil men do not sport tails with tridents or bare yellow fangs, so with Donovan was there no outward manifestation or advertisement of his genius. On the surface he was a regular guy. He pulled on his trousers in the morning like the rest of us. He hooked golfballs into water hazards just like you and I. Did Mr Donovan imagine that I did not know this?

They emerged from the bushes. They were still talking, and their conversation continued out of my earshot during the remaining holes of the round. I wondered what they were talking about, but as soon as I approached them they fell silent. It was obviously a private and important matter. Thus excluded from the talk, I concentrated on my game. I did well. By the end I had won six pounds.

Afterwards we sat on the clubhouse terrace, looking down on players putting on the eighteenth green. When I say 'we' I am referring to Mr Donovan and me – Donovan himself had rushed off immediately, despite his father's entreaties to him to stay. ('Stay Mikey, just for one drink,' Mr Donovan had said. 'Come on, we'll have a beer together. I'll buy. Come on, son.' 'I can't,' Donovan had said. 'I have to go.') I thanked Mr Donovan for the game. Given his forthcoming nature I expected him to reveal what had been said between him and his son on the course, but he said nothing on that subject.

Perhaps their exchanges had been insignificant, after all. Perhaps they had talked about golf or the weather in Ireland. (Such were the handicaps I laboured under; so often I simply had no way of telling what was taking place, even before my own eyes.)

We had a beer together in silence. Then I felt obliged to voice a complaint. I said that it was unsatisfactory that I had not been told that Michael would be coming. I told him it had prejudiced our relationship. Michael would now suspect, however wrongly, that inappropriate communications had taken place between us. I wanted to know why this little meeting had been set up, I said.

'What?' Then Fergus Donovan caught up with what I had said. Last night, he explained tiredly, he had, for once, got through to his son, and he had asked him to play with us. He couldn't see anything wrong with that. As for all this stuff about prejudice, he did not know what I was talking about.

I was about to argue my point of view when I saw that Fergus Donovan was distressed about something. He was shaking his head and muttering something to himself. Now I felt ashamed about my niggardly outburst. This was an old man who had travelled a long way to see his son, to lend him a helping hand. Judging by what had happened that day, it looked as though there were communication problems between the two. Donovan, it looked like, was not giving much away to his father. Judging by his early exit after the golf, he was not giving him much of his time, either. And then, of course, there had been the spectacle of his son weeping. No wonder Fergus Donovan was upset.

I offered the old man a beer, but he declined. As we said goodbye he handed me my six pounds' winnings which Donovan had forgotten to pay. 'I'll not have it said that the Donovans don't pay their debts,' he said.

I think it is worth mentioning what happened next. I left the golf course wrapped up, enseamed, in thought. I was not dwelling on anything in particular, just giving myself over to deep, unspecific contemplation of the morning's goings-on.

Donovan's breakdown, if I can call it that, had really unsettled me; and just as out on the course I had had trouble believing my eyes, now I found it difficult to trust my recollection. Had I really seen Donovan cry? Was it possible – Professor Michael Donovan QC? In tears?

My disbelief was fairly understandable. I had never, until that day, seen Donovan show any vulnerability at all – I had never seen him be anything other than *himself*. This sudden, extreme jump in his identity – from top lawyer to weeping golfer – was too much for me to accept. But accept it I did (I was forced to, I could not very well reject the evidence of my own eyes), and in the car I turned my mind over to a deep analysis of what had happened. It was, I am afraid, a typically fruitless exercise. The memories, theories and figurings all cancelled each other out so that my intense preoccupation came to naught. A cartoonist would have suspended a blank, cloudy bubble over me and linked it to my head with a chain of snowballs.

The caption following after that would show me staring around from behind my steering wheel with a baffled frown on my face and three exclamation marks and a question mark in the thought-bubble: because the next thing I knew I was driving around in side streets, tower blocks everywhere, lost.

I snapped out of my reverie. I had driven in completely the wrong direction: instead of going south, I had gone north. The discovery shook me up. What was going on here? How could such a thing happen? Panicking slightly, I quickly switched in to a thick flow of traffic and came on to a main road. Then I put my foot down. I speeded, I urgently needed to get back, and not long afterwards I was crossing the river over Battersea Bridge, as good as home.

FOURTEEN

I am afraid that I allowed the afternoon's goings-on to affect me unduly, because when I finally pulled up in front of my house I came to the conclusion that enough was enough. Sweating, sticky, smelling of my car's smoky interior, I decided that the time had come to get to the bottom of things. There was a word, a blunt, pocket-sized word, that I could no longer get around: why?

This is not, I should say, a question I often ask myself, certainly not in relation to the behaviour of my fellow men and women. Rarely will you catch me looking into whys and wherefores. As I see it, either you know something or you do not. If a mystery arises, you bide your time, because time, in my experience, clarifies. If the mystery persists, take care of it with a robust presumption. Choose a reasonable analysis and stick to it. Only if, for some reason, the presumption is not enough, should Why? be considered, and then only as a last resort. This approach is, I think, a sound one. Not only is Why? generally an unproductive and inefficient interrogation, but most of the time, you will find, it is positively counterproductive – it actually sets you back. Why? Because once the word makes one appearance it makes thousands more, it proliferates and consumes everything before it: start asking why and you start sliding down a slippery slope, suddenly everywhere you look things cry out for explication, elucidation and unravelment. What I am saying is this: ask why and you ask for trouble.

This is what happened to me on the night of the golf game. Three hours after I had decided to crack the day's mysteries I was to be found sitting at my desk, a scratch pad in front of me and biro in hand. I was smoking a cigarette and I was nonplussed. The Donovan affair did not add up. I mean this almost literally. I had written down the principal elements of the case and, like a corny sleuth sweating over clues to a murder, I had placed plus signs between them and an equals symbol at the end – an equals symbol that was followed by *Donovan cries on golf course?* For a long time I sat there regarding the question mark, darkening and thickening it by superimposing it with still more question marks. Why had Donovan cried on the golf course?

My sinuses ached as I racked my brains. No luck. No matter how I figured it, I drew a blank. The equation – Arabella leaves Donovan + Donovan silent in court + Donovan's journals + Donovan fighting the divorce + me + Arabella's ansaphone message + Fergus Donovan + Donovan's new book – led me precisely nowhere, because each element, each addendum, was itself a mystery. Why had Arabella left Donovan? Why had Donovan broken down? Why was I so interested? And so it went on, one why leading to another. It was not that I sought a mathematical solution, because plainly the actions of human beings are never going to work out that way. They are never going to be susceptible to infinitesimal calculus, trigonometry or arithmetic. The answers to the problems are never to be found, like they were at school, by flipping to the back of the text-book. Nevertheless, a certain amount of computation must be involved. Things must eventually tot up; not to the nth decimal point, of course not, but roughly, give or take a few digits. But with Donovan nothing worked out. So many things remained irredeemably and tantalizingly obscure that, rather petulantly, I crumpled up the paper and threw it across the room.

I lit another cigarette and tried to clear my head. I tried to stand back and look at things from a distance, to gain a fresh perspective – maybe that was all that was needed, maybe the case was like one of those trick close-ups of everyday objects: you turn the page upside-down, hold the snapshot away from you and squint, and suddenly the strange, blurred image is transformed into the corner of a Hoover. Maybe everything would suddenly focus into unmistakable familiarity.

I got nowhere. The fact of the matter was that I was no longer involved in the case, I was completely embroiled in it. Whereas in other cases unresolved puzzles were a matter of complete indifference, in *Donovan v. Donovan* they fretted and nagged at me. Edgily, in a state of excitement, I paced about my room and rubbed my chin. What tormented me was that I knew that, just around the corner, all sorts of answers and discoveries awaited me. Tantalized and impatient, I wanted to fast-forward the action, to skip out the middle bits and get to the end, to the fireworks. It is not that I anticipated the kind of finale you get in adventure movies, with detonations and sizzling cars. But I did know that the answers, when they reached me, would not be run-of-the-mill: I knew that something out of the ordinary was going on, something big. And I could not wait to find out.

I did what I often do in these situations: I ran myself a bath. Almost as soon as I stepped into the foggy, clammy bathroom I felt better. I drenched my face in hot water and leaned back neck-deep in the icebergs of bubbles that rose aromatically from the water. I rested my feet on the taps. Then, after I had slowly soaped my neck and arms and the tensions drained away from me, my patience and methodology returned. This rage for order was premature. I was being unprofessional, jumping the gun. At present I simply did not have enough facts at my disposal. There were xs and ys and zs that remained beyond me, but only for the time being. There was no need, as yet, to go and probe and question too deeply. Also, there were many things that I did not strictly need to know, many things which were irrelevant: I was, was I not, trying to understand *Donovan v. Donovan*, not Donovan (although, admittedly, the two were not entirely distinct –

already they were beginning to intertwine). I had no doubt, in any event, that eventually, as ever, most things would fall into some satisfactory kind of order.

In this state of relaxation, something occurred to me about Donovan's remarkable tears: London's buried rivers. In olden times, I remembered reading somewhere, a series of urban rivers ran between the houses down to the Thames. Perhaps rivers, with its connotation of broad, surgy waterways, is the wrong word. Streams, I think, would be more accurate, because I am referring to trickling feeders of the Thames like the Fleet and the Tyburn. These streams no longer figure on any maps. One by one they have been buried alive by the city, vanishing deep under the cement and asphalt coat that covers the London earth. Nevertheless, you can still tell where they once flowed, their old beds revealed by the shallow valleys that dip perceptibly through certain streets and circuses. This does not mean that the streams have disappeared entirely. No, they are not to be suppressed so easily; they are still there, forcefully springing from the subsoil, making their way through pipes and underground channels; and yes, they still make their presence felt, crushed as they are by the city: after heavy rainfall cellars in Islington start flooding, the current in the Serpentine suddenly picks up. This is why Donovan's tears on the golf course made me think of them: somewhere inside him there had been some sudden downpour.

Even as this quaint parallel came to me I knew that it would not take me very far. What I needed was information, not metaphors. Even so I derived comfort and a measure of illumination from it. In the absence of factual progress it reassured me to make this dreamy type of headway.

My wait-and-see approach was rewarded three days later, on Tuesday 6 December, when I received a fat and rather intriguing envelope from Philip Hughes. Inside it was a letter and a wad of correspondence. The letter was marked 'Without Prejudice' and it contained an offer: Arabella would accept a lump sum payment of £50,000 in full and final settlement if

Donovan consented to the divorce petition. All things considered, it was not a bad offer. A bit of negotiation could lower the payment by £10,000, and given the uncertainties of a trial and the distress, inconvenience and expense that it would cause, leaving aside the substantial financial award which Arabella might receive, I would have warmly recommended it to Donovan in normal circumstances. But his instructions on this point were clear: he would not consent to the divorce, not at any price.

I turned to the second paragraph. Donovan, Hughes alleged, was molesting Arabella with the enclosed letters. Such correspondence was to cease immediately or an injunction would be obtained.

Hughes's threat was over-dramatic, I thought, and not to be taken too seriously. If Donovan had threatened physical violence of some sort or had camped outside her house or bombarded her with telephone calls it would have been different. To complain of epistolary harassment was taking things a little far; no one forced her to read the letters. Then I thought, Wait a minute: letters?

I picked out the bundle from the envelope. My sticky fingers leaving faint fingerprints, I removed them from the elastic band and counted fourteen enclosed in airmail envelopes bearing colourful English, Swiss and French stamps. They had not been opened. I fingered them. They crackled in my hands. They gleamed and slid around in my fists like clean plates. Then I put them to one side. There was no question of examining their contents. These were private communications, I had no business with them. They were strictly between Donovan and his wife.

Why, then, if that was so, was I to be found five minutes later in the office kitchenette, bent over a grumbling kettle, holding envelopes over the plume of steam?

I only unsealed three letters. There was no time to do any more and I was receiving strange glances from my workmates. June, though, had no qualms about asking me what I was doing. It is part of her charm, this directness.

'James, what on earth are you doing?' she said.

'I'm working,' I said boldly. 'What does it look like I'm doing?' I yelped as the steam scalded my hand.

'It looks like you're opening mail you shouldn't be,' June said. 'That's what it looks like.'

I gave her a reassuring smile, and continued steaming.

June said, 'Well, I just hope you know what you're doing.'

The first letter I unsealed was dated 28 September 1988, about a week after Donovan had received the petition and – again I consulted the chronology of the case that I had drawn up – the day after he had finished those rather curious exercises in his notebooks. (At that point I noticed something else for the first time: that Donovan had started his notebook exercises – his comeback, in other words – the day after he had received the petition. What was I supposed to make of that?) It was a strange letter. I had anticipated a billet-doux of some kind, some sort of plea from the heart: instead it read uncannily like the pleading in a statement of claim. Reading through it, I half-expected the short, pithy paragraphs (each making a distinct point) to be numbered and broken down into sub-paragraphs marked by Roman numerals.

The letter started by giving some facts as Donovan understood them. They had been married for just over twelve years. During that time they had had their ups and downs (I am paraphrasing, of course; I cannot reproduce that agreeable, eloquent voice which Donovan projected in his writing). Problems, difficult problems, had presented themselves and had been overcome. Why? Because the two of them had always valued their marriage. It was a precious thing which, until recently, they had always striven to preserve. So much, Donovan said, could not be in dispute. Then he moved on to his next point. Recently fresh difficulties had arisen, difficulties which had prompted her departure. Quite what those difficulties were Donovan was unable to say: Arabella had not voiced any specific grievances, she had merely packed her bags and left without a word, refusing to have any contact with him. Then, out of the blue, he had received her petition, filled with wild accusations of cruelty and neglect and unreasonableness. Why, if she set any store by their marriage (as she had often claimed) had she not discussed her grievances with him? If he was in the wrong about something (which he was forced to deny, not knowing exactly of what it was he was accused) then he would make amends. He would meet her complaint.

Then Donovan took an alternative scenario. Let's say, he said, that Arabella no longer desired to save the marriage. Did that justify her not speaking to him? No; no, because it represented a fundamental development which needed to be discussed: it was a serious matter that affected both of them and it was only fair that, as a party to the marriage, he should be heard. Whichever way you looked at it, Donovan concluded, her refusal to speak to him was unfair and unjustifiable and accordingly her petition was ill-judged and overhasty. Besides, he loved her. He wanted to see her. She only had to telephone his clerk and, subject to his not being tied up, he would put her straight through to him, no matter where he was in the world. He counted on her to come to her senses. He loved her, Donovan said again. He loved her with all his heart.

I carefully replaced the writing papers (six sheets) in the envelope and re-sealed it with glue that I keep handy in a desk drawer. It was not possible, outside of a forensic examination, to tell that I had broken the letter-flap, that I had – let me make no bones about it – broken Donovan's trust.

Once I had covered my tracks I gave the letter some thought. There was no doubt that, on paper, it expressed a powerful equitable argument. A neutral bystander armed with the bare facts would have to agree that Arabella should not, as a matter of fairness, have left Donovan in the lurch without any explanation or notice. To take a legal analogy, it was arguable that he had been unfairly dismissed: the procedures of consultation and warnings which a husband of twelve years might reasonably expect had not been followed. It might well be that Arabella was right to leave Donovan: but that did not mean that he was no longer entitled to a hearing, especially as there was a possibility that, after such a hearing, she might have a change of heart.

To my mind, the letter showed that Donovan had something of a contractual approach to marriage. He saw it as an organic, mobile bundle of undertakings, reciprocal duties and implied terms. One of these, it seemed, was that a benefit to one party gave rise to a debt to the other. Arabella had obtained a benefit when she left him, but she had also incurred a debt: in return for her new freedom she owed him reasons and a chance to put his case. These letters from Donovan, I reflected, could be said to boil down to marital bills of exchange. Or maybe (this was playful conjecture on my part) Donovan saw marriage as a type of treaty, a bilateral agreement concluded between two sovereign persons – a concordat of love containing provisions and articles and reservations that could be invoked and enforced. (The law, I should say, took a different view of wedlock to Donovan. In its eyes, marriage was not a species of contract but a state of affairs. Quite whether this distinction clarifies anything I am not sure.)

I must say that in all the matrimonial cases I had ever worked on I had never come across a letter making an appeal to justice quite like this one. At first I did not know what to make of it; surely this legalistic approach, this reliance on objective standards of fairness, was, well, inappropriate? Surely the heart ruled the head in these matters? Then I remembered: these letters were not written by just anybody, they were penned by Professor Michael Donovan QC. If anyone knew what they were doing it was he. If he considered that this tack would succeed, then no doubt he was right; quite apart from his natural tactical gift, did he not know his wife better than anyone?

The second letter that I opened, dated 29 October, was relatively brief. It began with a definition: an irrational course of action is one which plainly will not achieve the result which it is intended to achieve. It is irrational, for example, Donovan patiently explained, to scramble eggs in order to reach the moon. Similarly, Donovan said to Arabella, your actions are irrational on two planes. The petition was irrational because its weakness at law meant that it would not succeed in bringing about a divorce; and bringing about a divorce was irrational because it would not succeed in bringing her happiness. On the contrary, it would bring her nothing but misery. Surely she must see that? And if she did, surely she would act upon that insight?

There was one more thing (I continue to paraphrase). Should they not see a marriage guidance counsellor? Donovan was ready to put in as many sessions as it would take. Perhaps that was what they needed, a bit of expert advice. They could air their grievances, they could listen to each other afresh and maybe even really hear each other. What did she think about that? Would not a calm, rational third party be helpful in this complicated and inflamed situation? He asked her to think about it, in her own good time. He loved her.

As I glued up the envelope I gave a little smile. It was revealing that Donovan should suggest an arbitrator to cure the problems, and it was also a smart move. It was an arrangement he would naturally feel very comfortable with, addressing arguments to a presiding authority.

I opened the last letter of the series. It was dated 28 November, the day of the pre-trial review. It was completely different to the others and after I had read it once I told June, rather dramatically, to hold all calls. Then I read it again.

You should have spoken to me this morning, Donovan started. You shouldn't have run away like that, I wasn't going to eat you up, I simply wanted to talk. Arab, the least you can do is answer my letters. Write to me. Please, Arab, my darling. What is there to lose? At least acknowledge receipt, because – and here he began to read like a poor man's lawyer, emotively pleading personal injury (heartbreak, nervous shock, hysterical aphony, distress) and loss of earnings (his work had been terribly affected). Then he failed to sound like a lawyer at all. He sounded like the man on the street, like absolutely anybody. Come back, Arab, he begged. Give me one last chance. So disturbed was Donovan that he actually had started a sentence and discontinued it. The sentence which started *Remember everything we have done together, remember when* had been scratched out with a bold, undulating line and abandoned, which was most unlike Donovan, who wrote without any modifications or corrections. I kept reading. The letter continued along clichéd lines, finishing with the words (and here I quote), *I am desperate, Arab. My love, just tell me what I have to do and I'll do it.*

I must confess that I found all of this rather disappointing. It was unworthy of Donovan to resort to such shabby emotionalism. He was squandering his natural intellectual advantages and advancing exactly the sort of points that someone like myself, an ordinary man with merely ordinary ideas and words at my disposal, might advance. And I experienced another sensation, namely resentment. It bothered me that he should wade about in this way, in this mire, that he should humiliate himself like this. A man like Donovan, a noble spirit, begging and scraping to a woman like Arabella? It shocked me, if the truth be known.

Then I realized. Then the penny dropped. This was the cleverest ruse of all. Donovan, having sensed that his old line was not securing results, had decided to adopt a completely different tack altogether. Cogency, good sense and dignified requests for fair play had gone out of the window. In their place had come irrational supplications for clemency and forgiveness and emotional pressure. Donovan, in a last attempt to bring Arabella around, had got down on his knees to tug at her skirt and heart-strings. I could see his reasoning: Arabella was unbudging so therefore he would *move* her.

I put away the letter with a grin. You had to hand it to Donovan. He did whatever it took to win. If it meant demeaning himself then he demeaned himself. If it meant masquerading as a man at his poor wits' end, then he would conduct that masquerade. He was a true professional, the advocate's advocate.

That said, there was a slight problem here. There was

something even Donovan had not foreseen: Arabella had not read any of these letters.

I went to lunch feeling better about the whole business, more clear-headed. The letters might not have worked as far as Donovan was concerned, but they did help me, they did advance my understanding of the case. Arabella's strange message on Donovan's ansaphone, for example, could now be seen as a reference to the letters: stop sending me letters, that was what she had meant. I realized, of course, that Arabella could equally have been referring to something else, and that there was no way of verifying my assumption. But the important thing was that I now had fresh facts which, given a certain analysis, were consistent with, and explanative of, facts that had previously baffled me completely. Until I had read the letters, to take another example, I had wondered what Donovan was doing to prevent the case from coming to court: now I knew. Yes, things were beginning to fall into place. And what also heartened me and sent me to lunch happy was that I had been confirmed in the back-seat approach that I was taking not just to the whole business, but to the narrower matter of the litigation itself. I could rest assured, Donovan was on the case.

When I returned from lunch I lit a cigarette and reached for my biro. I told June to forward the letters and the settlement offer to Donovan, and got on with my work.

FIFTEEN

There was a lull in the Donovan case in the weeks leading up to Christmas. Nobody was around. When I gave Donovan back his letters to Arabella and received no response, I rang Rodney to find out where he was. This was in mid-December. Vienna, Rodney told me. He had flown out on the 9th and would be gone until Christmas. After that he would go to Ireland for a short vacation.

After a moment's hesitation I telephoned the Savoy and asked for Fergus Donovan. I wanted to tell him that Donovan had attempted to correspond with Arabella but had failed to get through. Hopefully this would cure his misapprehension that nothing was being done. Maybe then he would leave me in peace.

Mr Donovan? He checked out over a week ago, the receptionist said.

This took me by surprise. Old Fergus Donovan was not the type to throw in the towel so easily. And if he had made up his mind to leave, why had he not telephoned to tell me? I did not understand it at all.

But then, after a moment's reflection, I saw that his departure made sense. He must have realized that nothing he could do would change the way things were heading – that it was too late now for a last-ditch patch-up. For there could be no doubt, even in that oily calm before Christmas, that things were flowing in a certain direction, that below the surface propellers were turning. Now, suddenly, the trial was just seven weeks away – and seven weeks was nothing, seven weeks would arrive in the wink of an eye. Fergus Donovan must have sensed this, sensed that we were being carried inescapably to that February hour.

For it to be appreciated how things were – to appreciate how powerful the tug of events had suddenly become – I think that resort must be made to the world of films: action films. Often, in these movies, the protagonist ends up on a raft in a river, escaping from pursuers. He traverses gulches and deer-crossed shallows and then, just as it seems that he is home and dry: rapids. White-water rapids.

He shoots the rapids. By the skin of his teeth he has zigzagged the boulders and made it through the torrents. The sun reappears, he smiles, in the cinema we all relax. We have made it.

Suddenly the camera pans in on the man's face. He has heard something. He listens. We, in the cinema, we listen too. We lean forward in our seats, all ears.

At first, nothing. The water tinkling, a bird breaking from a tree (by now we too are on the raft, down there alongside the hero). Then, there, there it is: a distant, constant roar. What could it be? What could that sound be?

Then everybody notices something about the river: the water: it has whitened and quickened, and the raft is really moving. The current, it is suddenly clear, is far too powerful for us to jump overboard or to steer ashore. Meanwhile the roar is growing louder and louder and the raft is travelling faster and faster towards it. Then camera closes in on the hero's face, on his horrified, wide open eyes: it has dawned on him.

The camera withdraws to a safe spot up in the woods, whisking us away with it. Down on the raft, in the booming air, there is nothing the hero can do about anything. Inexorably his vessel is sucked towards the edge of the huge waterfall . . .

I shall stop that story at this point, because what happens next is irrelevant. The significant moment in it, as far as I am presently concerned, is that moment when we all realize that the hero is at the mercy of the muscular water, that he is being borne wherever it wills. So it was with the Donovan case. The trial date loomed like that roar downriver and an irreversible onrush drove us all towards it.

Now it may be objected that the comparison I have just drawn is misleading: the Donovan story may have been a drama, yes, but it was a real-life drama, utterly distinct from your picture show. But to that I say: it is not so simple, this distinction. Just as, at the cinema, there is the illusion that what you see is not just a fast series of consecutive photographs of, say, a foaming river, just as it can seem that the river is foaming right there in the auditorium, so the reverse can sometimes be true: sometimes, in real life, it can feel as though *you* are being flashed up on some screen, as though somewhere rows of eyes are drinking in *your* magnified actions. I once went to a play (Susan had bought the tickets, there was no way out of it) where, out of the blue, the actors ran into the stalls and began involving the audience in the action, grabbing us by the sleeves and forcing us to our feet. I did not know what was going on, whether I was a viewer or a participant or what. At times, these last months, to my confusion and exhilaration, it has been the same. And right now, looking back at it all from my desk, I feel like a movie goer as the touched-up, superreal action rolls before my eyes . . .

With the trial closing up on me, I embarked upon an analysis of how it might go and what tactics to employ. Usually one leaves these things to the last possible moment, but in this case I began my preparation well in advance. I did not want to be caught out by Donovan should he suddenly fire me some question. I fetched the pleadings from my file and looked again at the allegations.

Boiled down to its essence, Arabella's complaint was that Donovan had cruelly degraded and neglected her.

The accusation of cruelty I found rather old-fashioned. The

law had moved on since the days when a wife had to show cruel behaviour which threatened her health. It was an unwisely harsh allegation to make, I thought – all that a wife needed to show these days was behaviour on the part of the husband that would make any expectation of continued cohabitation unreasonable.

Still, the question of cruelty had to be gone into. What was meant by 'cruel'? Some guidance was to be obtained, I saw, from the case of *Le Brocq*. Cruel means cruel, Harman CJ defined. I looked at the facts. The husband was found to be a morose and withdrawn man. This was not due to any wilful malice on his part but due to his 'make-up' – 'his conduct flows from a personality for which he is unable to help himself,' the judge held. It could not be described as cruel. Petition rejected.

That was a possible line of argument, I reasoned. Donovan may have ignored and therefore degraded Arabella, but he did so unwittingly. He could not help it that he was so absorbed in his thoughts, and surely you could not describe absent-mindedness as cruelty? Or could you? The categories of cruelty, another authority informed me, like the categories of negligence, are never closed. Nor was there any requirement of evil or malice, I read somewhere else. Confused, I looked at the dictionary definition of cruel: disposed to inflict pain, it said. Was an unmalicious disposition to inflict pain possible?

By this stage I was beginning to have difficulties in distinguishing and cohering all the various dicta on the subject, so I put away the books. Donovan would have the legal side of things wrapped up, there was no need for me to go into the matter too deeply. The facts, too, he would be on top of: had he not assured me that Arabella would be unable to prove her contention? The important thing was that I had identified the question which lay at the heart of the case: had Donovan been so preoccupied with his work and himself that it would be unreasonable to expect Arabella to live with him?

My money was on Michael Donovan. I knew my man. In a

case like this one, a winnable case, he always did the business. But that is not to say that I relished the prospect of the trial. No, I feared the worst, I feared what Donovan might do to his wife during cross-examination. *Donovan v. Donovan* was a mismatch, and no sensible person could look forward to it.

Around Christmas-time most firms of solicitors hold an office party or a bash of some kind to mark the occasion. Batstone Buckley Williams is no exception, and just before the break everybody clears up their room and decks it out with the tinsels and shiny fripperies you always see at these sorts of festivities. Work stops early and the fun and drinking begins. Before long crackers, whistles and other items of revelry are in evidence, and as the evening progresses there is loud music and a disco.

I must confess that it is only after I have had a lot to drink that I feel entirely comfortable in the conical, brilliant hat which someone has insistently placed on my head, and that I am able to forget the redness of my face and the perspiration patch along my spine. And it is only then, when I have drunk enough to forget myself, that I am able to take to the dance floor, and even then it is only to participate in the communal dances – the ones where everyone holds the person in front of them by the waist and, having formed a tight, warm human centipede, we shuffled around the room cheering and singing. At moments such as this, in the midst of this joyous chain-gang, I am suddenly aware of how interlocked we all are at Batstone Buckley Williams and how integral and fortunate my position is there, and also how contented I am just to be around in the rowdy, glad night.

As a partner I am allowed to invite a handful of guests (preferably persons with some useful connection in the law). If Donovan and his father had not been abroad I would have considered inviting them, but as it was my thoughts turned to Susan. Poor Susan! Maybe she would appreciate an invitation, it was not often that she enjoyed a carefree night out . . . And then I abandoned the idea. I remembered our last meeting; I remembered that it might not be a bad thing to be unencumbered by a female partner at an office party (not that I had definite aspirations in that regard, but one never knew . . .). So in the end I finished up by asking Oliver Owen.

'James, I must say that it's very kind of you to think of me.' Oliver sounded a little perplexed. 'But I don't think I'm free that night.'

I said, 'Well, it would be nice to see you there, that's all. Don't worry if you can't make it,' I said. 'I know how it is – family and all that.'

'Exactly,' Oliver said.

On the afternoon of the 23rd I packed up my things and watched as the Christmas tree was brought into the room. For some reason – maybe because of the twinkling view it affords of the Strand – my room always hosts the Christmas tree. This leaves me with the wearisome task of having to decorate it with the usual baubles and angels and electric stars. Luckily for me, June does not trust me with this important task and takes it upon herself to weigh down the tree with the trinkets. I am left to spray on the snow and to cover the drooping branches in glistening aluminium tassels.

As evening approached most people went home to change and eat something before the party, but I just popped out for a quick chickenburger and a glass of milk to line my stomach. When I returned to the office one or two people had started the celebrations, so I took up a position behind the drinks table and acted as barman. It is a job I am happy to do because it clarifies everything. Usually at parties my identity is fuzzy around the edges and it is unclear exactly how and where I come into things. When I am behind the bar, though, my role and my responsibilities are clear and there can be no mistake about what I am doing and why I am there: I am there to pour the drinks. This is not a negligible responsibility, and it must be said that I enjoy the status it confers upon me for the evening.

On this particular night things went particularly well. I fell into a nice rhythm of sloshing and mixing and icing and pouring and before long the party around me was in full, sweating swing. People were enjoying themselves and one ripple effect of this was that they were very friendly to me – perhaps even over-friendly. People I hardly knew roared with delight at the sight of me and pounded me on the back as I handed them their liquor. So when, at around eleven o'clock, I heard a voice shout out jovially, James! James, old boy! I barely took notice, I took it to be yet another of the exaggerated greetings I had been receiving that night.

'Come on James, come on! You're slacking!' the voice cried. 'Two bloody marys, pronto!'

When I saw it was Oliver and a friend I immediately wiped my right hand on my shirt and extended it.

'Oliver!' I said joyously. 'Oliver! I thought you couldn't make it! Here,' I said, furnishing the two of them with big, red doubles, 'knock these back, there's plenty more.'

As I leaned over to hear what he was saying, Oliver suddenly let go of his glass, splashing my shirt with juice. He looked at me apologetically and grinned.

'Shit,' he said. 'You're going to have to top me up.'

I laughed. Oliver is a charming, if mischievous, drunk and it was no bother at all to replenish his glass. I was aglow with the encounter; there is nothing quite like unexpectedly running into an old friend.

'Let me introduce you,' Oliver said. 'James Jones, meet my pupil, Diana Martin – the apple of my eye.' Oliver said to her, 'Did you know that James here was once in your shoes? So near we came to taking him on, and yet so far.'

I flushed. I tried to cover my face with my drink.

'He washed his hands of us,' Oliver said. 'And how wise he was. Look at James, my child, indeed look around you, and learn: there is more to life than the Bar.'

We looked. On the floor a line of drunken men and women were pretending to be rowers. They were chanting and shouting and throwing objects – shoes, pens – at the ring of laughing onlookers. Usually such a spectacle – the sight of people so clearly enjoying themselves – would have warmed my heart, but this time I felt ashamed. I felt like disowning them.

'Why did you turn down a tenancy?' Diana asked me.

I looked at Oliver. He had placed me in an embarrassing situation.

I said, 'Well, I didn't exactly turn it down, not exactly . . .'

Oliver said to Diana, 'Well, it's a rather unfortunate story. You see, a vacancy arose, and James wasn't around to take it up.'

I was confused. 'Vacancy? What vacancy?'

Oliver was not listening. He was explaining to his pupil what had happened. 'Just after James here had finished his pupillage, Lord Tetlow went to the Bench, and so there was an extra space in chambers. We tried to get hold of James to offer him the tenancy, but no one knew where he was. We tried everywhere; I remember manning the phone myself and ringing up every chambers in the Temple to get hold of him.' Oliver put his arm around my shoulder. 'No one thought of ringing up this firm, which is not surprising because no one had even heard of it. James?' Oliver looked at me. 'Are you all right?'

It rocked me: Oliver's news knocked me off my physical equilibrium. It actually batted me across the head; my cranial nerves were signalling the same dizzy, tinny pain that I had felt once when, hurrying along my dark corridor at home (the telephone was ringing, there was no time to switch on the lights), I had walked straight into the edge of the half-open door and my skull had given off a great crack.

'I'm OK,' I said to Oliver. I said, 'Look, excuse me, will you,' and rushed off bent almost double.

The lavatory floor was wet with urine but I slumped down on it all the same. I had to, my legs could not hold me up. My whole body, in fact, felt liquid and powdery, and it suddenly came home to me that that was all I was made of, water and dust. That is not all: I also felt misshapen, mashed up. I felt like a cartoon animal that has fallen with a whistling noise

155

down a mile-deep canyon to crunch face-first on the road at the bottom, only to be immediately mown down by a whizzing truck: flattened and splatted, my torso a pancake with tyre-patterns all over it.

On my knees, I vomited into the lavatory bowl. I must have stayed there like that, my head sunk in the bowl, for quite a while, because the next thing I became aware of was hammering and shouting at the door.

'Open up!' somebody was yelling. 'What are you doing in there, open up!'

I got to my feet, wiped my mouth with my sleeve and went to the door. A bunch of people were waiting outside. I pushed past them and headed for the exit.

'Gross!' a man shouted. 'Look at that puke! Gross! Jones, you're sick!'

I caught a cab and crashed out as soon as I got home. I did not even bother taking off my clothes or pulling back the duvet; I just kicked off my shoes and slumped out on the bed. I was floored.

The next day, Christmas Eve, I spent in bed. When I woke up, from dehydration, at eleven-thirty, I stumbled over to the bathroom to swallow three aspirins, filled a bottle with tapwater and went back to bed, this time first slipping off my smoke-scented, drink-stained clothes. It was like this, burrowed in the duvet, with the curtains drawn and the room half dark, that I spent the daylight hours, occasionally leaning over to take a swig from the bottle. I did not feel terrible, I felt nothing. That was the whole idea, not to feel anything at all.

By the time the room was fully dark I was ready to make myself a cup of tea and watch television. I must have watched three or four films back-to-back before I returned to bed. I fell asleep at once. I fell into a bear's sleep. When I awoke and switched on the radio, the Queen of England was rounding off her Christmas speech. Then I watched some television and, suddenly famished, rang my local Indian for a chicken tikka and nan bread. Then, feeling a bit better, I rang up my parents and my brother Charlie and wrote a Christmas card to Susan.

Afterwards I soaked in a sweet bath and tidied up the place. I brought the duvet from my bedroom and a bottle of red wine from the kitchen and spread out on the sofa to watch some more television. Boxing Day morning found me still there, watching breakfast television. All in all, not that bad a Christmas. I have known worse.

I must leave the story there and swing back to the present for a moment, because there has been an important development.

It happened this morning. A man came storming into my office, pushing June aside with a brusque movement.

'Jones, I want to talk to you,' he shouted.

I was working on this Donovan story at the time, on the above section to be precise, and for a number of days it had almost completely overtaken my work. This was grossly irresponsible of me, I know, but that was the way my priorities worked out.

I looked up. I failed to recognize who this man was.

'Jones, I've had it up to here,' he shouted. 'I must have rung fifty times, and every bloody time I get your secretary here trying to palm me off with some bollocks about a meeting.'

He advanced purposefully towards my desk. It was not until he grimaced unattractively that I recognized him: that stone in my shoe, Lexden-Page.

I said nothing and looked blankly at him. My mind was on my work.

Lexden-Page leaned over my desk, knocking books and papers across with his hand. He was raging. He could barely contain himself.

'Get out my file,' he said, the words escaping slowly through his gritted teeth. 'Get it out. Now.' A great force exuded from him which raised me up: I felt as though I was being grabbed and hauled to my feet. 'You heard me, Jones,' he said. 'Get out the bloody file. Right now, Jones. Right bloody now.'

I saw June in the background, clutching a file and waving her finger to attract my attention. She was distressed, yes, but even so she had the presence of mind to dig out the file. What a dear she was! What a treasure!

I looked at Lexden-Page. He was towering over me in an intimidating fashion, his top lip curled into an angry strip of fur. He was physically frightening.

'Fuck off,' I said. 'I'm working. June will show you out. June?'

Lexden-Page was stunned. He was transfixed. His feet were stuck to the floor.

'You heard me, Mr Lexden-Page,' I said, returning to my papers.

June hesitated, then came forward. 'Come on, Mr Lexden-Page,' she said gently. 'Mr Jones can't see you right now. Let's get you a cup of tea. Maybe he'll be able to see you in a moment,' she added, giving me a significant look.

'June,' I called as the two made their way out, 'please tell Mr Lexden-Page that I am busy for the remainder of the day. Should he wish to see me at another date, please arrange a meeting.'

They went out and I stretched my legs with a feeling of exhilaration. Was that me? Had I really dismissed him that easily?

Five minutes later, I went to see June. I confess that a gloating smile played on my lips.

'Well,' I said. 'That takes care of that.'

June did not reply. She turned her back to me and busied herself with something. I was about to go back to my desk when I noticed that her shoulders were trembling.

'What's so funny,' I said, grinning. 'June, what's so funny?' She shook her head and stayed turned around. 'June,' I insisted. I touched her shoulder.

June screamed. 'Nothing!' she screamed.

She was crying. Her face was streaked with tears, it ran with tears like my windshield in the Colford Square rain. I stood and stared. My eyes focused on the picture she had framed on her desk, a picture of her jumping for England. She is just splashing into the sandpit, her outstretched arms and legs are bright black and glistening, the sand is spurting around her as she arches forward; her eyes and mouth are wide open and she looks shocked. What a strange activity, I thought, jumping for your country.

'Nothing!' she screamed again. 'Now get out, you pig!'

I ran out of there. I made off thinking, My God, what have I done? What have I said? I was expecting her to be grateful for having expelled Lexden-Page so quickly, now here she was upset. I could not understand it. My June, whom I liked so much!

Back at my desk, I started thinking. I thought about June crying, and about Lexden-Page. I thought about the terrible workload that awaited me, the telephone calls, the letters, the effort. I thought about Donovan. I thought about June crying. All these things flashed through my mind.

I cleared my desk.

'Goodbye, June,' I said as I passed her. 'I'm off.'

It is only a short walk to the senior partner's office, no more than twenty paces, and yet when I got there I was out of breath. My chest was tight and fisted-up.

I knocked and walked in. He was talking to a client. I interrupted him.

'I'm taking a few days off,' I told him. 'I need the time to sort out some private business,' I said. I left immediately, before he could say anything. His face wore a dumbfounded expression, but I did not care, I was too angry. I was too angry to give a damn.

That was only a couple of hours ago. Right now the telephone is ringing. When it finishes, I will take it off the hook. Meanwhile, let it ring. Let the damn thing ring.

SIXTEEN

The telephone is disconnected and it is time to get on with my story. But I cannot. I cannot go on, not when I am in this state, not while my mind is ringing like this.

What fills my head, what tintinnabulates between my ears, is an outcry, an outcry composed of these cries: Why? Why? Why had I not got that tenancy? Why had circumstances conspired so freakishly against me? The omissions, near-misses and close shaves that had ganged up to foil me were fiendish. They were outrageous. First of all there was the fiasco of my failure to apply in writing for a tenancy, then there was the one-in-a-million scenario of the chambers failing to contact me when Bernard Tetlow had moved on. What could have been simpler? There was a demand and there was a supply: I wanted that job and they wanted me to have it – so what force had come between us, and why? The cruelty of it! It breaks my heart to think of it! Here I am, an unregarded small-time solicitor, up to my neck in small potatoes, surrounded by the second-rate, the mediocre and the so-so, my days a mindless sequence of deadlines, petty conversations and tiny facts. Look at what has become of me: a nobody, a human nothing. James Jones has turned out to be no one at all.

I know what you are saying here. You are saying, My God, what a self-pitying, bellyaching, unpleasant little man. He's behaving like a spoiled brat. Why doesn't he grow up? Why doesn't he get a grip of himself?

Well, I do not buy that, I am afraid. I do not buy all that stoical stuff, taking the rough with the smooth and letting bygones be bygones. To hell with all of that, to hell with getting a grip of myself! I have a legitimate grievance here. I worked myself to the bone for that tenancy, and what did I get? Nothing. I was robbed! Let bygones be bygones? Why should I?

It makes me despair. When I think of what I have become, when I think that I used to be a *lawyer*. I used to have analytical faculties, powers of cerebration, ratiocination. And now . . . now I cannot even understand a simple legal concept; even a notion as straightforward as marital cruelty makes me struggle. That is not the worst of it. To think that I could, that I *should*, right at this moment, be someone else, that I should now be *something* – that is the worst: that my name should be up there on that blackboard in Essex Court, that *James Jones* should be there, figuring in the law reports and newspapers, in the periodicals and the footnotes: that instead – instead we have this rubbish.

Why? And why me? This is what I want to know. Why should I be the one to end up this way? Why, of all people, me?

I have mopped my face, dropped a fizzing disc of aspirin into a glass of water and swallowed the solution. It has worked, and I have calmed down. I have regained my sense of proportion. I have stopped crying (yes, for the first time in two decades I have cried, you can see the tears where they have landed on the page and made words run) and I have pulled myself together. It is vital that I do not allow myself to be side-tracked by such irrelevant emotional outbursts. Why I did not get taken on at 6 Essex is neither here nor there. It does not go anywhere towards meeting the question in hand, which is this: why did the Donovan affair end in the way that it did?

The sooner I am able to answer that query the better, because the sooner I will be able to return to work. That does not mean that I am in any great rush to get back. No, I will say this for my job: as a partner I am allowed a certain flexibility. I have certain freedoms. If I want some time off, I can usually take it. There is a theoretical danger of being voted out of the firm by the other partners – of being fired – but I know how rare this is and how much leeway I have. This leave without notice that I am now taking is against the rules, but the transgression is not grave enough to put me in any real hot water. Eyebrows will be raised and subtle reprimands will be forthcoming, but that is all. If there is one thing I still do know about in this maelstrom, it is the tolerances of Batstone Buckley Williams.

Going back to Christmas, 1988, I holed up in bed for a day or two afterwards. Cushioned by duvets and extra pillows, waiting for the new year, I managed to put a lid on the Oliver Owen revelation. Forget it, I told myself. It's over. It's not important. It's all turned out for the best.

Then, as I began to feel better, I actually drew strength from Oliver's news. It occurred to me that I had been paid a great compliment: when that vacancy arose at 6 Essex, they had gone to great lengths to contact me. Of all the young barristers in the Temple, I was the one they had *singled out*. To do that they must have really rated me. They must have thought that I was quite something.

A thrill of gratification ran through my limbs. Then I thought, Maybe I still have some of that old brainpower. Maybe there are grey cells that can still be salvaged.

Excited by this possibility, I decided to put myself to the test. To start with I reacquainted myself with the principles of international law. Yes, they still made sense. Then, during four sleepless days, I reread all of Donovan's writings (which is not to say that I took in every word). I looked again at the notes and observations I had made about them over the years, often surprising myself with the perceptiveness I had shown in those days. Was I really responsible for that acute note in the margin? Was that mine, that penetrating aside?

Gradually, after a week of fruitful concentration in front of the blazing gas fire, my confidence in my mental abilities began to return. I began to make something of an intellectual comeback. I began to apply my mind seriously, less tentatively, to the themes of *Supranational Law*, trying to understand how and why Donovan had arrived at the prescriptive conclusion that international law should, in the final analysis, be more than just an expression of the relations of sovereign States. I had already seen that Donovan would have to come to terms with the principle of the self-determination of nations and autonomy generally, that he would have to look at the function and rationale of the State; and instead of leaving those frightening subjects alone and waiting to see how Donovan would deal with the problems, I took them on personally, head-to-head. I went to the library and boned up on philosophical texts, perusing Locke, Rawls, Nozick and the rest of them in record time. I am not saying that I understood or appreciated everything I read, or that I did not rely heavily on secondary texts. Of course I did. But what was extraordinary was the facility with which I grasped the concepts that these great minds bandied about – I actually understood what they were saying, where they were going. Needless to say, it thrilled me to be there, alone in the library's reading room, involved once more in academic pursuits, shadowing difficult ideas along their steep, breathtaking routes. Yes, I said to myself as old thought-patterns and insights came back to me from the past, Yes, I remember now. And then I thought, This is it. This is what it's all about. This is the life.

When, after three weeks, this idyll came to an end, I felt refreshed, as sharp as I could remember. Shaving on the morning of my return to work, I looked forward to tackling the demands of the weeks ahead. Then I suddenly remembered.

The trial. The Donovan showdown. I had forgotten all about it.

As my blade curved around the contours of my face, carving tracks of fresh skin through the shaving cream, I counted the days until February the 1st: eighteen. The trial was just two and a half weeks away and still Donovan and I had not talked about, let alone decided on, such things as the evidence, the lines of argument, the problems that we might face. I had not heard from Donovan since the game of golf and it was vital that we went into these matters. It would be the first thing to attend to when I went to the office.

Rodney gave me some disconcerting news.

'Mr Donovan? He's in Rio de Janeiro isn't he?'

Because I was a little tense I said, 'I don't know, Rodney, you tell me.'

'That's right, sir, he's in Rio,' Rodney confirmed. 'Due back on February the 14th, if I'm not mistaken.'

This took me aback. It did not make sense: how could Donovan be at his divorce trial in London if he was in South America?

Rodney gave me Donovan's hotel number in Rio. After a number of attempts June finally put me through. Mr Donovan was not replying, the receptionist said. It was 6.10 in the morning, she said. Take this message, I said: *James Jones phoned.* (I thought about phrasing the message in the imperative − *Phone James Jones, urgent* − but decided against it.)

I received no reply that morning and when I returned from lunch there was no message for me. This was no laughing matter, I thought. This was serious. Something had to be done, I had to find out what was going on. Just then, just as I was wringing my hands in anxiety, I received a telephone call. It was from Philip Hughes. He made no sense at all.

'Well,' he said, 'I must say that I expected it all along. I could see it coming a mile off.'

I really did not know what to say to this.

'Yes,' I said. 'Now, what can I do for you?'

'Well, the ball's been in your court for about six weeks now,' Hughes said, 'and I think it's time we heard from you.'

'What about?' I said.

'The money,' Hughes said. 'The fifty thousand.'

I asked Hughes what he was talking about.

The settlement, he told me. The settlement fee. The case had been settled, he said. Don't say I had forgotten? The case had been settled back in December, the 9th of December to be precise. That was when Donovan had accepted his offer, when he had signed the agreement. Surely I remembered now?

'Yes,' I said. 'I remember. Yes, of course. The settlement. The fifty thousand.'

Donovan was no longer fighting the divorce. He had given up the ghost. Behind my back.

'Mr Donovan's in Brazil,' I said.

'I know,' Hughes said. 'But the agreement specified payment of the first instalment within thirty days. Thirty days elapsed a week ago, Mr. Jones.'

I told Hughes that I would look into it and hung up. The divorce was on. The trial was off.

Why had I not been told? Why was I always the last to find out? I was the solicitor, for God's sake. I should have been the first to know. Nothing should have been agreed without my say-so.

June came in. 'Mr Lexden-Page to see you,' she said. 'It's about this morning's hearing.'

'What? Ah yes.' I remembered. The pre-trial review of *Lexden-Page v. Westminster C.C.* was scheduled for eleven o'clock. 'Yes, I'll see him, June,' I said.

In he came. In came Lexden-Page. He was, as usual, bristling with anger.

'Come on, Jones,' he said. 'Let's get a move on. We're going to be late.'

We took a taxi to Westminster County Court, and ten minutes later we were seated around the registrar's table. Not unpredictably, the Council was trying to strike out the action on the grounds that it was frivolous and vexatious. I could think of little to say to this. At best our damages amounted to a pound or two, and it would plainly be a waste of court time to pursue this amount in this particular case. To make matters worse, Lexden-Page refused to settle for any amount. He wanted his day in court.

I said, 'I see the force of my friend's arguments.' I paused. Lexden-Page glared at me. I said, my voice lacking conviction, 'But this case does not simply revolve around a scuffed shoe and a stubbed toe. It involves an important principle.' I looked at my papers, trying to think just what that principle might be.

The registrar and my opponent regarded me with curiosity. 'This may be a frivolous matter for the Council, with its millions of pounds of resources, but for the Plaintiff, an ordinary citizen, it goes to the very heart of his liberty as a pedestrian. This case also goes to the root of the responsibilities which the Council bears towards its rate-payers and towards visitors to its borough. These are not matters to be brushed aside. The Plaintiff has a substantial complaint which must be heard.' The registrar and my opponent looked at each other in mild amazement. I leaned over to Lexden-Page. 'Anything else?' I whispered. 'Anything else you want me to say?'

'Say it as if you mean it, damn you,' he said furiously.

The registrar struck out the claim. Lexden-Page began spluttering and reddening. Once outside, he found his voice.

'I'm appealing,' he said. 'This isn't going to end here. I'll take this to the highest court in the land. It's an outrage. It's a scandal. And you,' he said to me, losing his voice half-way through the accusation, 'you . . . I want a new solicitor. I want someone who . . .' He could not continue. He was choked up with emotions.

'Mr Lexden-Page,' I said. 'You're upset now. That's understandable. Why don't we talk this over at some other time, when we've regained our objectivity. Go home now and phone me tomorrow to make an appointment. How does that sound to you?'

I put my protesting client into a taxi and hailed another one for myself. As we groaned away from the kerb I forgot all about the morning's hearing and began thinking about Donovan, about his sudden consent to the divorce. It had me in two minds.

It made sense and yet it did not make sense. On the one hand he was quite right not to contest the case. On that hand he had seen reason, he had seen that there was little to be gained from fighting the divorce. There were two possible explanations for his change of tack: either he had foreseen all along that he would probably not manage to dissuade

Arabella and had planned this last-minute concession; or he had understood, for the first time (maybe when his letters had been returned), that his marriage was irretrievably lost, that nothing he could do would bring Arabella back: thus prompting his sudden decision to settle.

Looked at in this way, the case fell into place. There was nothing superficially baffling about it, there was nothing that could not be fitted into the picture. It left one or two question marks – the episode on the golf course, for example – but nothing that could not be explained away or dismissed as irrelevant. On the face of it, then, the settlement made sense, it was susceptible to a consistent analysis. But, in another, more profound way, it did not make sense. That was what bothered me in the taxi back to the office.

The arithmetic of events was unconvincing. In the equation you had Donovan's determination to fight the divorce, plus his conviction that Arabella would not be able to prove her contentions, plus his father's deep anxiety to save the marriage, plus Donovan's great skill as a litigator, plus the relative weakness of Arabella's case; even given certain minuses (the distress of the trial, the question as to whether Arabella was really worth it, the generous terms offered by Arabella) these elements did not, by my calculation, equal to a settlement. Which meant that either the settlement was a ruse of some kind or, more likely, that there was a factor, an x, which still had not been revealed to me. But what could that be? What did the x stand for?

I will briefly go into this question, because it may be important. A while back I videotaped a magic show on the television. It was an old-fashioned show. There was a man in chains in a water-tank, there was a man in a top hat sliding blades and saws through a leggy girl lying flat-out in a box. That was the kind of show it was. The performer who really interested me, though, was a magician. After spending a few minutes flapping handkerchiefs into doves, he performed a trick – a simple, unspectacular trick, but all the more intriguing for that – which really got to me: he put his palm to the camera and produced card after card in his hand from thin air. How had he done it? To this day I do not know. I replayed the scene twenty times in slow motion and twenty times I drew a blank. It was not because of my eyesight that I did not see what was going on; no, it was a question of angles. The magician had ensured, in a cunning, subtle way, that certain of our (the viewers') lines of vision were blocked: so that no matter how hard or how often we looked, we would see only one part of what was happening, the trick part. Something like that was going on in the Donovan case, or at least that was the impression I received – an impression that I was seeing only a portion of the action; that something was going on behind the scenes.

So what? it might reasonably be said. We cannot know everything, and since when do our lives tie up like shoe-laces, into bows? You learn to live with loose ends. You have to, otherwise you go crazy.

Now, normally speaking, I would be the first to agree with this. I myself am quite happy to wrap up a case in ill-fitting paper and leave it bulging and unwieldy – as long, that is, as I am satisfied that the case *is* wrapped up. This is what worried me about *Donovan v. Donovan*. Much as I might have wished it to be over, I had a feeling that we were not yet out of the woods – that matters would not, indeed could not, end there. Surely the case, surely this whole affair, could not simply fizzle out in this way? It was all too lopsided: Donovan's theatrical breakdown, his father's dramatic arrival from Ireland, the eerie diaries, the scene at the pre-trial review, the tears on the golf course, the fast-approaching trial: surely all this momentum, all this mass times velocity, could not just evaporate – could it? The physics of it was all wrong. What is more, I still picked up that roar in the air, a roar getting louder with every moment. Something told me that we were still on the river with the waterfall ahead. Something told me that the cameras were still rolling.

SEVENTEEN

I did not dwell for long on the Donovan settlement, at least not immediately. I was not able to, I had to get on with my other work, of which there was plenty. I am, it must not be forgotten, a junior partner. Whatever denigrations I may have heaped on it, it is not a negligible position. It is we junior partners who really keep the firm going. While the senior partners are on long lunches with clients, back in the office myself and my contemporaries have our shoulders to the wheels. Our clients may well be small people with small problems, but they are numerous and their hundred and one demands must be dealt with efficiently. That is the challenge, to dispose of as many of these pint-sized cases as quickly as possible. It is not as easy as it looks. They can pin you down, these lilliputian chores, and you have to watch yourself; otherwise you wake up one morning and find yourself guyed down and tied up by hundreds of unattended tasks that have crept up on you while you slumbered.

So the next time I gave the case my full consideration was 25 January 1989. I received, out of the blue, a fax from Donovan. He was still in Rio de Janeiro. The fax said: *James, as you probably have gathered I am consenting to the petition. Participate in any consent proceedings on February 2nd. Instruct junior counsel. Copy of settlement agreement attached. M.D.*

So. On 2 February consent proceedings would take place. The judge would be asked by Arabella to pronounce a decree nisi, and we would not oppose the application. It was cut-and-dried stuff. I glanced at the settlement: nothing noteworthy, the payment of a lump sum in three instalments. From a legal point of view the case was no longer special. From now on it was simply a matter of administration.

The morning of 2 February was freezing cold. The wind scorched my head as I tramped down the Strand and by the time I reached the court my ears were bright red and hurting. I met up with the counsel I had instructed, a young woman called Rebecca Gibbons, and we wandered over to speak to Philip Hughes and his counsel, a Mr Brooke Sulman. Hughes handed me a copy of an affidavit sworn by Arabella wherein she detailed what she had suffered at the hands of Donovan. It was an unusually bland statement which could have been made by anyone. It added little to the Petition. Arabella complained of loneliness, lack of communication between herself and Donovan, his indifference (an example was given of a time when he had gone away for two months without so much as telephoning her) and so forth. It was a terribly ordinary affidavit which made terribly ordinary points. An uninformed reader would have never been able to guess at the dramatic subtext, that history was moving through those stilted paragraphs.

The judge pronounced the decree nisi in record time.

The marriage was as good as dead. In six weeks Arabella would apply for a decree absolute and that would be that. One stamp from the court office and no more Mr and Mrs Donovan.

When I arrived back at the office I made a little scene of blowing my hands and stamping my feet. By the time I sat down at my desk I had a cup of steaming coffee and a digestive biscuit waiting for me. Whenever June sees me come in shivering in my overcoat with my red ears, she always puts the kettle on and brings me a boiling brew. 'There,' she says. 'Drink that. It'll make you feel better.'

'June,' I say. 'You shouldn't. That's not your job. You've got enough on your plate as it is. You shouldn't, June,' I say.

I pick up my cup happily and June purses her lips and looks all business. I feel her standing there as my eyes dip down to my cup. Her shoulder leans against the jamb and she is regarding me, making sure that all is well, that there is nothing she can do for me. My June. My summer month. I would be lost without her.

(I wonder what she is doing now? The poor thing probably spends her days deflecting inquiries from irate clients, cancelling meetings, securing time extensions, re-distributing my work. If anyone will clear up the mess I have left behind, it is June. She will know that I am in some kind of trouble. She will have recognized the symptoms. All the same, I feel guilty at having burdened her with the consequences of my actions. I must remember to get her some kind of present when all of this is over, some token of my appreciation.)

When I came back from court and sat back with my coffee, I pushed at my iron desk with my feet and swung around to look up at the sky. Seeing nothing but the sky makes me contemplative, and on this occasion I began meditating upon the consequences of Donovan's divorce. By now I had become used to the idea and had overcome my dismay at not having been consulted; and although the sudden and mysterious end to the matter still left me uneasy, I had pushed all of that aside. I had also got over the feeling of anti-climax mixed, it must be said, with regret. I knew that the end of the case did not mean the end of me and Donovan. Quite the contrary. Now we were only just at the beginning. Now our futures looked more closely bound than ever.

Let me explain. It came to me, sipping my coffee that morning, that the divorce would benefit Donovan. Now his time would be his, from now on he would be free to finish *Supranational Law* in peace. And the more I thought about that book, the more excited I became. If ever a book was made for its time, this was it. The frazzled world was crying out for a jurisprudence to cope with the environmental crisis, it was crying out for someone to step into the breach. Donovan would be that someone. In *Supranational Law* he would supply that jurisprudence. When the historians of the next century came to look at the factors that turned around the present crisis, they would dwell long and hard on the name of Michael Donovan. They might even (my God, if only this were true! If only!) feel compelled to read *Michael Donovan: An Appreciation*, by James Jones.

Yes, gazing up at that white, foggy sky, I saw the situation growing rosier by the minute. When Donovan's *Supranational Law*, with its brand new regime for the critical resources of the planet, came to fruition, then the parallels I had drawn with Hugo Grotius would become irresistible. My thesis would take off. Just as Grotius provided the much-needed concept of the High Seas in *Mare Liberum* back in the seventeenth century, a concept which lasts to this day, so Donovan would provide its modern-day equivalent. It was all so neat, it all fell so spookily into place, that I sprang to my feet, shivering. Yes, I was destined for greater things! There could be no more doubt about it, not now, not after everything that had happened: Donovan was heading for the history books and so, on his coat-tails, was I. My pupillage with Donovan at 6 Essex, my years of research thereafter (only made possible, it dawned on me, by my failure at the Bar), our reunion through his divorce, my uncanny discovery of his manuscript, all of these pointed to one thing: Donovan and Jones were in this together. The two of them were going places.

Here I took a hold of myself. Enough, no more dreaming, the time had come for hard achievement. I determined there and then to bring off my Grotius thesis. Whereas previously during my studies I had never quite known what I was doing or why, now my intentions were clear. I would do it, even if it meant taking a sabbatical from Batstone's. I would write that paper.

That night I quit work early and quickly walked the dark streets to the Middle Temple library. I climbed the winding stairs to the international law section and took out a fistful of periodicals. Then, at a lamplit desk, I hunted down any references to Donovan and any material that had a bearing on his work. There was plenty. By the time the bell rang to signal the library's closing, I saw that if I was going to catch up on the years of research that I had neglected, it would take many evenings and weekends of homework, not that easy when you are putting in eight or nine pretty tiring hours a day, five days a week. Yet still I found the prospect enticing, and on the underground home, slithering under Waterloo and down beneath the Oval, I was bursting with anticipation. I could not wait to sit down and get on with it.

I got on with it. Where I found the energy I do not know, but for five weeks I was red-hot. I clocked in early at work and concentrated. There was not a moment to lose. No more daydreaming, no more dawdling. I turned those papers over at top speed. I had June on a non-stop merry-go-round of typing, telephoning and running in and out. Not that she minded, not June: she thrived. She was also intrigued. She wanted to know why it was that I burned through the day and smoked out of the office on the dot of five o'clock.

'What's the matter with you?' she said. 'Why are you in such a rush?'

'Rush?' I did not look up. I continued scribbling at a sheet.

June waited for me to say something else. Then she said, 'Yes, rush. You're going flat out. I've never seen you like this.'

Again I said nothing. I had a letter to finish. I was a busy man, I had no time to sit around and chew the fat.

Then June said slyly, 'It's a woman, isn't it? You've got a woman, haven't you?'

I looked up and gave her a memorandum and a mysterious smile.

'I can't think what you're talking about,' I said.

She stepped away with the papers. Then she stopped at the door and turned to speak, the way they do in films for dramatic effect. 'James, you don't fool me. I know the look of love when I see it.'

I laughed and went back to work. It was amazing how

wrong people could be. Still, if that was what she wanted to think, that was fine by me. It was a perfectly harmless, even handy, illusion. It saved me a lot of explaining. That said, I must admit that nothing would have given me greater pleasure than saying, a modest smile on my face, 'Actually, if you must know, I'm working on a book. That's why I have to get away in the evenings. To work on my book.' (My book! How it chimed, that phrase! My book!) But I knew that the best thing to do was to keep quiet; they would not understand my project at Batstone Buckley Williams. No, I was a man in love. That was my story. I dashed off my work and grabbed my coat as soon as I could because I was a man in love.

When I got home it was more of the same. Pumped up with adrenalin, I worked and I worked. And it worked. Each night I struck gold. Each night some bright new insight would gleam in my notebook. I felt fantastic. Ideas came to me from I do not know where.

That is not all. Sometimes, leaning back from my papers for a minute's rest, I would close my eyes and see myself as I must have looked to others, a young scholar working through the night, my desk-top an island of light in the dark room. This is what I mean when I say that sometimes it is hard to keep the film world at bay. With everything going according to the script, I stopped watching television. I started watching myself instead. I tuned in to me.

Then Thursday, 9 March 1989, came around. That was the day when I telephoned Butterwells, Donovan's publishers. I had done just about as much preparation and preliminary studies as I was able to, and the time had arrived to take things a stage further: I needed to read *Supranational Law* – all of it. So I decided to ring up Butterwells.

I was put through to the publicity department. I thought the voice of the woman who answered was not unfamiliar.

'Excuse me,' I said politely, 'who am I talking to?'

'This is Diana Martin,' she said. 'How can I help you?'

I have always been proud of my ability to remember people, but on this occasion I surpassed myself.

I introduced myself. Then I said, 'We met, if I'm not mistaken, at the Batstone Buckley Williams Christmas party. You came with Oliver Owen.' There was a pause, and I added, 'I was the one behind the bar. The one pouring the drinks. That was me.'

'Yes,' she said hesitantly.

I got down to business; I did not want her to think that I was a heavy breather of some sort. I explained that I was doing some scholarship on international law and that I wanted to know the date of publication of Donovan's new book; also, if it was not asking too much, perhaps it would be possible to have a proof copy?

Diana Martin relaxed. 'Let me see,' she said nicely. After a significant interval she spoke again. She sounded in difficulties. 'Mr Jones, it does not look as though Michael's book will be published for some while.'

I said, 'Well, can you give me a rough date? Three months? A year? Ten years?'

She hesitated. 'I can't, I'm afraid.' She stopped again. 'It's very hard to say.' She was trying to be helpful, that was clear from her voice; but she was constrained by something.

'It's very important to me,' I said. 'Are you sure there's nothing you can tell me? I'll keep it to myself, if that's what you're worried about. Don't forget,' I said confidentially, 'like you I'm a lawyer. I know all about secrets.'

She relented. 'All right, I'll tell you what I know. It sounds a bit funny, I know, but Michael destroyed his manuscript. He burned it, it seems. For the time being, at least, he's abandoned the book.'

'Burned it?' I asked. I kept my voice calm. 'How curious. You mean he actually set it alight?'

'Well, that's what he says in his letter. He says that he's thrown it in the fire.'

'What date?' I said. 'What's the date on the letter?'

22 February 1989, Diana Martin told me. That was the date.

I thanked her and hung up. I felt strangely calm. I distanced myself from what she had described. So Donovan had burned his manuscript? How interesting, I thought. What an interesting development that was.

Then I sat still for a while, staring ahead of me at the wall where a 1989 calendar hung open. It was a Canadian calendar, and its pages depicted the scenic natural transformations brought on by each fresh month; forests all golden in autumn, horizons of wheat in the summer, that sort of thing. How it got up there, on my wall, was a mystery. June had no doubt hung it up there for decorative purposes, because I had enough gadgets in my office – annuals, almanacs, logbooks – to keep me up to date. That day the calendar displayed a photograph of a curve of snow, a snowfield sparkling under a hard, dark blue sky. Something bothered me about the picture. We were in the month of March; that calendar was not up-to-date, it was showing a winter scene, a January or February scene. So I walked over to the calendar to flip over a sheet, but just as I reached out I saw that it was in fact on the right page: this was a picture of an Ontarian field in March.

I went back towards my desk but I did not sit down. I stayed on my feet, looking out of my window at March in London. It was a fine spring day; as far as the weather went, everything was fine. The shoppers were out, the roads were blocked with black cabs, the workmen were back on their buildings. I could not breathe. My lungs just could not grip the slippery air. The motes, the atoms of oxygen, just slid in and out of my body. I ran out and drank a glass of water. My chest was hurting me; more precisely, my chest was burning me; it was as though something had ignited in there, as though my thorax were ablaze. I gulped down two glasses of water, and then a third. It did not help.

I panicked. Fire! I felt like shouting. Fire! I lost my head. I felt like ringing up the fire brigade to go to Colford Square on the double, to send up a ladder to the study window and aim their hoses at the pile of papers smouldering in the hearth. Maybe something could be salvaged, a few brown-rimmed, heat-curled pages, a few scorched-off sentences, even. Maybe . . .

I rubbed my face. Why? Why? Why should Donovan do this, why should he commit this arson? It was horrific: a masterpiece of jurisprudence and political philosophy rubbed out, reduced to ashes. It was a catastrophe, a disaster. I could not understand what had led him to commit this folly. And the actual gesture of incinerating the manuscript – that was far too theatrical a thing for Donovan to do. Desperately I reviewed the previous six months, checking and rechecking his actions, his words. Not a clue. There was not a single reason that I could find to explain what had happened. What had I missed? What had I missed?

Then I saw a glimmer of hope: the disc, the software which stored the book: perhaps that was still in existence. Yes; he would hardly have burned the disc; or would he? And maybe this phrase he had used about throwing the book on the fire – maybe that was just a figure of speech?

I stopped thinking about it. Disc or no disc, figure of speech or not, it made no difference. I saw that. What mattered was that the book was not coming out. And that was the matter.

There followed a period of waiting. I set about my work in the usual fashion and waited. Precisely what I was waiting for I did not know; but I lived in the expectation that something would come along, that eventually some beam of light would stray in my direction. In the event, nothing happened, nothing became clearer – if anything, things became more obscure. No new facts turned up. My firm received a cheque from Donovan for my services – there was no accompanying note – but that was not what I had in mind. I was just waiting for things to turn around, as per usual. Then one day it dawned on me, not dramatically but in a dull, tired way, that nothing was going to turn around. That was it. There was no more to come. The End, as they say in films, had been reached; somewhere, in a scene I had not witnessed, the cowboy had ridden off into the sunset.

This was in April. I stored away the *Donovan v. Donovan* file in my office and, at home, made a package of my abortive thesis and put it back where I had found it, in an old box in the attic.

Unfortunately, not everything ended there. For a while I went about my work with reasonable efficiency, but then, as I have said, things took a turn for the worse. First of all, lethargy crept in. All day I would trudge around the office in a state of exhaustion and apathy, struggling to fight off sleep at my desk. Then, in the evening, when I returned to my flat, I would be restless. I would sit down on the sofa to read and end up by throwing down the book or newspaper in irritation; television became unwatchable, and the nights – the nights became an ordeal of insomnia. Insomnia! What an affliction! In the middle of the night I would look over the edge of my bed at my radio-clock and calculate with horror that, even if I fell asleep *immediately*, I would get at most three hours' sleep. For feverish hours I smouldered in my bed until, at last, I heard the birds singing outside and saw the curtain lighten with the dawn. And while I steamed under my duvet, my imagination, too, would start overheating. In my terrible half-sleep, vague fantasies and wild notions would take hold of my fuming brain, exhausting and distressing reveries populated by Donovan and Mr Donovan, by Arabella and Susan and Oliver Owen. And so it went on, this awful pattern of sleepless nights and listless days.

It did not take me long to work out something about what was going on: I may be uncomprehending but I am not stupid. I knew what the trouble was – Donovan. I had tried to forget about him, to put the whole thing behind me, but I had been unable to. I thought that time would clarify, I thought that time would heal. But I was wrong, time did nothing of the sort. Time stood still, time took time off, so that weeks later nothing had moved on, and I was still asking myself, Why had Donovan burned the book? What had led him to it? Arabella? His father? His divorce? Something else? Something had gone on, something big – but what? What had gone on?

I could not work it out. I had clues to work on, I had strands – I had Donovan's breakdown, his break-up, his journal, the introduction to his new book, I had my researches, I had Donovan senior, I had the sudden divorce – but they had me tied up in knots. My leads led me nowhere. And there was something else: surely it could not end this way? What about all that momentum I had discerned, that inexorable drama? What had happened to that? Was it all to come to this – to nothing?

No, I decided. It was impossible that the Donovan adventure could just dematerialize. I had missed what had really happened, somewhere along the line I had missed a trick. And it was at that point that I decided to straighten things out once and for all, that I picked up my pen and embarked on this narrative. I would set it all out clearly, I determined. I would replay it. That would be enough – was not description supposed to be revelation? – to pick out whatever it was that I had missed. That should do it, I thought.

So, here I am then. It is 9 July 1989, and I have done what I set out to do. I have looked back on the last year and related everything there was to it. All the facts of the matter have been set out and now, at last, I am in a position to understand what has been going on. Now all I have to do is read carefully what I have written and, if everything goes according to plan, hey presto – all, or at least enough, will be revealed.

EIGHTEEN

I read everything that I had written, every word; and then I read it again, carefully, like a lawyer, satisfying myself that nothing had escaped me. I read the small print and I read between the lines. Then I closed my eyes, sat back in my chair, and waited. I waited for revelations, dénouements, clarifications, answers.

Nothing happened.

Imagine watching a film on television, a thriller maybe, something which really has you riveted to your sofa. The final reel is approaching, and the action is on the point of that tangy resolution you get in the best films. Out of the blue, your screen goes snowy. So you follow your usual routine: you bang the television, you check the aerial, you fine-tune the channel. You do everything you have always done. Then excitedly you resume your position on the sofa – there is still time to catch the ending – and hit the *on* button. More snow.

Imagine the fury that you feel at that fraudulent moment: that is how I felt. Cheated. All that writing, all that time off work, all for nothing.

I smoked an angry cigarette. Then I resolutely got to my feet. The time had come for action. If answers were not going to surface, then I would have to retrieve them myself. I knew how to get at them, with that sharp little screwdriver of a query, *Why?* It was time to go into the geneses, rationales and determinants of what had happened, to look at causes, not effects. It was time to open up the television.

Then, almost as soon as I had made that determination, I

became discouraged. There was no point in fooling myself any further, this *why* business was clearly not my strength. My knowledge of psychology and the inward workings of humans was on a par with my knowledge of television interiors, and the mysteries of the Donovan story loomed before me like an electronic thicket of encoders, circuits and image orthicons. I was out of my depth. Why Donovan had married Arabella, why she had left him, why he had suddenly acceded to the divorce – I passed on those questions. Donovan's dumbstruck collapse in court – what was I supposed to do about that, look it up in medical text-books? Look under *a* for aphony? What about the last time I saw him, on the golf course, the time he wept: who did I call in on that one? Why he burned his book? How should I know? *Why* should I know?

Yes, this is the problem with whys: ask why once and you never stop asking why. Why this always leads to why that, and everything unscrews and comes apart. This is exactly what happened that day. I fell into a line of questioning which dismantled everything: why was it I was so hung up on Donovan? What skin was it off my nose what happened to him? Why was I unable to work any more? Why – really – was I writing this stuff? It did not end there (as I have said, it is a slippery slope) – why had the fates conspired to deprive me of my tenancy at 6 Essex Court? Why was I a solicitor? Why should I care about my career? Why should I care about anything any more?

I could not see what was going on any more. My mind started blooping and rolling, like a man lost in a cathode-ray blizzard. I lost the picture completely.

Suddenly I felt terrible.

Then the telephone sounded (I had just put it back on its hook) and when I picked it up I uttered my first word for a week and a half.

'Hello?' I said.

'Thank God you're in,' a female voice said.

The last time I had spoken to Susan Northey was – let me work this out – 22 November 1988.

'Where have you been?' she said impatiently. 'You've had everybody worried.'

'Susan,' I said. 'How are you?'

Susan said, 'I got a phone call this morning from your secretary – Jane? They're trying to get hold of you at work. She thought maybe I knew where you were. She told me you'd gone off on some frolic with a woman.'

'It's June,' I said. 'Not Jane, June.'

Susan said, 'You're wanted at work, Jimmy.' She paused. 'Jimmy?'

'Yes,' I said. 'I know,' I said.

Susan waited before speaking again. Then she said, 'Look, are you all right?'

I reassured her that I was. 'I'm fine,' I said. 'Don't worry about me, I'm in good shape. How about you? How are you, Suzy?'

Susan sounded decisive. 'Look, stay there, I'm on my way.'

'No,' I said. 'Really, I'm fine. I'm just getting away from things for a while, that's all. Don't worry about it.'

Susan hung up half-way through my protests.

I did not want to see Susan, not right at that moment. She would demand explanations from me and what was I going to tell her? Also, I had just finished reading these pages and – I have admitted it – I was in a bad way. It was not easy, re-living those ups and downs, those hopes dashed left, right and centre. It had pretty much wiped me out. I was in no mood for company.

Later, the door-buzzer rang. I stayed put on the sofa. Then the buzzer sounded again and I dragged myself to my feet. Through the spy-hole I saw a gigantic face: Susan.

When I opened the door I stood around uncertainly – what was I supposed to do, give her a kiss?

Susan walked past me into the living-room. 'My God,' she said. She gesticulated at the mess. 'What's all this about?'

I went to make coffee. From the kitchen I could see through to the living-room. Susan was doing some tidying up. She had opened a window and now was plumping up cushions, emptying ashtrays and picking up, with the very tips of her fingers, buckets of chicken bones, pizza cartons and silver curry containers. I felt a dull glow of affection. Susan.

'Jimmy,' Susan said softly after we had sat in silence for a moment, drinks in hand. 'What's the matter? Hmm? What's the matter?'

'It's nothing, Suzy,' I said. 'It's just that . . .' I discontinued my sentence. I was exhausted, I just could not come out with the words.

'Tell me, Jimmy.' She was still looking at me with her bright grey eyes. 'Tell me,' she whispered.

I looked at Susan. Perhaps I had not properly appreciated her, I thought. Perhaps, with the benefit of hindsight, I would see her in a new light. So I looked at her again.

There was nothing new there. It is true that, sitting next to me for the first time in seven months, she had a sheen and freshness about her. But otherwise she looked just the same to me. She looked just as she had always done. She sat there with her serious grey eyes, giving off the same old sad, brave emanations.

'I've been working too hard,' I said. 'I just needed a bit of time off. Suzy, it's that simple. There's nothing funny going on – I'm not having an affair or a nervous breakdown or anything. I don't know what they're getting so worked up about at the office.'

She looked at me sceptically – and tenderly. She was not sitting very far away from me on the sofa. I sensed her breathing body near by, within range of my arms.

I said, 'Shouldn't you be back at work now?'

At that moment a breeze snared up the curtain in the open window and Susan stood up to free it. While she did this she explained that she had taken the afternoon off. Although she was still at the office equipment company in Hounslow, they had promoted her, so now she worked flexihours. She could come and go pretty much as she pleased. Even so, she told me, she was trying to get away. She would be looking for something new in the autumn round of jobs. Maybe something in advertising, or PR. What did I think?

I was happy that the conversation had taken this turn. That sounded promising, I said. Her new seniority would stand her in good stead on the job market, I said.

'I definitely want something else by the new year,' Susan said. 'I want to start the nineties on a good note.' She crunched a crisp – I had brought out a bowl of crisps and a pack of beers – and said, after a pause, 'You know, it's funny, isn't it, how little fuss they're making about the eighties coming to an end. You wouldn't think we were coming up to the end of a decade. A decade, Jimmy! You'd have thought there'd be a bigger fuss about it.'

Yes, it was funny, I said.

Susan, I thought once more, this time tiredly. Susan.

'I wonder what they'll call the eighties? It won't be easy, finding something to call the eighties,' Susan said. We stopped to think about it but neither of us could come up with the word to encapsulate the decade. 'It's sad, isn't it Jimmy,' she said with a bright, dolorous smile: 'Another ten years, gone.'

Yes, it is, Suzy, I said. What a pair we made, I thought.

Then, in a strangely matter-of-fact way, Suzy kicked off her shoes and moved over and took hold of me. She burrowed into my body, hooped her arms around my chest and awkwardly tucked her head under my chin. I was taken aback. We were in the middle of a normal conversation and suddenly here she was, embracing me. I had not seen it coming at all. I thought that she was leaning over to help herself to another beer.

For a while I reciprocated. I squeezed her lumpy little body against mine and let her nestle her face against my shoulder. And while she pressed her short arms around me I hugged her gently: you have to be careful with Susan, she has these collapsible shoulders, and when you hold her tightly it feels as though you are folding her in half. But then, after a little while, I let her go. To be truthful, I simply did not feel like indulging in anything physical. This was not Susan's fault – it was nothing personal – it was simply that that afternoon I was not in the mood for any kind of hanky-panky or for anything lovey-dovey. Can I be blamed? Here she was, un-invited, expecting me to pick up as though seven months ago was yesterday and nothing had happened in the interim. Also – this has to be said – she was making a spectacle of herself. What kind of woman would want to have anything to do with someone like me, in my state? It was all too desperate.

I slid out of her hands and cracked open a beer. I said nothing. Then I looked around at the squalid room, at the cloud of bugs hovering under the ceiling lamp and the trash of meals brimming from bin-liners and the beer mugs choked with ashy butts and Susan next to me with a hole in her brown tights and a susceptible expression, and I only just suppressed the urge to cry out, Get out! Get out of here!

Susan moved still closer to me on the sofa. I sensed her chunky knee resting against mine and her arm coming around again. 'Jimmy Jones,' she said.

I could take no more. She was a nice girl, but I just could not take any more. I gripped her and pushed her away. 'Look, don't do that,' I said. I hissed the words, I did not want to raise my voice. 'I'm not in the mood. Can you understand that? I don't feel like it.' I sat on the edge of the sofa and drank down some more beer.

She stiffened. I could feel her legs go taut as I looked down at the floor between my knees. After a moment of silence I threw her a quick, furtive glance. Her face was white.

She had flown into a rage. She got to her feet and stood back. 'You bastard,' she whispered. 'You think you're the only bloody person in the world. You haven't changed one bit. Have you ever stopped to think about how I might feel? About why I'm here?' Suddenly she shouted, 'Have you?'

Then I shouted too. I shouted, 'I don't want to know! I didn't bloody invite you here, did I! It's over between us, Susan! Get that into your head!'

She screamed, as her face turned patchy with tears, 'Over? Over? What's that supposed to mean?'

I shouted. 'Over! We're finished!'

She began sobbing but she still managed to cry out, 'You're so stupid! I'm never going to speak to you again!'

Then she ran out of the house. She tried to slam the front door but it jammed on a pile of mail.

I stayed where I was, breathing heavily.

Then a draught made the curtain flap out of the window again and a door clacked shut and I remembered that the front door was still open. When I cleared away the post I saw that among it was a letter from Batstone Buckley Williams. I took it back into the living-room, took a slug of beer, and opened the envelope.

Dear James,

It has been decided to call a meeting of the partners to discuss your recent departure from, and performance and conduct at, work. It is only fair to warn you that some of the partners are minded to question your future at the firm. We would be glad to hear any representations that you may wish to make on your behalf. You will appreciate that it is with great regret that we find ourselves in this position. The meeting will take place on 12 July at 2.30.

Yours sincerely,

The Partners, Batstone Buckley Williams

I finished my beer and switched on the television. Then I rang for a curry and, stretched out on the sofa, opened another can. Afterwards I drank more beer and watched more television until the moment came to haul myself to bed.

In the morning, when I lay there under my duvet, I reviewed the situation. It did not look good; it looked as though everything was on the slide. Donovan and me, my thesis and me, Susan and me, Batstone Buckley Williams and me – it looked all over between all of us.

There was something else. The luminosity seemed to have

changed. Although a great beam of July daylight blazed down through the curtains like a spotlight, there was a terrible lack of illumination about the room. Later, outside, when I went to buy some beers and cigarettes, it was the same. This fierce gold was pouring down from every corner of the sky, yet nothing lit up.

I went back to bed. Surely this could not be it. Surely things could not really be like this. Surely the clouds would pass.

And yet the next day, Wednesday 12 July 1989, the day of the partners' meeting, nothing had changed.

I caught the tube to the office. I used to like taking the tube, it made me feel like a Londoner. London is a world-class city and I liked to think that something of its status rubbed off on its citizens. Also, by catching the tube I was chipping in, doing my bit for the city. Without people like me, underground travellers, London would not work. If the subsoil did not seethe with trains, did not suck in and circulate a huge population of its own, the superficial metropolis – the landmarks, double-decker buses, skyscrapers and fountain-filled squares – would grind to a halt. London's heart is under its earth, and some days catching that Northern Line made me feel essential, like blood. I think that those days are over.

Yesterday morning I was numb. I sat out the journey staring at the dark walls of the tunnel rushing by. I was not thinking of what lay ahead, and when I stepped from the elevator into the office it suddenly struck me where I was and I began shaking. But I walked steadily to my room, disregarding the looks I was getting from everybody. Thanks to June they probably thought that I had made a fool of myself over some woman. I did not care what they thought.

My room had not changed. I had half-expected to come back to a transformation of sorts, but, no, everything had stayed just the way it was. Only the calendar had changed. Now it showed Vancouver in July – breakwaters, a beautiful ring of mountains.

Then I heard the noise June makes on her computer

keyboard with her long, black, brilliantly nailed fingers. Tip-tap, tip-tip-tap. I began shaking all over again. I had this moment planned and I was all nerves. I stood up and walked slowly over to her. She could not see me coming, but she could hear my footsteps, and even if she had not been told of my return, she would know that that was me walking towards her. I stopped in front of her desk. She looked up, but at my stomach, not at my face. Then she tilted her head downwards so that I could see the back of her long, elegant neck.

I said, 'June, I'm sorry about everything that's happened.' I paused and swallowed. 'I've had some problems,' I said. 'I shouldn't have let them affect me in the way they did. From now on, things will be back to the way they used to be,' I said. I moved my hands from behind my back. I handed her a bouquet of roses.

(If I can just come in here: those flowers – they were not really my idea. I had bought them as a result of a tip I received years ago from Simon Myers, my first pupil-master. If ever you have woman-trouble, he told me, buy them flowers. It always works. They know it's a trick, you know it's a trick, but they love it all the same. So I bought June roses.)

June accepted the flowers in silence. I stood there for a moment with my hands in my pockets, but I received no response. Then, as I turned away, she spoke.

'So,' she said. 'You're back.'

I gestured by raising my arms, Here I am, as you can see. I gave her an apologetic smile.

June said, turning to look me in the eye, 'Did you have a good time? I hope so, because it's been a complete nightmare here. I've had the worst couple of weeks of my life.'

I felt bad about what I had put June through, but I was not ready for this kind of conversation. I said in a soft voice, 'Don't say any more, June. You don't know what happened. Things have been difficult for me just recently.'

'Well, they're going to get even more difficult from now on,' June said. 'What are you going to tell the partners?'

'I'm going to tell them the truth,' I said.

In the middle of the conference room at Batstone Buckley Williams is a large egg-shaped table bearing four decanters filled with water. I was seated at one tip of the egg, the twelve partners were seated at the other. They were all looking down at the portion of the table in front of them and toying with pens and paper-clips. Directly in front of me, fourteen feet away, sat Edward Boag, the senior partner. Just above his left shoulder the sun shone straight in my eyes through a gap in the venetian blinds. I was hot, and I knew that my damp forehead was glistening in the rays.

The meeting was called to order. Boag looked embarrassed. Mumbling anxiously and tugging at his big ears, he stated the purpose of the gathering: to hear and consider the explanations I had to offer in respect of certain complaints made against me.

Boag put three matters to me. The first matter was the complaints the firm had received from various clients – some of whom had long-standing connections with the firm – who alleged that I had neglected their cases. He read out the clients involved and the gist of their allegations (these complaints, I realized, related to the work I should have been doing when I was writing about Donovan). The second matter was the Lexden-Page incident. Tugging hard at his ear, the senior partner described the incident as he understood it. It was to be noted, Boag mumbled, that Lexden-Page had taken the matter to the Law Society, and they were demanding an explanation from us. Then he moved on to item three, my abrupt departure from work eleven days ago. Boag coughed delicately and asked me whether I agreed with the facts as he had stated them. I said I did. Then he coughed again and said that this was a most regrettable matter. Only once in his forty-two years at the firm did he recall a meeting of this nature. Unfortunately, the conduct in question was on its face so serious as to require immediate investigation and, if necessary, action of a disciplinary nature. In considering what action to take, the partners were keeping all options open. Did I understand the gravity of my situation?

I did, I said. Then I put my side of the story to the partners. I explained to them how my brother Charlie had been seriously ill with intestinal cancer, and how my inability to concentrate on my work came as a result of my worry for him. The perpetual hospital visits, the operations, the chemotherapy . . . (Here I asked the meeting to forgive me for a moment and paused to gather myself. I took a deep breath and continued.) The incident with Mr Lexden-Page, I said. Yes, that was truly unforgivable. All I could say about that was that I had received the news that morning that my brother had slipped into a coma. That said, there was no excuse for the way that I had spoken to Mr Lexden-Page. My departure from work was to visit Charlie. (I coughed before continuing.) I could reassure those present that I would not be seeing Charlie on the firm's time any more. Charlie was dead, I said. Three days ago he had passed away.

I cleared my throat and stole a look up the table to see how the story had gone down. Pretty well, it seemed. No one was moving a muscle.

After a profound silence punctuated by the sounds of pens dropping, Edward Boag spoke up. To my surprise, he seemed irritated. 'Yes, thank you, Jones. It's a pity we didn't hear all of this a bit earlier, though, isn't it? Never mind,' he said, not waiting for a reply, 'it can't be helped now.' He picked at his ear. 'Thank you, Jones, you can go now unless anybody has any questions.'

I went back to my office. Half an hour later I received notification from the partners that in view of my bereavement I should have some days off. A final decision about what action, if any, they would take would be made on my return.

NINETEEN

I did not react to the news of my reprieve. I did not move from my chair. My body felt heavy, as though it had been leaded down for some underwater journey. I weighed a ton.

Then I thought: this time off that I had been given – what if it was to give the firm time to check up on my story? Any private eye worth his salt would find out inside a couple of hours that I had told a pack of lies, that my brother Charlie was as fit as a fiddle, working in a bank in Chester.

Of course they would check up on my story. They were not stupid.

I forced myself to my feet. An idea, a long shot, had occurred to me. I would look in my personnel file and see if there was any indication there of exactly how much trouble I was in. You may think it ridiculous, that the confidential deliberations and decisions of the partners should be placed in such a vulnerable place, but it is amazing how often bungles of this nature occur in organizations like Batstone Buckley Williams. There was always a chance that I would find out something.

I stepped into the personnel office and walked nonchalantly over to the filing cabinet. I opened my folder.

There was nothing which bore on my current position. But then I saw something else. A letter with a 6 Essex Court stamp caught my eye. It was signed, Michael Donovan.

26 October 1978

To whom it may concern:

I can confirm that James Jones was my pupil for six months. My recollection, so far as it goes, is of an industrious and capable young man. I can recall nothing to suggest that he would not be an asset to your firm.

At first, I thought nothing about this curious little discovery – at the time I was too numb to think about anything. Then, that evening, something puzzled me. The reference was dated 26 October 1978, about a month after I had finished my pupillage with Donovan: why, then, did he give the impression that he was racking his brains to think of something to say about me? If he had been referring to a pupil of some years past, or to someone he barely knew, then it would have been understandable – but we were talking about someone who, until thirty days previously, had seen him more often and more regularly than anyone. We were talking about me, not some fly-by-night. Why, if that was so, did he have such difficulty in bringing me to his mind?

I did not give the question more thought, but now, a day later, at home, that letter makes me angry. No, it makes me furious, I am pressing down hard on my pen in my fury. Donovan! He was supposed to be my referee! Was that all he could come up with, this mealy-mouthed reference? What was all this about 'my recollection' and 'I can recall'? Was I no more than a feat of memory? Did I amount to nothing further than the contents of one of his precious engrams? I am made of flesh and blood! He knew that! He knew that I existed independently of his recollection of me! So why, then, did he not simply and unequivocally affirm my qualities – James Jones *is* a capable young man, James Jones *will be* an asset to your firm?

I deserved better. I am not saying that the man should have lionized me, but I was due an accolade, a proper pat on the back. That he failed to do this, to do his duty by me, is a black mark against his name. You may say, Well, he's an important man, he has a hundred and one things to do every minute of the day, he cannot be blamed for falling short on matters of detail. Tell that one to the marines. If he was a genius, a man of history, then I might buy that – but Donovan, it has transpired, is nothing of the sort.

Yes, if *Supranational Law* had appeared as planned, I would not have minded how Donovan treated me. It would not have mattered, my association with him, even if painful, would have been worthwhile. I could have said, Those footsteps on my back are where history went striding by, those bootprints on my neck are the treadmarks of progress. But I cannot say that. All I can say is, I've been walked all over. I've been trampled on. And betrayed, too. I know this is a strong word, betrayed, but am I not right to use it? I was banking on Donovan. If he came good, I came good. Whatever he went on to I went on to also, in my own way. My road ran on to his road.

But Donovan's road has gone nowhere. Donovan's road is a dead-end. He has not come good, he has gone bad. All he has ended up as is an overworked divorcee. A socially inadequate, self-centred man who has nothing to say for himself, a man so one-dimensional that he is unable to write a love-letter to his wife without striking the stiff, ridiculous note of the lawyer.

(I pause there to note that I have just opened a bottle of Bulgarian wine, downed a glass in one mouthful, and refilled it to brimming.)

Something has occurred to me about one of those letters, about the last one, the incoherent, emotive one where Donovan begged Arabella to come back to him. Let us think for a minute about what was *not* said in that letter, let us home in on that scratched out, unfinished phrase *Remember everything we have done together, remember when* . . . Well, I have been visited by a moment of lucidity. It has come to me what that uncharacteristic little correction is all about. The answer arrived just now, as I put down my wine glass and picked up my pen. I felt it prickling its way up through my legs and down through my wrists: Donovan had quit on that phrase not because he felt that its sentiment would be out of place, or because something else had occurred to him, but because he simply *could not remember* anything he and Arabella had done together. That was it. He had no memories of himself with Arabella.

Yes, I think that I am right. I think that, for once, and at last, I have hit the nail on the head. Donovan had wanted to woo Arabella by reminding her of the good times they had had together, unforgettable magical moments and blissful dawns; but he had simply been unable to: he had not stored away any such times. When he had tried to dig up a few episodic souvenirs, a telling memento of his love for her, his mind had gone blank. For once that beautiful memory of his, that golden bin, had let him down.

It all makes sense: that is why he had not recognized me at that party and yet still was able, years later, to remember my name and the name of the firm I worked for. His mind was too crammed with words to accommodate the face of James Jones. *James Jones* and *Batstone Buckley Williams*, yes, that was no problem, he could slot those appellations in with all the other case-names, theories, laws, languages and other semantemes he had stashed away – but James Jones himself, the little guy with the bald head, chubby neck and wrinkly suits? The fellow who leaned towards kebabs, daydreams and late-night taxis? Sorry, full up. The same thing applied when he came to write my reference: once I had finished my pupillage, out came the mental eraser. He had rubbed me out of his life.

Donovan does not even know who I am!

Now I am beginning to see how Arabella must have felt. If she formed no significant part of Donovan's memories, how could she be said to exist for him? She could not, is the answer. Donovan had reduced her to a thing of naught. Yes, and if I think about it, that is how Donovan has made me feel about myself. Like a zero, a nullity, because whatever I did for the man glanced off the surface. It was as though he was composed of bumper rubber – you bounced off him, nothing you could do could leave a dent. And if you cannot leave a dent somewhere, who is to say you are anywhere at all?

It is the middle of the night and rays are arriving in my room. A new day – and, it might be thought, the time to say, Enough. That is enough about Donovan. No more. The water has flowed under the bridge.

I agree. I too think that it is over between us, that it is time for a divorce. But although I am letting Donovan go, I am not going to let him off. No; he may think that everything is hunky-dory, but most assuredly I do not. There is one last matter to deal with before I acquit him: he has to face the charge that he, Michael Donovan, did ruin the life of James Jones. Yes, it is time that the action of *Jones v. Donovan* was commenced.

Members of the jury, I am the plaintiff in this matter. I am the one who has suffered loss and damage – look at me, look how I have ended up, writing furious nonsense in the middle of the night, my career in ruins, my favourite women alienated, myself in turmoil, my world flat and lustreless. Members of the jury, I will show that the cause of all this sits over there – Michael Donovan.

Donovan comes in at this point. I can see him getting to his feet to make, in his warm, inevitable voice, two points. Number one: my life was not ruined. In fact, I had suffered no lasting loss at all. My career was recoverable, as were my friends. The turmoil of the past months I would soon get over. Number two: there was a problem of liability. Even if my life was in ruins (which he denied), he, Donovan, was not to blame. My downfall was my own fault. The facts spoke for themselves: he came to me as a client and, unbeknown to him, this triggered off a whole set of ridiculous and destructive fantasies on my part, which fantasies had led me to my present position. The problem here was not Donovan, it was me. Donovan could not be blamed for the fact that, when he met me, I was full of dammed-up desires and memories. He could not be blamed for the neurotic symptoms I was displaying because this repressed material had suddenly been released. That was his case: why should he be responsible for my character deficiencies?

Here Donovan regains his seat, an amiable, confident look on his face. I say nothing to this, but I do allow a mysterious smile to play on my lips.

I call my first witness. He comes striding across the court, a good-looking, well-dressed man in his early thirties. I clear my throat and start to my examination-in-chief.

Is your name Oliver Owen?

It is.

You are a barrister in the chambers of the defendant, Mr Donovan, are you not?

I am.

Mr Owen, can you describe the responsibilities of a pupil-master to his pupil barrister – in outline only – please?

Certainly. It is the responsibility of the pupil-master to instruct the pupil in the skills of a barrister. It is also his responsibility to take an interest in the career of his or her pupil.

Thank you, Mr Owen. And would you say that the pupil-master's responsibilities extend to informing the pupil of the tenancy application procedure in his chambers?

I would.

Unequivocally?

Unequivocally.

Would it be fair to say, Mr Owen, that a pupil who failed to apply timeously to his chambers for a tenancy because he was unfamiliar with the procedure could hold his pupil-master responsible for the detriment he suffers as a consequence?

All other things being equal, I would.

Now, Mr Owen, I would like you to cast your mind back to September 1978. It is a long time ago, I appreciate that.

I remember that month well, it was the month I was taken on as a tenant by 6 Essex Court.

You recall, do you, my own departure from 6 Essex?

I do. It was in the second half of September.

Did, shortly after my departure from your chambers, in 1978, a vacancy arise in your chambers?

Yes. Bernard Tetlow, as the late Lord Tetlow of Herne Hill then was, was appointed to the bench.

(Here the judge intervenes: May I say that it was the start of a most distinguished career on the bench by the Noble and Honourable and much-regretted Lord.) Quite so, my lord, and may I respectfully express my agreement with your lordship's sentiment. Mr Owen, did the chambers attempt to fill the resulting vacancy?

Yes. We attempted to contact you to offer you the place.

You're quite sure I would have been offered a place?

Yes. It was the view of chambers that you clearly possessed the necessary energy and intellectual ability.

When did you attempt to contact me?

Throughout October, I believe. We rang every chambers in the Temple, and every firm of solicitors we knew of.

And what were the results of these efforts?

We were unable to find you. It seemed that you had left the Bar. No one knew where you were.

Not even Mr Donovan?

Not to my knowledge.

(At this point I produce Exhibit 1, a letter, and pass it to the witness.) Mr Owen, could you read out the letter please? (He does. It is my reference from Donovan to Batstone Buckley Williams.) The letter is dated 26 October 1978, Mr Owen. Was it at this time that you were searching for me to offer me the tenancy?

(Oliver looks put out.)

Yes, I . . .

And what is your response to that fact, Mr Owen? (Again, Oliver looks uncomfortable.)

I must say, I am very surprised to read this letter. Mr Donovan must, or in any event should, have known that we were trying to locate you. He should have told us where you were.

Thank you, Mr Owen, I have no further questions.

(Another glass of wine while I watch Donovan cross-examine. Having long since scrubbed from his mind the business of my tenancy, he has been caught napping. He feebly puts a few questions to Oliver. They are the usual questions – can you be sure of all of this after such a length of

197

time, etcetera – and they cut no ice. Donovan sits down with an expression of bafflement on his face: how could this be happening to him?)

I call my second witness. A rumble goes around the courtroom when he takes the stand, because he bears an uncanny resemblance to myself. Were it not for the fact that he is slimmer and more prosperous-looking, he would be my spitting image.

Could you give the court your name and occupation?

Certainly. James Jones, barrister.

Could you tell us something about your practice, Mr Jones?

I am a successful international lawyer based at 6 Essex Court. It will not be long before I apply for silk.

I see; and could you reveal your earnings to the court?

Yes: £180,000 per annum.

And could you describe to the court your room in chambers?

I work in a large room overlooking a Middle Temple courtyard. The walls are decorated with beautiful old paintings of horses and some interesting items from my collection of contemporary art.

What about your desk?

My desk? Well, it is a large Georgian walnut secretary.

Its cost?

Well, I don't know; about £15,000, I should have thought.

Do you belong to any clubs, Mr Jones?

Only three; the Garrick, the Wig and Pen, the MCC.

Are you married, Mr Jones?

I am.

Do you have a photograph of your wife on your person?

Well, yes, as a matter of fact I do.

(He takes a snapshot of Mrs Jones out of his wallet and passes it to me. A gorgeous, raven-haired, soft-eyed woman is depicted. I raise the photograph for the jury's inspection. After they have settled down I shuffle my papers and clear my throat for effect. Then I wait. I wait for absolute silence before I continue my questioning.) Mr Jones, do you actually exist?

No, I'm afraid to say I do not.

Then who, or what, are you?

I am the person you would have been had events taken a different course.

Let me see if I understand you, Mr Jones: you are the person I would have become had I been taken on by 6 Essex?

Correct.

I see. Mr Jones, the court will have noticed the difference, indeed the gulf, if I may describe it that way, between you and me – you are successful socially and professionally, you are blessed with a wonderful wife and so forth. I am none of these things. Can you be sure that, had I been taken on by 6 Essex, I would have gone on to become like you?

Yes. You undoubtedly possessed all the talent and determination necessary to succeed as a top commercial and international lawer. You were cut out for it, Mr Jones, you were meant to be me – Mr Jones, I am the real you.

Thank you, I have no further questions. Mr Donovan?

A flabbergasted Donovan shakes his head. No cross-examination.

Now it is for Donovan to present his evidence. He has only one witness: himself. He puts himself in the box and takes the oath.

He can say nothing. He stands there in silence, tongue-tied. Well, Mr Donovan? the judge asks. Aren't you going to say anything?

Yes, I . . . says Donovan.

The judge raises an eyebrow. You are unable to speak, Mr Donovan?

Donovan says, Well, I . . . He stops again. Then, after a pause, he says, I have no evidence to give, my lord. I have nothing to say. He steps out of the box.

Just a moment, Mr Donovan, I say dramatically. Everybody looks at me: suddenly I am the centre of attention. You forget, Mr Donovan: I have yet to cross-examine you.

What happens next does not bear transcription. I tear Donovan apart. I do a Donovan on him: I pin him to the ropes and sock him with body-blow after body-blow. I cut him and outpoint him, I mash him in and knock him out: I Tyson him. The admissions come spilling out: Yes, it is my fault that you are not the James Jones you should be, the James Jones you were meant to be; yes, I take the blame for what you are presently suffering, I should have put chambers in touch with you in November 1978; yes, I have acted in a selfish and uncaring way towards you. I have been cruel, I admit it. I have ruined your life.

I let Donovan go. He is in pieces, and reels dizzily to his seat. I stand to address the jury.

You have just heard the Defendant, Mr Donovan, admit liability in this matter. There remains only one thing for you to deal with: the quantum of damages. Members of the jury, I want compensation for dismemberment, for that is what we are talking about here. This may sound heartless to those who have lost real legs, but I, too, feel as though something has been chopped off. I am attacked by impalpable pains in regions I cannot locate, pains like the pains amputees are said to feel in the thin air their hands once would have occupied. Members of the jury, let me make plain what I am saying. Let me explain what has been sundered from me.

Before Donovan came along (and it must never be forgotten that he was the one who entered my life, that he made the first move), I lived happily from day to day. I had no regrets, and if I looked forward at all, members of the jury, it was to more of the same. I was at peace with myself.

Then he showed up – Mr Donovan, the man you see sitting over there. It was not me he wanted, it was a solicitor – a solicitor he could manipulate and dominate. He did not care about the effect he might have on me, the disturbance he might cause by suddenly reappearing in my life. And what was the effect of his come-back? I will tell you. He dug up my old future. Not my recent future, ladies and gentlemen – not the times awaiting me at Batstone Buckley Williams – but my old future, the one I looked forward to as a young man: the James Jones, international lawyer, scenario. And the hopes which this future contained, hopes which until then were safely underground, suddenly came to light again, more vivid than ever.

These hopes were dashed, members of the jury. Of course they were; how could I, now, at this stage of my life, ever fulfil the desires of my youth? I did not have a hope of becoming an international lawyer or of writing a learned book, of taking part in the bright swirl of history: and yet I hoped. Because of Donovan, I hoped.

What do I mean, when I say that my hopes were dashed? Let me tell you: I mean that they were severed from me for good. Yes, severed, as though an axe had been put to them: because these kinds of dreams, these youthful skylines, they are connected bodily to you, members of the jury, they are hooked deep into your insides like anchors jammed in rocks: move the anchor and you move the rocks. And this upheaval, ladies and gentlemen, this rumbling of hearts and guts, is painful. Especially when, as in my case, it is unjust – I could have been, I *should* have been, an international lawyer and learned author. But I am neither of these. I have been deprived of what I had coming to me, a deprivation I can lay at the door of Mr Donovan. If the Defendant had not been so self-centred, he would have alerted his chambers to my whereabouts at Batstone Buckley Williams, and I would now be a different man with different horizons. But I am not. The old me-to-be, the man of my dreams – you heard him giving evidence earlier, members of the jury, the other Mr Jones – he and I have split up for ever. It is over between us, it is over between my real self and me – for there can be no doubt, members of the jury, that the person I now am, and the life I now lead, worthy as they might be, are not the real thing. The real life, lustrous and significant, has been lost to me, and that is as bad as losing a limb. Anyone who thinks that I am going too far is wrong. I would give my right arm for those vanished years, even now.

(I stop there to let the jury take in what I have been saying. I look over at Donovan. He is sitting silently, in a daze. I know what he is thinking; not, My, how selfish I have been, but, My

God, James is good – *really* good – how stupid I was never to have spotted his talent when he was my pupil! I resume.)

Members of the jury, Mr Donovan himself has admitted that he has ruined my life. It happened a long time ago, it is true, over a decade ago – but it happened. He deflected me from my rightful path. It may be that you think that I am feeling a little too sorry for myself, that I should show more backbone and face the future like a man, and you may be right to feel this. Perhaps I am not as strong a man as I should be and perhaps, in this sense, I have contributed to my loss. That may be so. But Mr Donovan here, he should have known that before he started to ruin my life. He should have realized what stuff I am made of, he should have realized (he is a lawyer, he is familiar with the eggshell–skull principle) that I was a vulnerable party. Members of the jury, I ask not just for a compensatory award, but for exemplary, punitive damages. I ask for justice.

I sit down. Donovan has nothing to add. While the jury deliberates, I finish my bottle of wine. I see that it is 8 a.m.

TWENTY

I never heard what the verdict of the jury was. The next thing I knew I was waking up on the sofa in the mid-afternoon with a hammering dehydration hangover, my rashy face hanging pale and swollen in the mirror on the wall. It sounded, from the gurgles and rumbles that tremored down my chest to my stomach, as if trains were running through my body's tunnels.

Sweating a little, I lit a cigarette and glanced around me, at the living-room. It did not look good. Empty wine bottles, junk food cartons, newspapers, fat-crusted dishes, socks, cigarette packs, underpants, rotting flowers and garbage of all kinds stood out in the harsh daylight. Dust particles swam around in the air and a big bluebottle jangled against a windowpane. I stubbed out my cigarette: my throat was too sore to smoke it down to the butt.

Then, after I had guzzled at a stream of lukewarm tapwater in the kitchen, I made a discovery. I felt lighter than I had done for days; I felt as though some freight had been unladen from my body.

I felt all right.

I pushed my feet into shoes and headed for the door. I had no special destination in mind, I just needed to get out. I did not bother to change, or to shave or wash. I just stepped out of the house the way I was.

I caught a bus. I sat on the top deck and smoked a cigarette. It was yet another cloudless, sunshiny day, and when, at the Elephant and Castle, the bus stood still for ten minutes in a tangle of traffic, it came to me that, yes, I was not mistaken, I was feeling better. Down below throngs filled the pavements and two guys in sunglasses in an old purple sports car were blasting out opera and setting everything to music. It was a shot in the arm, and for the first time in a while I envisaged being part of all that action down there.

Then a small smile visited me: something struck me: all at once, on top of this bus, I was seeing daylight. The knots and kinks that had roped and snarled up my mind had ravelled out, and suddenly the whole of the Donovan business looked different. I was seeing it in a new way, from a distance, from the vantage point of someone looking back. It looked as though I had moved on: moved on from the Donovan part of my life.

Yes, I thought. What Donovan saw in Arabella, why he had collapsed in court, why he had burned his manuscript, why he had not contested the divorce, why Arabella had left that message on the ansaphone, why his father had come and suddenly gone, why he had cried on the golf course – who cared? Not me, that was for sure. Me, I had lost interest. Whether Donovan threw himself off a cliff or scaled great heights, it was all the same to me. Good luck to him. During the boiling, therapeutic night I had disentangled my life from his, and that was that. This was not a case of forgive and forget: this was just a case of forget. Anyway, there comes a moment when forgetting *is* forgiving – amnesty, after all, flows from amnesia.

Yes, I was letting it pass, all of it. Bygones were bygones. I knew that if I looked long and deep enough into the vehement events of the past year – events which had, as far as I could see, expired suddenly and inexplicably – they would no doubt yield profound and interesting meanings, illuminations of the downfall of genius and of the mysterious causalities of history. But I did not want to know. I had cut the cord, and that was that.

The bus freed itself from the traffic and sped off. I lit another cigarette and settled back in a tingling frame of mind. I felt quickened, the window-framed scenes outside flitted by like a strip of film. We swerved up to the Strand via Trafalgar Square and the crowds, the jetting water, the flocks of pigeons; my cheek flattened against the window, I watched a baby in a pram, a policeman giving directions, a teacher waist-deep in schoolchildren and a couple holding each other and laughing, the woman tossing her head upwards and backwards in my direction.

It was Arabella, and the man – I had to lean over to check – was Michael Donovan.

At first I did not respond. Then, as the bus was stationary, I left my seat to look at them out of the rear window.

They were still there, walking along holding hands and kissing each other. They looked delighted. They could have been celebrating something, they looked so happy.

The bus started up and left them behind, amongst the crowds.

I could not believe it. They had got back together. Whether or not Donovan had dissuaded Arabella from finalizing the divorce, whatever the details of the matter were, one thing was clear: they were back together again. The Donovans were reunited.

Well, I said to myself, that was a matter for them. Me, I was not going to spend any time working out the hows and whys of their reconciliation. I had fish of my own to fry.

But when I returned home I had a small argument with myself. One part of me said that I should forget all about what I had seen, that it made no difference anyway, that I did not want to risk becoming involved with Donovan all over again. The other part said, Why should I dismiss the incident? Why shouldn't I think about it? I would put my mind to it in the same way as I might mull over any other item of curiosity. There was no need for me to apply special prohibitions or security measures vis-à-vis Donovan; now that I had said boo to his ghost, I was able to contemplate him on equal terms, man to man.

The second part of me won the argument.

How had Donovan done it? How had he managed to turn Arabella? What kind of offer had he made?

No sooner had I asked myself this last question than something hit me, something slapped me across the face. It was not an offer that had won Arabella, it was an offering: he had burned the manuscript of *Supranational Law* for her.

Of course, I was speculating, and it was quite possible that the two mysterious events which I had brought together – the Donovans' reconciliation and the conflagration of the book – were wholly unrelated. But my theory, my intuition, made sense. It added up.

I flicked a fresh cigarette out of my pack, lit up, and began walking quickly around the room; suddenly these currents, these juices, were flowing through me . . .

Everything was topsy-turvy again. So Donovan was a hero after all. Viewed in the light of the sacrifice he had made for Arabella, his story was a shining chapter in those great antagonisms, life versus art, man versus woman: faced with the stark choice of pursuing his love or his genius, he had gloriously and chivalrously chosen love. This might not have been history I was seeing, as I had originally thought, but it was certainly a love story. The boy had got the girl. I could see 'The End' rolling across the final frame, a frozen shot of the two of them together, handsome and laughing, on the Strand.

I pulled out another cigarette. So this is what had been happening all along. This is what had been significant about the Donovan story – not international law, not history, not me, love.

I recognized that this final version did me no favours. I preferred the original scenario, with me as a player, as a footnote in the history books. Now, it transpired, I was a minor, dispensable character, with no part in the final, crucial reel, where the Donovan drama had come to a climax, where Donovan had somehow saved his marriage. My story – a hard-luck story – was by-the-by. In the end, in the final cut, I had been edited out.

I did not mind. This was the wonderful thing. I was not bitter about the outcome. I looked on the bright side: it had been an adventure. That was what was important, that was what I took away from it: for a few months, I had lived vividly; for a few months, my obscure little life had been lit up.

I looked around at the debris everywhere and rubbed my hands and rolled up my sleeves. The Donovan story had ended. The lights had come on and it was time to put away the popcorn and head for the foyer. Time to clear up this mess and get on with my life. I went into the kitchen and fetched a bin-liner and began filling it with clinking, smelling objects. Then, when I had loaded up the bag and knotted up its mouth, I ran into a problem: I ran out of bags.

Two minutes later I passed out in bed. Too tired to go out to buy more bin-liners, I had undone the full one and had tried cramming it with more stuff. It had not worked. All that had happened was that the bag had ripped open along the side and some sour, coagulated milk had dribbled out on to the floor. It was too much to face. I had been through enough that day. There was always tomorrow.

The next day I hoisted my dripping body out of the tub and got ready to face the world. I shaved and washed and knotted a tie around my neck. Then I caught the tube up to the north bank of the river and wandered down the sunny Embankment gardens to the Wig and Pen, a drinking club on the Strand. I am not a member there but, as my face rings a bell, I am taken for one. Over the years I have come to befriend some of the boys who go in there in the afternoon, and on this occasion I was optimistic about running into someone I could talk to. By the time I stepped into the bar I was in a nice, uncomplicated state of mind, looking forward to my first normal conversation for weeks.

There was hardly anyone around. Two barristers were huddled in a corner and an old red-faced fellow was reading a newspaper at the bar. I took my glass of wine and sat a few chairs away from him. One hour and several drinks passed and, although the place had started to fill up, no one had spoken to me. Then joyfully, I recognized a face.

'Barman, two bloody marys!' I cried.

Oliver Owen regarded me. 'Well, I must say, you're looking more, shall we say, more substantial than the last time we met.' He pointed at the shirt stretched tightly over my stomach. 'What are you hiding in there, a basketball?'

'Do not mock me, sir,' I said flamboyantly, handing him his drink.

'Correct me if I'm wrong,' Oliver said, 'but the last glimpse I had of you was of your fleeing rump en route for your office bog. Not an attractive spectacle, if you'll permit me to say so.'

'You refer to that ornament of the social calendar, the Batstone Christmas party,' I said. 'I remember the moment well. You had just dropped your bombshell when the drink suddenly got the better of me and I was forced to take flight. Most embarrassing.'

Oliver wore the look of amusement he invariably wears in my company. He stands up straight and looks down at me with a sly, discriminating smile. 'What bombshell? You're not talking about my female pupil, are you? What was her name?'

'Diana Martin,' I said. 'No, I use "bombshell" not in the sense of a knockout beauty, but in the sense of an item of devastating news.' He kept looking at me, forcing me to elaborate in a casual, jolly tone. 'Remember. You told me how 6 Essex tried to get hold of me to offer me a tenancy when Tetlow had gone, but couldn't find me? Well,' I said, 'that came as a bit of a surprise. Hence my use of the word "bombshell". Comprendo?'

Oliver frowned with a smile on his lips. 'Did I say that?' Then he looked at me and started laughing. 'You didn't actually believe me, did you?'

I said, with will-power, 'No, no, of course not. Of course I didn't. Don't be ridiculous,' I said.

Oliver kept laughing. He tossed his head back and just went on laughing. 'You did believe me, didn't you? You thought that we'd turned the Temple upside-down looking for you, didn't you?'

I said nothing. I tried to come up with a smile and voice a denial, but I could not. The muscles around my mouth had collapsed.

'Don't get angry with me, James, it sounds like I was doing you a favour.' Oliver was still laughing. 'You wouldn't want my pupil to think that you'd failed to get into chambers, would you?'

There was a silence as Oliver swallowed his chortles and straightened his face. Then he spluttered into his glass and began laughing again.

I finished my drink. 'I've got to go,' I said, knocking my stool to the ground.

I lurched through the door and, stunned by the sunlight, reeled for a moment on the pavement. Then I waved down a passing cab, fell into the back and nodded off, my head rolling around on my chest as we took the corners.

I awoke in my living-room at half-past seven (it strikes me, looking back on these last days, just how much sleeping and waking I did). I had a go at standing up. I felt sick. Close your eyes, pirouette a few times and then open your eyes: that was how I felt. Events had whipped me around at such velocities and from such acute, unexpected angles, that I was turning like a top.

When the spinning passed, I went into a daze. There is only so much shock and setback and realignment a man can take in a day. I stared at the television for a while and fell asleep on the sofa.

Nothing had changed in the morning. Everything was still the same, the flies, the drizzling dust, the mess. So this was it. This was my new, post-Donovan world. This was my life. A house filled with trash, a dead-end, soon-to-end job, and at their centre, me, James Jones. James Jones, I thought. James bloody Jones. Solicitor, bachelor, small-timer, loner. He had me trapped, the bastard. He had me locked up. I felt like that unfortunate fellow in the story, the one who woke up one morning to find himself imprisoned in the carapace of an enormous, despicable insect. Jesus Christ, I thought with a sudden, lucid horror, I was stuck with him – I was stuck inside that fat, failed, unloved bastard.

In pain, I rolled off the sofa and started walking around the house to empty out my mind. Like a zombie I just wandered around for a few minutes, trying not to think. Then I saw that I had received a thick envelope in the mail, and that it was from the *International Lawyer*. I remembered: the article I had sent them early in the year, when I had revived my studies. They had finally got around to returning it to me. What a joke, I thought. To think that I imagined that the learned editors of that journal would ever consider an article by a nobody like me. To think that I imagined that I could ever grasp, let alone master, the problems of supranational law – and in two weeks. (And yet, when I fingered the letter, I was pounding . . .)

I ripped open the envelope.

Dear Mr Jones,
Thank you for your paper on the problems of developing a supranational law. I read it with great interest. Unfortunately, the International Lawyer *already has a piece on this very subject, written, I am afraid to say, by myself (I have enclosed it for your interest).*
Yours,

Michael Donovan

I stood there for a moment. He had not even realized who Mr Jones was.

Then, slowly, I made a space at the kitchen table and looked at Donovan's piece: *Some Problems of Supranational Law.*

It read, needless to say, like a dream. Donovan explained how he had attempted to construct a jurisprudence of supranational law and how and why he had failed. He listed the obstacles he had encountered (more, many more than I had envisaged) and said that, as international law was adapting quickly to the new circumstances – he cited the Montreal protocol as an example – there was no need to develop supranational principles. He had fallen into the monist trap, he said. He concluded that the way forward was to describe and elucidate the developing rules of international co-operation rather than to seek to formulate a prescriptive, teleological jurisprudence.

I dropped both pieces, his and mine, into one of the bulging plastic bags that surrounded the dustbin. I gave a dry laugh. So much for Donovan as the new Grotius. So much for Donovan burning his book for love. So much for Donovan as the instrument of my downfall.

So much for all of it. Sitting there in the buzzing, reeking kitchen, I saw, for the first time, what had happened. Nothing had happened. The whole thing had come to nothing.

I began to feel unwell again, again it seemed as if the floor was tilting like a deck at sea, and I had to close my eyes and wait for the room to even out. When I opened my eyes I was sweating. Feeling panicky, I thought: the Donovan story, with all of its twists and mysteries, came down to this: he was a busy lawyer who had been through a difficult patch with his wife and who had tried unsuccessfully to write a difficult book. That was it. There it was, the long and short of it. As for me, my story was nothing special, either. It was not even the story of a hard case, a poignant tale of might-have-been, of a man unluckily deprived of his vocation and true self. No. I was simply a solicitor who, in the last year, had badly deluded himself. No more, no less. I had not been in any adventure, in any real-life thriller. When I had seen history and destiny and tragedy and love story in what had happened, I had been seeing things. There was no special link between Donovan and me, nothing other than the usual, flukey contiguities. My road was not a tributary of his road.

Then I took a grip of myself: Donovan's story? My story? What was I thinking about? People do not have stories, they have lives; they have a spell of sticking around in the flesh, and then they are no more: that is what people have. And I thought, Roads? Roads? Roads have destinations, roads take you to places, that is why we build them. But Donovan and I – we were not going anywhere. Even if Donovan published his book, even if he became the greatest jurist since Hugo Grotius, even if he lived happily with Arabella for the rest of his days – where would that get him? And even if I was sucked into his historical slipstream, even if every one of my dreams came true – where would that leave me? Dreams? You dreamed when you were asleep, or at the movies. Wake up, Jones, I told myself. You're not in some film here, this is the real thing. This is not Disneyland, this is Earth, a planet in an unremarkable galaxy in the suburbs of a universe in the middle of nowhere. No one was going anywhere. No one, not even Donovan, had anywhere to go.

I went to bed. I lay curled up there for the rest of the day and, the next morning, I stayed put. There was nothing to get up for. It was not that all the doors of my life had slammed shut, it was that there were no doors. I lay there feeling terrible, thinking, My future – where was my future? I pictured the forthcoming events, the passage of the calendar days, and no matter what I saw – myself at Batstone Buckley Williams or, if they threw me out, myself elsewhere, working away for years to come – I saw no future. Even if I envisaged myself as a heroic international lawyer I could see no future.

I thought of Susan, I thought of how she worried about just this point. Right then, I could have done with Susan next to me to warm me up. I could have done with her arms around me right then.

Eventually – how or why I do not know – I got out of bed. I felt heavy all over again, like an astronaut kitted out on Earth. But somehow I got around to cleaning up the house. I worked solidly for three hours. I scrubbed the kitchen, killed the flies and rejuvenated the living-room. I moved the dust and polished the silver and disinfected the sink. I took the rugs into the garden and beat great puffs of dirt out of them. For one reason or another, I just kept plugging away. I washed and shaved and walked slowly to the tube station and took the train up to the office. I felt empty as well as heavy, I felt scooped out.

I got into work and sat behind my desk. My job was on the line, but I was not afraid. I did not care, to tell the truth. It did not matter to me what happened. Then, after a while, I went to the senior partner's office and knocked.

'Ah, Jones.' The old fellow gestured towards the chair.

I sat down.

'Feeling better now, Jones?'

'Yes, thank you,' I said.

'It must have been a terrible shock for you, losing your brother like that. A terrible shock.'

I said nothing.

Old Boag looked me in the eye. 'Well, feel free to start whenever you wish,' he said. 'My condolences, and the firm's.'

'Thank you,' I said. 'I'm sorry I haven't . . . '

I did not finish my sentence. Old Boag was waving his hands. Forget it, he was telling me. Don't worry about it.

I went back to my office and looked down on the clattering street for a time. Everyone was rushing to and fro and up and down as though nothing was the matter. They were scurrying over zebra crossings, leaping off buses, honking their horns, pointing at displays and raising their voices. A wind blew through the street and everything fluttered and then went back to normal again.

I heard a thump behind me. It was June, June with her fire-engine smile. She had brought me a steaming cup of hot tea.

'Drink it,' she said. 'Come on, it'll do you good.'

I picked it up and took a weak gulp. 'Thank you, June,' I said. 'That's delicious.'

She watched me drink. 'If you need anything – *anything* – just ask. All right?'

Off she went, trotting back to her desk. June.

I picked up the telephone receiver – it weighed like a bar of lead – and made a couple of calls. First I rang my brother Charlie and told him what the score was. Then I rang Susan's office. No, she's not here, they said. I should have known better, but I felt a flicker of hope for her. I said, You mean, she no longer works there? She's found another job? No, they said. She's out for the moment, that's all. I wanted to leave Susan a message of some sort, and I searched around in my mind for something to say. I said, Say James Jones rang.

What now? I thought. Where to next?

I had to keep busy. I picked up the telephone again and dialled Lexden-Page.

'I'm terribly sorry, Mr Lexden-Page,' I said.

'That's all right,' Lexden-Page said unconvincingly. 'I heard you were going through a patch of trouble. I'm sorry about your brother, Jones.'

I said tiredly, 'Well, what are we going to do about your case, Mr Lexden-Page?'

Lexden-Page found his old tone. 'We'll fight it, Jones,' he said excitedly. 'I'm not taking this lying down.'

Poor old Lexden-Page, he did not have a hope in hell. Not only had his appeal to the county court failed, he had also been refused leave to appeal. He would have to get leave to appeal from the Court of Appeal (impossible) and, on top of that, win the actual appeal: also impossible. Even then, if he wished to continue fighting, he would be refused leave to appeal to the House of Lords, who in any event were bound to dismiss the appeal proper. The whole thing was impossible, an utter non-starter. Lexden-Page was going nowhere, and it was time that he got this into his head. It was time that he woke up, faced some facts.

His voice rang in my ear again. 'Well, Jones? Well, what do you say?'

'We'll appeal,' I said. 'We'll appeal right to the very end, Mr Lexden-Page. We'll give it everything we have, Mr Lexden-Page,' I said.

Also by Joseph O'Neill

Netherland

Longlisted for the Man Booker Prize 2008
A Richard & Judy bookclub pick
Winner of the PEN/Faulkner Award for Fiction

What do you do when your wife takes your child and leaves you alone in a city of ghosts?

Hans van den Broek chooses cricket. Alone in a terrorized city, struggling to understand the disappearance from his life of people, places and feelings, he seeks refuge in the game of his childhood. But New York cricket is a long way from the tranquil sport he grew up with. It's a rough, almost secret game, played in scrubby, marginal urban parks, by people the city doesn't see – people like Chuck Ramkissoon. Years later, when a body is pulled out of a New York canal, hands tied behind its back, Hans is forced to remember his unusual friendship with Chuck – dreamer, visionary, and perhaps something darker...

'Dazzling, told with great grace and daring'

KATE SUMMERSCALE

'Beautifully written'

MONICA ALI

'Mesmerising. I've not read anything recently that has quite so brilliantly captured the exuberant madness and cultural diversity of [New York]'

JEREMY PAXMAN

The Breezes

Fourteen years ago Mary Breeze was killed by lightning. It should have been all the bad luck that the Breeze family was due but, as John Breeze is about to find out, this couldn't be further from the truth. *The Breezes* is John Breeze's account of his family's most hellish fortnight, when insurance policies, security systems and lucky underpants are pitted against redundancy, burglary and relegation – and lose. John (a failing chairmaker) and his father (railway manager and rubbish football referee) are only feebly equipped with shaky religious notions, management maxims and cynical postures as they try to come to terms with the absurd unfairness of lightning striking twice…

'Using wonderfully extravagent prose, both lyrical and earthy, O'Neill pulls off that rare thing – poignant farce'   *Observer*

'Impressively, O'Neill handles tragedy and farce with equal aplomb…the book ends with an optimism as irresistible as it is hard won'   *Independent on Sunday*

'At once deeply affecting and extremely funny…This is a novel about losers forced to become winners'   *Guardian*

'A hilarious chronicle of life's crappiness'   *TLS*

Blood-Dark Track

A Family History

Joseph O'Neill's grandfathers – one Irish, one Turkish – were both imprisoned during the Second World War. The Irish grandfather, a handsome rogue from a family of small farmers, was an active member of the IRA and was interned with hundreds of his comrades. O'Neill's other grandfather, a hotelier from a tiny and threatened Turkish Christian minority, was imprisoned by the British in Palestine, on suspicion of being a spy.

At the age of thirty, Joseph O'Neill set out to uncover his grandfather's stories. He emerged with a tale of two families and two charismatic but flawed men – a story of murder, espionage, paranoia and fear, of memories of violence and of fierce committments to political causes.

'He uncovers fascinating parallels between the two men, illuminating the ways in which individual lives mesh with history'
Sunday Times

'This is a beautifully written and complicated book, in which difficult perceptions are expressed with forensic honesty'
Sunday Telegraph